In Them Days

A Novel
By Isobel Warren

CEDAR CAVE BOOKS
NEWMARKET, CANADA

WWW.CEDARCAVE.COM

In Them Days
Copyright © Isobel Warren, 2013
www.inthemdays.ca

Published by Cedar Cave Books
www.cedarcave.com
350 DAVIS DRIVE, #95511
NEWMARKET, ONTARIO, CANADA L3Y 8J8

Edited by Lorraine Hunter

Designed by Sandy Peic, Inspired Sight and Sound Inc.
www.inspiredsightandsound.com

Library and Archives Canada Cataloguing in Publication

Warren, Isobel
In them days / author, Isobel Warren ;
designer, Sandy Peic ; editor, Lorraine Hunter.

Issued also in an electronic format.
ISBN 978-0-920403-17-4

I. Hunter, Lorraine, 1947- II. Title.

PS8645.A766715 2013   C813'.6   C2012-908441-7

Acknowledgements

Only one name gets credit as 'writer' but many amazing and generous people helped to inspire, define and polish this, my first novel. My husband, Milan Chvostek, and our daughter, Annabelle Chvostek, top the list, having patiently read drafts and rewrites for two long years and never stinting in their moral support and wise counsel. Our son, computer whiz Paul Chvostek, continues to guide me through the technological wilderness. My long-time friend, Sheila Lyttle, an early reader of the manuscript, helped bring into sharp focus the tempora and mores of the between-wars era. Medical editor Terry Murray ensured that the book's medical sequences bore a genuine resemblance to reality. Dr. Joaquin Kuhn, a writer and teacher of impressive experience and generosity, was an unflagging source of wise advice and rich encouragement.

Editor Lorraine Hunter's cool judgement and skill helped shape the overall book into a more coherent and cohesive whole. Corrie Adams revealed a formidable talent for in-depth assessment of plot and character. Gail Sellers and Julie Achtermeier provided valuable feedback on the plot. Anne Martin of On Top of The World TV continues to be an invaluable source of advice on marketing and publicity. Sandy Peic of Inspired Sight and Sound applied her inimitable design talent to creating a simply beautiful finished product.

I sat down to write this book two years ago because I could not walk – I had broken my ankle. It was an idyllic summer and I spent it in the garden, laptop in hand, cats nearby. The real work began when I realized that random images triggered by high-octane pain killers do not necessarily ensure a well written book. That's when family, friends and top-notch professionals came to the rescue and it is to each one of these beautiful people that I owe a huge debt of gratitude.

How do I thank thee? Let me count the ways.

Isobel Warren,
NEWMARKET, CANADA

About the Author

Isobel Warren is a veteran Canadian journalist with credits in myriad Canadian publications, as well as radio and TV. She is the author of three travel guides and a soon-to-be-published children's book, *Gypsy on Ice*, the story of a Roma boy caught between his first love, hockey, and his family's historic passion for music. She has also compiled *'Them Days – The Cookbook'*, a 1920s recipe collection. She has taught Creative Writing at various post-secondary institutions for over thirty years. Warren was co-founder and past-president of the Travel Media Association of Canada and is now a member of the Writers Group of York Region and a director of the Newmarket (Ontario) Arts Council. She lives in Newmarket, Ontario with her husband and assorted cats.

How To Write A Book – First break an ankle. Immobilize leg with ugly, heavy pump-up boot. Retire to garden with painkillers, plenty of cats and gallons of tea, compliments of attentive husband. Set up laptop. Write. Write. Write. That's it. **Isobel Warren**.   *Photo: Milan Chvostek*

Contents

The Valley According to Lenny

Well, I'll tell ya this. The last thing I ever expected to be doin' in my old age was I'd be writin' a book. But then this here doctor lady from the city come along a few years back, pokin' around for somebody to recall the old days and some of the neighbours pointed at me. This Dr. Butters – she ain't a real doctor that fixes broken bones and delivers babies. She's some kind of high class doctor from the university there – anyways, I told her some yarns that she wrote down and she claimed they was grand stories and there was nuthin' for it but that I'd tell her more. Makes ya wonder what sort of stories them doctors like to read.

Well, you know, this here Valley is a real quiet place. Or it used to be, before the war. Most of us come from Irish or Scot roots, that come here back in the 1800s and got Crown land, and built log cabins and then when they could afford it, they put up their big red brick houses, from the brickworks down on the Bass River. And they bought their chairs and tables and beds from the folks up at Foreston from the Aikman family that was good at woodworking. Old Man Aikman, he told me one time that aik means oak in the old Gaelic so that made them men of oak, good at woodworking. Anyway, they brought more family over from Scotland and trained up the youngsters and before you knew it there was a whole town of people sawing up lumber and making furniture for every house in the Valley. If we needed cash, we'd saw down a few trees and haul them over to the lumber yard at Foreston. And if we needed a casket, that's where we went too.

We didn't have no electricity nor water in taps nor indoor toilets. Nor cars. We got around with horses and wagons or sleighs. Most houses had one of them big wooden telephone boxes screwed to the kitchen wall. The mouthpiece sticks out in front and the receiver hangs on a hook to the side of it. Women always had the phone put in down low so they could set in their rocking chairs, rock the cradle with one foot and talk on the phone all at once. We all shared the same party line so when you called anybody, the telephones all up and down the road let out a kind of burp like they's just et beans, so people knew to pick up and listen in, even if it was none of their business. Well, especially if it was none of their business.

'Course there was the war. The Great War, they called it but there was nuthin' great about it. Young lads sailin' off to France, coming home, if they was lucky enough to be alive, with lungs burned by mustard gas or missin' legs or arms. Never could figger what they was really fightin' for. But after 1918, that's when things started to change in the Valley. Adam Chandler brought home his new bride and she sure caused a stir. Them lads that survived the war come back with all their scars and problems. Girls chopped off their hair and their skirts and said they'd get educated and get jobs before they'd get married. Adam got a car and before long some farmers got tractors and sold off their horses. Nuthin' was quite the same. The war changed everything.

That doctor lady, she never let up. She even turned up with this here new-fangled recording machine with rolls of tape and a microphone, like the mouthpiece on the old telephones, so's I don't have to write stuff down on paper and annoy my arthritis.

So even though I only ever got half-way through grade school for having to stay home and help with the farm work and I hardly ever had a pen in my hand except to sign the registration papers for my Holsteins, here I am helpin' to write a book. With no paper or pen. Mucking out the stables or hauling in the hay was never as tough as this. But I'm too old for them chores now so I guess I'll just hafta set here in my rocking chair and harvest memories from them days.

Lenny

CHAPTER 1

The Fire

Fire is a terrible disaster on a farm. House or barn, it don't matter which, the loss is somethin' awful. Losin' the hay and the grain for feedin' livestock, or worse still, losin' the livestock – a farmer could lose his farm and the family could lose all they'd worked for.

Different from the city, y'know. In them days there was no fire truck screechin' down the lane. No fire hose neither – just water from the well, pumped by hand, carried to the fire in buckets. Even with them fancy copper lightning rods, many a farm building was struck by lightning and went up like a torch and not a soul could stop it. Them old wooden barns burn like kindlin' and the straw and hay inside feed the blaze.

Fact is, the hay and straw can be the problem. Just the least bit damp and they can start to heat up and finally flare up – they call it spontaneous combustion. You'd see us all winter long up there in the barns turnin' over the hay and straw to find warm spots. But sometimes we missed them, no matter how hard we tried. That's what happened at the Donovan farm one cold night that nobody ever forgot.

Lenny

Adam Chandler was weary of travel and grateful for his own bed after a busy week in the city. He stretched his lanky body and pulled the quilts up to his chin, ready for sleep. But sleep was elusive.

He thought back over the week in Toronto – the Winter Livestock Show, where farmers from across the province gathered, sharing new ideas, new crops and grains, new medications and treatments, new buggies and harnesses. And the horses! Oh how he loved those horses – the mighty draught horses – golden Clydesdales with their fluffy feathery feet, huge Percherons with massive necks and noble heads, Belgians and Friesians, black as night. But his particular weakness was the high-strung thoroughbreds, so sleek and slim, moving like dancers on feet as dainty as china tea cups. He'd made note of a couple of breeders whose stock he especially admired and vowed to himself to have one of those elegant little horses as his own one day soon.

And he thought about the girl he'd met there – Julianna – so exuberant and beautiful, ladylike, but not at all like the shy and awkward farm girls who lived in the Valley. He remembered her calling card, tucked into the breast pocket of his dark suit, and he determined to write her a polite letter after a suitable time had passed. But first it was time for sleep.

And that was when he heard the bell, clanging wildly, ringing out disaster. He leapt up and peered out the window but he could see nothing. It was past midnight and the Valley was in darkness. But the bell clanged on, an urgent summons for help.

His farm clothes were tucked away in the wardrobe but his town clothes still hung over the chair by his bed. He yanked them on and ran downstairs, through to the back door where he found his barn boots and a jacket. Out the back door, he could hear the bell ringing up on the hill and he thought he smelled smoke. Oh no, he thought. FIRE. At the Donovan farm.

He snatched up a halter and backed Brutus out of his stall. No time for a saddle. He leapt onto the smooth bare back and galloped furiously to the Donovan place, just a mile away.

The barn was burning. Already a line of men and boys had formed, passing buckets of water from pump to barn to try to quell the flames. Adam's horse began to snort and rear at the smell of the smoke so he hitched him securely to a post well back in the lane. He ran to the pump, to spell off Lenny Findlay who was furiously refilling buckets that smaller boys carried back from the front of the line. Pumping was hard work and before long Adam's arms and shoulders began to complain. When Olga Dietrich reached for the pump handle and took over, he was glad to relinquish the job and join the bucket brigade, though he wondered briefly at a woman doing a man's job.

The heat must have been building for many days and when it flared up that Sunday night in November, it swiftly became an inferno.

John Donovan was first to spot the fire. Past bedtime he was still awake, reading, as he often did, late into the night. He thought he'd smelled smoke and glanced out to see a red glow in his straw barn. His yell roused the household – his wife, Rachel, and the children, Willie and Betsy – and then he was out of the house and running toward the barn while Rachel urgently rang the big brass dinner bell that hung beside the back door. Its usual job was to call the men to dinner but when it tolled at midnight, the neighbours knew there was trouble and, like Adam, they came running, bringing their milk pails and slop buckets from home. But their bucket brigade was no match for the flames. The fire was up in the straw barn where a damp clump of straw must have heated up and burst spontaneously into flames – and it was spreading fast.

Built like most barns in the Valley, the barn was an L shape with a gangway leading up to the hay and straw barns and the threshing floor above, with stables and pens down at ground level. Knowing that livestock were at risk, neighbours rushed in to save them. Hector Hawkins and Joe Dunning ran up and down the cow stable, releasing the cows from their tethers and slapping their rumps to hurry them outside. Otto Dietrich and two boys braved the sheep pen and managed to persuade the sheep, who were even more confused than usual, to run to safety. As soon as their pen was opened, the pigs, already screaming bloody murder, took care of themselves, tearing out into the barnyard and as far from the barn as possible where they gathered in an grunting gaggle, suspiciously eyeing the fire. A bunch of barn cats sidled out of the cow stable and the group breathed a sigh of relief. That stable, at least, was empty.

But then one little mother cat struggled out, hauling a kitten by the neck. She dropped it just outside the door, and turned back into the smoke to bring another and then another, four tiny kittens in all, from whatever nest she had made for them back behind the cow stalls. Little Willy Donovan, who had a soft spot for animals, dashed to the doorstep and scooped up the kittens, clicking encouragement to the mother to follow him. She was a barn cat and wary of humans, but those were her babies and she wasn't about to abandon them. She followed him and her brood up to the house where his mother, Rachel, quickly lined a cardboard box with a pair of worn-out long johns. Purring effusively, the mother cat leapt in and nursed her brood.

Meanwhile, the horses, five of them still in their stalls below the hay barn, smelled the danger and started to whinny and stamp in fear. The onlookers knew the challenges of saving horses from fires – their panic at the smell of smoke triggered rearing and slashing hooves that presented real danger. The men hesitated but Liam Findlay, Lenny's son, was off and running and Adam followed him. Into the stable they raced, where two mighty Clydesdales, Sultan and King, were already snorting and prancing in terror.

Liam had seen those horses born – they were full brothers to his own father's fine team, Duke and Royal, from their brood mare, Mathilda. He'd laughed at their wobbly legs as they staggered to their feet for the first time, had watched their mother wash and nurse them, had taught them about halters and leads and oat mash – and missed them bitterly when they were sold. He loved that team as they loved him and he was not about to let them die. "Quiet, Sultan. Down, down. Quiet now,

King. Be still now lads. You're coming out with me. Don't make a fuss. We have to run for it. Quiet. Quiet." He never stopped talking and his familiar voice seemed to settle them somewhat. He wrapped his jacket around Sultan's eyes, slipped the leather strap around his neck and eased him out of the stall and into the yard where the great beast stood, still trembling and snorting. Adam brought King out in the same way, snatching two bridles from the harness racks as he passed. Two men took charge of them and led them down to the lower pasture, safely away from the barn.

The smoke was thickening and they were starting to cough but back they went. Liam headed straight for the back box stall to a terrified pair of Canadian horses – hard-working allies of the mighty Clydesdales in all the toughest jobs of the farm. Adam turned to the single stall where Princess, the gentle little mare that pulled the buggy and gave the youngsters bareback rides on Sundays, was whinnying and rearing in terror. Fearing her slashing hooves, he ran round to the front and climbed into her manger, which offered at least some protection. He peeled off his shirt and somehow got it tied over her eyes, loosening her rope and holding it firmly as he backed her out of the stall, talking to her every step of the way. At the door he grabbed his shirt and smacked her rump to set her running out of the barn while he turned back to help Liam with the team. Princess raced out into the night and several men reached for her but she wheeled suddenly, heading straight back into the barn. In her mind, it was home and it meant safety.

They heard Princess gallop back inside and both Adam and Liam went to her rescue. She was wild with fear but Adam snatched up a feed bag and again covered her eyes. Together they urged her toward the door, never letting go of her until one of the men could get a bridle on her and lead her, still bucking and whinnying, down to the lower pasture.

But now they had lost precious time. Liam turned back to the fire but his father was beside him, holding him back. "Ya can't go back in, Liam," he said. "Don't risk yer life, lad. Ye've already done all ya could."

But Liam fought him off. He wrapped his shirt around his own face and raced back inside. Adam rushed after him, driven by fear for the boy but also by his love of the horses. A wall of thick smoke almost drove him back, but Liam had already plunged into it. The beams overhead were crackling furiously and flecks of fire were beginning to fall into the stable. Adam heard Liam coughing and, following the sound, he found the lad on his knees at the entrance to the box stall. Seizing him by the shoulders, he half walked, half pulled him out the door, just in the nick of time. Fire was falling into the stable now, and they could hear the remaining horses screaming in terror and then in pain as they burned to death in their stall. The sounds tore at the hearts of the men who watched but they too were helpless. Beyond the smell of burning hay and wood, they began to smell burning flesh and several of them turned away to throw up. Adam steered Liam toward his father and the two men stood shoulder to shoulder with the lad, who was watching and listening in silent horror.

Little Willie, back from bedding down the cat family, heard the screams and smelled the smells. He began to cry, then to scream, his agony a fearsome counterpoint to the silent pain that all the neighbours felt for the horses trapped inside. Willie's father tried to pick him up and hold him but he was rigid and hysterical, his arms wrapped round his head and over his ears in a futile attempt to block out the dying cries of the horses. As if Willie's agony spoke for all of them, Adam turned to him and scooped him up, rigid as a statue, and headed up toward the house. But Olga Dietrich intercepted him, reaching out for the boy and slowly carrying him away from the fire and its terrible toll, into the house where she sat with him in the cozy kitchen, rocked him and sang little songs to him in German. Then she handed him over to his mother's arms where he fell asleep, still sobbing quietly. Rachel laid him gently on the couch and covered him with a quilt.

And from that day on, Willie did not speak.

Back at the barn, they watched, a grim little cluster of men, despairing that their efforts to quell the blaze had failed, a bit ashamed of not joining the rescue mission to save the horses. Their faces scorching, their sweat-dampened backs chill in the brisk November night, they shivered as the flames and sparks shot into the sky. There was a full moon that night but its light was pale before the brightness of the fire.

Overwhelmed with grief and his own helplessness, Adam moved away from the group and stood alone by the fence. His eyes still stinging from the smoke, he sensed the tears on his cheeks that no one must see. The men kept an eye on Adam but they could not approach him or offer any comfort. Alone there, in his ruined city suit, a lonely child grown into a lonely man, he had never felt so isolated in his life.

Suddenly another shout went up, this time from one of the lads. "Fire. Fire. The hen house." In their dazed concentration on the barn, the men had ignored the wooden pen, housing at least fifty fine Rhode Island Reds. A cinder that had landed on the cedar roof was already sputtering into flames. They could hear the frightened hens cackling wildly inside, imagining their frantic fluttering up to their roosts and down again, searching for safety. But no one wanted to go inside or release them into the confusion of the barn yard. Besides, their rooster, a giant old brute who weighed close to ten pounds, was known to attack and even once killed a fox that tried to make off with one of his plump brood. So in tacit agreement, they tackled that fire from the outside.

Instantly the bucket brigade formed again, with Olga Dietrich at the well, tirelessly pumping out bucket after bucket to be passed down the line. And this time they succeeded. They soaked the hen house and the roof and then kept a close eye on it in case another cinder fell.

Lenny Findlay looked around for Liam but he was nowhere to be seen. Then he remembered the horses he had saved, now down in the lower pasture. He walked down and let himself in the gate. Gleaming in the fire's glow, Sultan and King stood like golden statues, their long blond manes and tails shining in the flickering light. Liam was lying on Sultan's broad back, clutching his thick golden mane, sobbing his heart out. Sultan's head was bowed and his ears turned back to share the lad's grief. Beside him stood King, leaning against Sultan's shoulder with his broad forehead pressed against the boy's arm.

Lenny pulled off his heavy jacket and laid it gently over his son's bare back and left him there, figuring that those two great beasts whose lives he had saved, so faithful, gentle, loving, were more comfort to him than any human could be.

The barn burned quickly – it was full of straw on one side and hay on the other, and the wooden walls themselves were dry. Flames and sparks roared up into the sky and even as they stood and watched, helplessly, deeply sorry for the Donovans, the men were secretly thankful that it was not their own barn.

Liam hadn't come back so Lenny headed home to bring back bridles and leads and horse blankets. When he galloped back, struggling to control his own terrified horse, he hurried down to the lower pasture, slipped the bridles over the horses' ears, and laid the heavy horse blankets over their shivering backs. Liam still lay on Sultan's back and he stayed there, his slim young body sheltered by the same blanket.

Lenny and two other lads led the three horses back to the Findlay's barn and stabled them in a spare box stall. Velma Findlay, had brewed up a hefty batch of her warm oatmeal gruel laced with blackstrap molasses and other secret ingredients, rumoured to cure every ailment in man or beast. The horses sucked it up gratefully. In fact Sultan enjoyed it so much that he picked up his bucket and whacked it against the manger, demanding more. Liam joined the boys to brush and curry the horses, and comb out their golden manes and tails, talking gently to them. They brought them hay and straw and so put them to bed.

Back at the Donovan barn, the angry blaze was burning down. The heavy hand-hewn beams, a foot or more square, supporting the ceiling of the stables and the floors of the straw and hay barns, had fallen and continued to smoulder, occasionally flaring up stubbornly but soon dying again. Only the thick stone walls, taller than most men, remained standing.

The men fanned out across the barnyard and herded the squealing pigs and stolid cows into an empty drive shed, not as cozy as their pen in the barn, but better than a November night outside. Snug in their thick woolen coats, the sheep stayed outdoors. As dawn approached, several men grabbed buckets from the milk house and set to work milking the cows, perched on old cheese boxes because the milking stools had all burned. The cows were skittish and slow to let down their milk but at last the job was done.

Finally, well past dawn, they turned away. Up at the house, Rachel Donovan, exhausted and dazed, had hauled out the big copper boiler to heat water on the wood stove. Never was soap and water more welcome. The men sluiced their faces and hair and the steam from the boiler helped clear the smoke from their burning lungs. The neighbour ladies had pitched in to prepare a hearty breakfast – huge platters of fried potatoes, bacon and scrambled eggs, slabs of home-made bread slathered with butter and honey and Mrs. Donovan's strawberry jam, washed down by cups of hot strong tea.

It was over. They headed home to deal with their own chores, well fed but soul-saddened, wounded by the loss but blessed by the neighbourly goodness of everyone in the Valley. And they knew too that it wouldn't be long before there'd be a barn raising: neighbours helping neighbours to get back on their feet and the new Donovan barn ringing with the celebration of fiddles and the thump of dancing feet.

Few noticed that Adam had not joined them. Alone as always, he'd ridden home, carefully groomed and fed his still-skittish horse, ensured that his stable man was dealing with the chores, and, leaving his ruined suit in a sodden heap on the floor, crawled gratefully into bed. He was instantly up again, digging into his jacket pockets until he salvaged Julianna Brightson's crumpled calling card. Propping it up on his bedside lamp, he finally slept.

And little Willie, entrapped mutely in his grief, was more or less forgotten until Julianna arrived in the Valley.

CHAPTER 2

The Missing Bride

Well, sir. I'll tell you this. When Adam Chandler come home from his wedding without no bride, the buzz in our Valley was busier than a swarm of his own bees.

Adam Chandler took himself off to Toronto to marry a lady that none of us had ever clapped eyes on. Of course the folks in the Valley wasn't invited to the wedding – couldn't have gone anyways what with livestock to tend and crops to harvest and no money for the train. Nor the fancy togs ye'd need for showing up at a highfalutin' wedding. Not like Adam, who could hire men to do his chores and women to tend the house.

So we all stayed home and waited for him to get back and show off his bride.

But first, every family in the Valley was treated to a Wedding Announcement, printed up on heavy paper with fancy lettering. We still have ours after all these years and I'll bet nobody that got one ever threw it away.

Finally, two weeks after the wedding, off went his farm manager, name of George, in the fancy buggy with that high-stepping gray mare of his, and back comes Adam, looking very pleased with himself. With George. But no bride.

Well, now, I try to mind my own business. But sometimes curiosity gets the best of a fella. When I couldn't stand it no more, I trotted across the road to Adam's big place, to welcome him home.

Like always, he was polite and friendly. "We're all looking forward to makin' yer new bride welcome," I says, puttin' on my company voice. (Funny how ya go all lah-de-dah when you're talkin' to rich guys.)

So Adam says: "I'll be happy to see her myself."

I tried again. "I hope ya had a real nice wedding and honeymoon."

"Oh yes, indeed. Very small and quiet – just what we wanted. A few lovely days in Niagara Falls too. Amazing place, Lenny. You must pay it a visit. Millions of gallons of water pouring over those falls and tumbling on down the Niagara River. It should be one of the Seven Wonders of the World."

I was a lot more interested in the missing bride than I was in water falls, but we gabbed for a bit until finally I realized I wasn't going to get nowhere more so I said good day and plodded out his laneway.

"We'll be seeing you at the party," he yelled after me.

Party. What party? I couldn't hardly turn around and plod back so I went home and told my wife, Velma. She's a sensible woman – they say she can see around corners and this was for sure a dandy corner for her to take a peek at.

"Well, I agree, it's a peculiar way to start married life," she said. "But he don't seem upset, eh? There's got to be a reason. Maybe she missed the train. No, but then, he'd have missed it too. Maybe she hadn't finished her packing. She prolly has a heap of clothes and wedding presents galore.

"And this party. I'm guessin' they're havin' a party once she gets here and we're invited."

That seemed as far as we could go so Velma went ahead and informed the party line about what she knew so far. It only needed one call what with everybody in the Valley listening in. There was plenty of chat but they didn't figger nothin' out any better than my Velma did, except that it seemed a dang funny way to get married.

But Adam was different – and so was his bride. When Velma saw her chance, she ambled across the road to chat with Clara, the farm manager's wife. She was out in the garden pickin' beans. And it turned out that the bride was due to arrive in two days, to the train station at Paxton Ford, where Adam would meet her with the horse and buggy.

Well sir, I can tell you, the party line sizzled like sausages that night. Everybody in the Valley was waiting for Thursday and harvest be danged!

In fact it was remarkable how many of the men had to trim brush out by the roadside that day and how many of the women dilly-dallied by the clothes line pretending to check their wash for dampness but keeping an eye on the road. And finally we heard the sharp little hoof beats of Adam's pretty mare, Daisy, and the buggy come over the hill.

But we didn't see much. Adam tipped his hat to us but his bride was wrapped up in some sort of shawl that hid her face. We watched them pass by and that was that.

"She was wearing black," Gertie Biggar says to the party line. "Means she's in mournin'. What's she doin' gettin' married right after a funeral."

"Maybe somebody died at the wedding or right afterward. What if somebody dropped dead right there in the middle of the service. So she had to stay for the funeral and then wear mournin'." That was Lizzie Hawkins' pipin' up. Nice lady but thick as a maple plank.

And Gracie Morgan horned in too. "I seen in Eaton's catalogue where plenty of women in Toronto are wearin' black these days. It ain't just for funerals no more. It's stylish." Gracie seen herself as kinda our fashion expert, though to my eyes, she always looked like a witch, specially after she took to paintin' her face.

So the busy bees was buzzin' but we just had to wait and see.

Lenny

Julianna always dreamed of living in the country, far from the bustle and crush of the big city. But now as the carriage bumped along a swamp road that heaved and squirmed beneath its wheels, and the bushes seemed to reach out scrawny arms toward them, she wondered vaguely if she'd thought it all through.

Beside her was her handsome husband. She sneaked a glance up at his classic profile and again felt the thrill of love and physical attraction that had convinced her to say 'yes' when he popped the question. She knew he was moderately wealthy, college-educated and different from any other man she'd ever met – a deep and quiet man with a wicked wit. And, she thought to herself, he's tall, dark and handsome, with his six-foot frame, muscular and fit, his jet black hair, luxuriant moustache and piercing blue eyes. She settled back against the leather cushion, once again acknowledging the rightness of her decision.

"Sorry about the bumps," Adam explained as he reined in the lively little horse, slowing the carriage almost to a crawl. "We call this a corduroy road – like the corduroy velvet that ladies sometimes use for dresses," he added. "It's about the only way to build a road through a swamp – you lay the logs crosswise on the road, very close together, so the wheels bump over them as we go. Helps to keep you awake after a long trip. And it's certainly preferable to sinking up to our axles in swamp water." They laughed together.

Leaving the swamp behind, they trundled along smoother dirt roads sending up a long cloud of dust behind them. Now on either side, dense woods of long-limbed maples, their glorious autumn red and gold punctuated by tall black spruces and fluffy pines, reached over the road to form a mighty triumphal arch that seemed to welcome her to her new home. They gave Julianna a thrill of pleasure but a chill as well. She imagined wandering among the trees, losing her way, maybe encountering one of the black bears or mysterious antlered deer that Adam had told her roamed those woods. But at last they topped a steep hill and below them lay a view of the Valley so perfect that it took her breath away – rolling fields rimmed by zigzag rail and field stone fences, cows quietly grazing, wooden barns, weathered to a dark gray, with chicken coops and drive sheds nearby, and red brick houses set back from the road, snug amongst kitchen gardens and orchards, where bright red apples still glittered on the branches.

The day was golden. The fields where wheat and oats had recently been harvested were golden, the tall corn plants were golden, the warm September sun was golden. She felt a golden glow within herself – of happiness and anticipation for her new life, a chance to slough off all the grief and disappointments of the past few years. The rhythmic movement of the horse's gleaming haunches, the rocking of the carriage, the touch of Adam's body next to hers were delightful. So much to learn, she thought, so much to enjoy.

"Not far to go now," Adam commented, restraining the little mare who, knowing that home was nigh, aspired to cover the final mile to her stall and her oats box at breakneck speed. Julianna's knowledge of horses was limited to the tired nags that pulled milk and bakery wagons along city streets. They were dependable and intelligent enough to know which houses to stop at and wait patiently while milk or bread was delivered to the door, then clop onward to the next customer without so much as a cluck from the driver. But this sleek animal, so trim and neat, with its delicate feet and peculiar colour was a whole new experience. "Adam, this horse is such a strange colour," she commented. "I've never seen anything like it before."

"Daisy's a blue roan," he replied. "Equal parts of white and in this case gray hair in her coat produce that lovely blue tone. If she were a sorrel, she'd be a strawberry roan; a dark chestnut is called a lilac roan. Then there's the honey roan which is palomino – the ones with blond tails and manes. I like the odd colours. In fact, I like odd horses."

"Adam, why does she have those splashes of solid gray on her back?"

"When I bought Daisy at the horse auction, she was a sad broken-down horse, almost impossible to handle. She was terrified of people, kicking, rearing. That's why she was up for sale. The fool that owned her had given up on her. He'd tried to break her by brute force. And she had deep wounds on her back where he'd whipped her. When they finally healed over, only the gray hair grew back so they show as solid colour."

"But she seems so gentle now," Julianna remarked, remembering how the little horse had nuzzled Adam's hand as he adjusted her bridle at the station. "How did you manage that?"

'It's a long slow process," he explained, "but kindness can work wonders. You talk to them endlessly. You never ever startle them or frighten them in any way.

You spoil them a bit with treats like apples or carrots and try to touch them as soon and as often as they'll allow it. You never use a whip – in fact I had a horse once that would fly into a panic at the very sight of a whip. You treat them with respect and one day they come to realize that you're a friend. But the problem with a damaged horse like this one is that they always carry their fear deep in their hearts. They never completely regain their trust. And there's always a danger that something will suddenly frighten them and they'll rear or kick or take the bit in their mouth and run away."

Hmm, Julianna thought. Another challenge. Horses are the mainstay of country life. So I'd better start learning how to handle them.

Adam interrupted her thoughts. "Here we go, Julie. Running the gantlet. I see some of the neighbours out pretending to work but they're really watching out for you," he added with a grin. "There's not much excitement here in the Valley so right now, you, my dear Julie, are the centre of attention."

Suddenly feeling shy, Julianna shrank back and adjusted her shawl over her head. Adam touched his hat to the attentive neighbours but steadfastly headed for home, much to Daisy's relief and his neighbours' disappointment.

"Our neighbours are good folks," Adam remarked. "You may think they're nosy at first and a bit rustic but they take care of one another. I just hope they don't decide to do a chivaree."

"Chivaree? Do they disapprove of us?"

"Oh no, it's just a bit of tom-foolery to welcome a couple back from their honeymoon. What makes you think they'd disapprove of us?"

"Well, there are chivarees in England and Europe," Julie explained. "It's a very old custom that only happens these days in small villages where they want to shame people who've made an unfortunate marriage – or no marriage at all."

"No disapproval here," Adam replied. "It's all horseplay though the brides and grooms dread it. The neighbours wait until the lights are out and then they sneak into the front yard with anything they can find to make a noise – cow bells or whistles or old sauce pans that they beat with sticks. They start making a huge racket and they drag the bride and groom out of the house, preferably still in their nightshirts, to dance on the lawn. There's always a fiddler to keep the music going. Everybody has a bit of fun and then they present the couple with a gift, maybe a quilt or a pair of chairs. And off they go home."

Julianna chuckled. "What a relief. I'd hate to start off on the wrong foot."

Adam reined in the eager little horse and turned into a long laneway lined with huge maple trees, just beginning to display their rich autumn reds and golds. Set far back was the big brick house, where wild cucumbers and morning glories climbed the white railings of a broad verandah, creating a deep cool green haven. Julianna just had time to imagine curling up on the big hammock with a good book. "It's a dream house," she proclaimed.

"You're about to meet two exceptional people," Adam announced. "They came here to work for me…to manage the place…and they've become my best friends."

Two figures appeared at the side door and hurried down to the carriage. "Here they are – our right hand people," Adam commented jovially. He helped Julianna down from the high step. "George Cooper…and Clara Cooper… my wife, Julianna Chandler." She smiled and extended her hand. They seemed hesitant but they shook it, each in turn, and then turned their attention to the baggage. (Later Clara told her that no lady of the house in England had ever offered to shake hands with them.)

While the luggage vanished through the side door, Adam led Julie to the big front door and then suddenly scooped her up and carried her over the threshold. He held her there, gazing into her eyes and then kissed her deeply and warmly. "Welcome home, my love," he said.

The house was as inviting inside as out. In the big front hall, she saw a tall coat rack fashioned with a seat, a long mirror and a receptacle for umbrellas. The parlour on the right looked as parlours should: stiff, formal and rarely used. But to the left, the sitting room beckoned with deep couches and a round centre table, perfect for spreading out books, maps or afternoon tea. "Want to stop and get unpacked?" Adam asked. "Or continue the tour?"

"Oh I'd love to see the rest of the house," she exclaimed. "It's lovely." He led the way to the dining room where a long white-clothed table was ringed by a dozen chairs and ornately carved cabinets decked with blue and white dishes lined the walls. Beside the window overlooking the lawn, a small table and two chairs hinted at intimate breakfasts. The kitchen came next, with its big black wood burning stove and a scrubbed wooden table where loaves of fresh-baked bread were cooling, emitting a scent that sent Julianna's stomach into growls of hunger. In the adjoining pantry, well-stocked shelves and deep bins for flour, oatmeal, bread and other staples testified to the household's comfortable status.

Next to the pantry was the washroom. Adam showed her the trapdoor leading to a deep cistern under the floor and the creaking iron hand pump, providing a steady supply of water, heated on the wood stove, for washing and laundry. But water for drinking and cooking, he explained, came from the outdoor well in hefty buckets that had to be lugged into the house.

Beyond the kitchen, spanning the whole length of the house was the summer kitchen, headquarters during summer months for cooking and laundry, to keep the heat out of the house. One end of that space was given over to honey production – a crank-operated separator, and tables equipped with huge trays and vicious-looking knives for capping the combs so the honey could be released.

Finally at the back of the house, they peeked into a massive woodshed. "Come winter, it'll be packed to the roof with split wood, to keep all the stoves going until spring," Adam explained.

Such hard work, Julianna thought to herself. Hauling logs, cutting wood. She caught herself nostalgically recalling the coal-burning furnace in her father's house in Toronto. Country living is for the strong, she decided.

But she had no time for memories. From under the back steps, there emerged a massive black dog, the biggest dog she had ever seen. She found herself shrinking back behind Adam but the dog neither barked nor snarled. With his vast brush of black tail wagging briskly, he greeted Adam with a gentle snuffle and a paw in the hand. "Well now, Fogo," Adam said. "Say hello to my beautiful new bride." He turned to Julianna. "Give him your hand, Julie. He's very friendly." Tentatively she extended her hand. The dog solemnly filled it with his huge paw and gazed up into her face. "How do you do, Fogo," she managed, feeling a bit silly about shaking hands with a dog.

"He's huge," she gasped. "What kind of dog is he?"

"He's a Newfoundlander," Adam explained. "From the Dominion of Newfoundland, down east. I met a breeder at the Livestock Fair in Toronto – the same fair where you and I first met. So I bought a puppy from him and here he is. He's actually a water dog – he even has webbed feet – and this breed is famous for saving people from drowning. Though we don't have much demand for that here on the farm.

"He's a fine chap," Adam added. "If you get hurt, he'll sound the alarm, but he only barks in emergencies. If anyone threatens you, he'll attack, and at 160 pounds he does tend to strike terror into the hearts of villains. If you go out in the woods and get lost, he'll find you and bring you home. He's the smartest animal on this whole farm. He's a working farm dog but he'll be your best friend."

Oh my, Julianna thought. My first day here and my education is already advancing. She gave Fogo a tentative pat on the head and earned a grateful wag of his bushy tail.

The house was handsome, but not lavish. Clara Cooper, speaking with an appealing English accent, showed Julianna up a broad centre staircase which on the left opened to the master bedroom wing, and on the right, to four more bedrooms, two of which served as the Coopers' sitting room and bedroom. She opened the vast clothes cupboard and offered to help unpack. "I'm fine with the unpacking," Julie responded "but" she paused shyly, "I need to use the toilet."

"Of course," Clara smiled. "I do apologize. I should have thought of that." She opened the door of a small washstand and revealed a lidded chamber pot that matched the blue and gold ewer and bowl on top. "Here you are. It's the closest we can come to indoor plumbing, I'm afraid. Now I'm off to get you some hot water so you can freshen up before dinner." She picked up the pitcher and exited discreetly, returning minutes later with steaming hot water.

"Supper is usually at about six," she announced. "We're very informal here so don't feel you need to 'dress' for dinner. Just come on down to the dining room or the kitchen when you're ready."

"Mrs. Cooper," Julie called her back. "Where do I empty the chamber pot?"

"Oh just cover it and tuck it away. My helper comes in each morning and either she or I will empty it when we do up the rooms."

Julianna was uncomfortable. The idea of Adam's good friend emptying her toilet slops was offensive. 'I have a lot to learn about country life,' she told herself, 'especially doing household chores without running water.'

Perched on the bed, she contemplated her new circumstances. Her thoughts turned briefly to the flush toilets in her father's house, the taps running with hot water and the warmth from the basement furnace. Such a big change – farms and forests, blue horses and hand-shaking dogs, wood-burning stoves, coal oil lamps, chamber pots, for heaven sake. How would she cope? And where would she fit in?

Julianna had always tended to tackle life on the run. "Slow down, dear, or you'll have permanent scars on your knees from so many tumbles," her mother used to admonish her.

As a child living in Oxford and later Berlin, where her father joined medical teams that studied malaria and venereal diseases, Juliana was quick to acquire languages and make friends. But her mother's longing for home finally brought the family back to Toronto and the big house on Jamison Avenue where Dr. Brightson opened his medical practice and clinic while maintaining a small research laboratory near the University.

The house buzzed with the energy of two young people and their friends along with the conversation, commitment and arguments of medical and scientific colleagues, who regularly settled in around the dining room table for fine meals and lively debate.

But when Julianna was seventeen, two tragedies struck. Pneumonia claimed her mother and Europe's war killed her only brother, burying her in a pit of black depression that blotted out school, friends and her own family. Later she was to realize and regret that her self-absorption had excluded her father whose grief was compounded by the bitter awareness that despite his medical skills, he was unable to save the lives of the two people he loved best. Father and daughter walked parallel paths of dark isolation, occasionally penetrated by Dr. Brightson's sister, who sized up the situation and decided to take action.

Auntie Margaret had been a force in the Brightson's lives since Julie could remember. She lived directly across the street from her brother and, now retired from teaching, she frequently visited to help out in the medical clinic or take charge of the children or just for a pleasant chat and a cup of tea.

She chose the garden as her first antidote to Julianna's depression. "Julie, dear," she called one day. "I desperately need some help in the garden. Could you come over and lend a hand? Spring is just around the corner and I'm finding the garden a bit too much to handle."

Julie listlessly joined her to dig and snip where she was instructed to do so. "This rose bush," Auntie Margaret pointed out. "It's so very special and it needs extra care because it's the one that your Mother gave me for my birthday two years ago."

Julie remembered that rose – a deep pink tea rose that even in its first year had produced an array of fragrant blooms. Together, they approached it reverently and examined each twig, trimming back those with blackened tips, removing one that seemed to have died back to the root. Gently they worked the soil at its roots and added fertilizer.

"Horse manure – best food for roses," Auntie Margaret stated.

"Where did you get it?" Julianna asked.

"The milkman's horse," her aunt replied. "Straight from the source."

Julie imagined her neat little aunt, armed with broom and dustpan, trotting along behind the milk wagon, sweeping up horse manure in the street and she smiled and then chuckled, for the first time in far too long.

As they stood before the rose bush, Auntie Margaret slipped her arm around Julie's waist. "Now we have something beautiful to help us remember your lovely

Mother," she said and Julie turned to her, sobbing, the memories overwhelming her. But the blanket of darkness had been penetrated. She visited the rose bush every day, watered it as the earth demanded, fussed over each bud and carried home a single rose every few days.

"I hope the roses don't bring back too many sad memories for your poppa," Auntie Margaret ventured. "He has been suffering so much." The insight struck Julianna with the force of a blow. Yes, her father had also been suffering too and she had done nothing to help him.

At that instant she decided to become a doctor, to work alongside her father in his practice and his research, to somehow compensate for her failure to offer emotional support when he needed it most. He greeted her decision with surprise and then reserved enthusiasm.

"I'd be proud to have you as a colleague," he told her. "But be warned. There's a mighty wall of discrimination against women in the medical profession and you could be bruised when you bang into it."

And she was.

Some cited her poor marks in her final school year, the year that in her mind she called the 'double-death' year. Some replied that medicine was not a suitable profession for women. The University of Toronto, on which she had pinned her hopes, suggested that she transfer her application to the Faculty of Domestic Science, a more suitable place for a woman. Some simply refused her without explanation. But the sum of her efforts to enter medical school was zero. Inspired by the newly founded Women's College Hospital, she dreamed of being part of its team of women doctors treating women patients. But without that elusive degree, she was cut adrift.

"Degree or no degree, I'll be glad to have your help right here at home," her father exclaimed. "I can't grant you a framed certificate, but I can teach you more here in our practice than you'll learn at medical school. Work along with me, Julie, and you can re-apply next year."

It was a mixed practice, serving not only the comfortably affluent population of west Toronto, but some nearby working class and slum areas too. Of course those latter categories, often money-strapped, waited for dire emergencies before turning up at the doctor's door and frequently had no funds with which to pay. But they were never turned away and Julie came to realize the depth of her father's commitment to health care for all. She also began to view the plight of women, especially poor women, as the lowest in the pecking order of both medicine and politics.

Julianna met Adam two years later as they sat side-by-side at a gala dinner celebrating the opening of the Winter Livestock Fair in Toronto. Her father served on the board of directors; Adam represented the farmers of his county. It was a pleasant evening and Dr. Brightson suggested that Adam pay them a visit when he was next in the city. Their friendship grew. Adam and Julie began exchanging letters and finally realized that their friendship had turned into love.

And now here she was, his bride, queen of his heart, seriously wondering if she really belonged in this strange new world. Time would tell.

CHAPTER 3

A School for Willie

We wasn't too bookish nor schoolish in them days. Farmers needed strong backs more'n readin' an' writin'. The schools was closed for July and August to let the youngsters help on the farms but many a lad left school in April and stayed home til October to help his pa with the crops. That's why the girls got better educated than the boys – they was in school longer. But if the ma got sick or died, the oldest girl always left school to tend to the household and the younger ones.

We had a school house within walking distance of most farms in the Valley and one teacher taught all eight levels. Teachers never lasted long in our school – they always hired the youngest ones that never taught before and once they learned their trade, they high-tailed it to a bigger school.

Some teachers was meaner than others but we was taught to spare the rod and spoil the child. We'd all had the whip applied to our behinds at home and the strap to our hands at school. But we never thought nuthin' of it – school was for learnin' to read and write, whatever it took.

Or so we figured, until little Willie Donovan, who still couldn't talk, started school.

Lenny

When Willie turned six, it was time to go to school. His older sister, Betsy, took him by the hand and walked him to the one-room schoolhouse where all the youngsters from the valley were taught by a single teacher.

That year, the new teacher was Miss Alberta Malone, a recent graduate of the six-month course that passed for teacher training. Only slightly older than her oldest student and considerably smaller than several of the grade eight lads whose commitment to book learning was ephemeral at best, she was nervous on her first day. But as she surveyed her new domain with its wall of blackboards, the cast iron wood stove, the smelly oiled floor and the battered desks, she concentrated on one piece of wisdom she'd learned at teachers' college: "You MUST maintain order and discipline, to ensure your authority over such a large group. You must be stern and unsmiling, always insisting that students obey your instructions. You must always be prepared to apply the strap for bad behaviour." She had already located the strap – in the top right hand drawer of her desk. She took a deep breath, grasped the bell with both hands and headed for the door to summon the children inside.

Betsy took full advantage of her big sister role to lecture Willie on rules and etiquette as they walked to school. "You'll have to sit with the little kids," she advised him crossly. "That's the small seats up at the front. I sit with the big kids. You mustn't make any noise in school and you mustn't kick your seat or squirm. Teachers don't like that." She didn't need to warn him against talking out loud – Willie didn't talk.

Before long, Christine Dunning caught up with them. She was two years older than Willie but younger than Betsy. "I'll be sitting close to you, Willie, so don't worry. I'll take care of you," she promised.

When the teacher rang the bell, they deposited Willie in the boys' lineup and moved over to the girls. The children began to shuffle into the school but Miss Malone's sharp command startled them. "March," she yelled. "March like soldiers. Heads up, shoulders back, pick up your feet." They did their best, aware of the teacher's unfriendly surveillance but not sure how to obey her orders.

Inside, Christine showed Willie where the youngest children sat and she chose a nearby desk for herself. He sat down and began to study the underside of his desk but she reminded him to stand beside his desk until the teacher arrived at the front of the classroom.

So far, so good. "Good morning, children," the teacher began. "Good morning, Miss," the children mumbled.

"My name is Miss Malone. From now on you will say 'good morning, Miss Malone'." There was silence.

"So you may start by greeting me correctly, right now," she snapped.

"Good morning, Miss Malone," her students intoned.

"That's better. Now I want each of you to stand and tell me your name and age and what grade level you are starting. We'll start over here with the highest levels."

One by one, the students rose and, some shy, some cocky, some nervous, answered the roll call. All except Willie. When his turn came, he stood obediently, but said not a word.

"Speak up," the teacher snapped. "You have a voice. Now use it."

Willie gazed at the teacher, his throat muscles moving spasmodically, his face registering a mixture of fear and confusion, but no words emerged.

"Name, age, form." Miss Malone's voice sharpened. Willie looked from her to his feet and back again.

She marched over to his desk, towering menacingly over him.

"You will obey my instructions NOW or you will feel the strap," she snarled.

Christine's hand shot up but the teacher ignored her, still glaring at Willie.

"Please Miss," Christine intervened. "Willie can't talk."

"Be quiet," Miss Malone roared. "I did not give you permission to speak."

"But Miss," Christine persisted. "He hasn't been able to talk since their barn burned. He. . . "

"Be quiet," the teacher shot her a venomous glance. "When I want your opinion, I'll ask for it."

"His name is Willie Donovan, Miss. He's six and he's in grade one," Christine ventured bravely.

"Come here – both of you," Miss Malone ordered.

She marched them back to her desk and opened the dreaded top drawer. "Hold out your hands," she ordered. Christine obeyed and received two sharp cracks on each hand. Willie stepped back and hid his hands behind his back. "Hold out your hands or you'll get even worse," the teacher threatened. He looked at Christine. There were tears in her eyes as she rubbed her sore hands together in a vain attempt to reduce the pain but she nodded to him and gestured to hold out his hands. The teacher's blows were swift and sharp – two smacks to each hand – and Willie burst into tears, sobbing loudly.

"Well, at least you can bawl out loud," Miss Malone taunted. "So now you can talk. Go back to your desk and tell me your name, your age and your form. Now!"

Back at their desks, both children wept. Christine's tears spilled silently down her cheeks, Willie sobbed. But he did not speak.

Miss Malone pointed to a tall wooden stool that stood in the corner to the left of her desk. A hand-lettered sign identified it as 'The Stupid Stool'. "I see," she barked. "So if you refuse to obey, you'll just have to go sit on the stupid stool and think it over. Come on, up here. Face to the wall."

Willie obediently stumbled up to the stool and sat.

The classroom was silent, except for his sobs. Over with the bigger students, Willie's sister Betsy kept her head down – she had no intention of crossing the teacher. Besides, she was quietly relishing Willie's punishment – he got all the attention at home. Christine too kept her peace. She wanted to run to Willie and comfort him but she knew the result would be more strapping for both of them.

"We'll start with arithmetic," the teacher instructed. "You there," she ordered the biggest boys. "Take these arithmetic problems and copy them on the blackboard. And mind you write good n' clear."

She moved to the blackboard that faced the newest students and began to write the numbers from one to ten with chalk. Then pointing to each number with a long wooden pointer, she read off the numbers and instructed the children to repeat the words after her. "One," they intoned obediently. "Two. . . Three."

"One, two, three, four, five, six, seven, eight, nine, ten," a merry older boy suddenly rattled off. "Quiet," the teacher commanded. ''Come up here."

Petey Smith, now scared, stumbled to the blackboard. "You are going to write this one hundred times to remind you to speak only when you're spoken to," Miss Malone explained curtly. She wrote 'I will not talk in school' on the board and handed Petey some chalk. "Get on with it," she ordered, pointing toward the black board. Awkwardly, he began to write. His punishment lasted most of the morning, frequently interrupted as the teacher counted his repetitions and erased them with a brush, admonishing him to hurry up or he'd get no lunch.

"Now juniors take your slates and copy these numbers," the teacher ordered. Little hands awkwardly grasped chalk and tried valiantly to replicate the numbers on the board. "Middle grades – I want each of you to sit with a junior and help them learn their numbers. The rest of you can get to work on the arithmetic problems you've just been given."

Willie was still perched uncomfortably on the high stool. The teacher continued to ignore him.

The morning wore on with older students coaching younger ones, and correcting their mistakes as Miss Malone tried to determine the level of arithmetical expertise amongst the seniors. It was approximately the same as her own but she barked and blustered her displeasure to ensure that they did not realize that their ignorance and her ignorance were about equal.

At last she announced that it was lunch time. Willie was afraid to climb down from his stool but Christine again defied the teacher. "Come on, Willie," she called. "It's time for lunch." The teacher eyed them both balefully but said nothing.

Outside with their tin lunch buckets, the children split up – the girls sitting on the grass beneath a huge oak tree, the boys further off under a maple. Willie wasn't sure where to go but Christine motioned for him to join her with the group of girls. But he wasn't safe there either. As the boys headed for their chosen spot, a safe distance from the contaminating influence of girls, their taunts began. "Yer brother's simple," one of them yelled at Betsy. "Willie Witless," another yelled and then warming to his own brilliance turned it into a rhyme that the other boys were quick to pick up: "Witless Willie. Witless Willie. Comes to school and acts real silly."

Christine moved closer to Willie and whispered: "Don't listen to them. They're the silly ones." Finally hunger triumphed over bullying and they moved on. She noticed that Willie was fidgeting and whispered: "Do you need to pee?" He was shy but he nodded yes. She took his hand and led him to the outhouses behind the school. "You go to that one, Willie. It's for boys. This one's for the girls."

Willie came back, visibly relieved, and they finished lunch. Before the bell rang, they lined up at the iron pump in the yard and took turns drinking cold water from a tin cup that hung there for all to use. Then once again, they filed solemnly through the cloak room, empty of coats and scarves in the warmth of a balmy September, and back to their seats. Willie looked up at Christine and pointed to the 'stupid stool' but she nodded to him to go back to his own seat.

Now it was time for reading. Those who could already read were directed to their school readers, which contained collections of action stories and cautionary tales, designed to teach young minds the difference between right and wrong. One girl from grade eight was assigned to read to the primary grades. Christine, who was an enthusiastic reader, was leafing listlessly through her book when she noticed that Willie was fidgeting again. His discomfort became more and more pronounced and he looked round at her worriedly and gestured in the direction of the outhouse. "Pee?" Christine mouthed the word soundlessly. Willie nodded.

Christine raised her hand and after a suitable delay, the teacher recognized her. "Please Miss," she said, "Willie needs to be excused."

"He didn't ask me," Miss Malone replied. "Cat got his tongue?"

She stared at Willie and he nodded vigorously, pointing toward the toilet. "Speak up," the teacher ordered. "If you want to be excused, you raise your hand and then say 'Please Miss Malone, may I be excused.'"

Willie stood but he was silent.

Miss Malone was adamant. "Sit down until you're ready to ask properly," she snarled.

Willie sat. Christine ached for him, seeing his look of desperation. Suddenly he began to cry again, his whole being suffused with shame as the urine trickled down his bare legs to form a puddle on the floor. The youngsters around him began to point and giggle.

The teacher leapt forward like an attack dog. She was shaking with rage.

"This is disgusting," she roared. "Didn't your mother potty-train you? Stand up."

Head hanging, shoulders slumped, Willie stood for all the school to view his disgrace.

"You're going to clean up your own mess," Miss Malone persisted. "Go and get something from the cloakroom."

Willie stumbled out to the cloak room, still blinded by his tears but he could find nothing. Tapping her foot in frustration, the teacher glared at the students, scaring them into silence. Finally, she could bear it no longer.

"Christine, since you're so fond of this…creature, go and find him and help him clean up his mess."

That's precisely what Christine wanted to do so she hurried to the cloakroom, found a pile of newspapers intended for fire starting, and gave Willie a handful of them. Back at his desk, she helped him mop up the puddle, and bundle the soggy newspapers, which they took back to the cloakroom, stuffing them into the iron stove. She took hold of his hand and they stood together for a few moments, steeling themselves to return to the classroom. Suddenly Christine turned, snatched her own and Willie's lunch buckets from the shelf and headed out the door with Willie in tow.

When she heard the outer door slam, the teacher rushed toward the cloakroom. But Christine, still holding Willie's hand, was already running for home. "You get back here right now," the teacher screamed. "Christine…Willie…you get back here."

The children heard her but they fled all the same. When they were out of sight of the school, they slowed to a walk, panting and scared. ''Willie, we're likely going to get it when our folks find out," Christine warned. "but I'm going to tell them what that teacher is really like so maybe they won't be so mad at us." They scuffed along in silence for a while.

"Miss Wainwright was our teacher last year," Christine recalled wistfully. "She was real nice and everybody loved her. She used to play the piano and sing with us and she taught us lots of songs. Like Row Row Row Your Boat. Do you know that one?" Willie shook his head.

"I'll sing it for you. It goes like this:

'Row row row your boat, gently down the stream.'

And immediately she noticed a change in Willie. He began to march in step with the music.

"Merrily, merrily, merrily, merrily, life is but a dream," she continued, matching her steps to his.

She sang it again and again.

And so with the song to comfort them, they marched bravely, hand in hand, all the way home.

Retribution

They was a rough bunch, them Dunnings. Everybody in the Valley knew they used their fists and their boots to think with cuz they didn't have no brains. But nobody interfered. In them days, we was taught that family troubles should stay in the family. We might gossip about them behind their backs but we'd never butt in. If men hit their wives or their youngsters, they was just bein' men and heads of the house – it was none of our business. Besides, we was brought up to obey our parents and the teacher and feel the strap if we didn't. And nobody wanted to risk being on the wrong side of Old Joe and his son. Only Rachel Donovan had the nerve to stand up to them.

If you'd asked me then, I'd have said Christine's parents was in the right and Rachel Donovan was wrong to interfere. Well, it's took me a lot of years but now I know, I'd have judged wrong.

Lenny

Willie and Christine walked right past her folks' place and on to Willie's, without attracting any attention. When they reached the Donovan place, Christine was about to knock, but Willie walked in and Christine followed, remembering that it was, after all, his home. His mother was in the kitchen and she was startled to see them. "Willie…Chrissy…what's wrong?"

"I brought Willie home," Christine replied bravely. "Mrs. Donovan, that new teacher is so mean. She gave us both the strap because Willie couldn't say his name and she got mad and when I tried to tell her about him, she got mad at me too. And she made him sit on the stupid stool all morning and then she wouldn't let him go to the backhouse and so he wetted and so I brought him home." She was breathless from the urgency of her story.

"Why don't you both wash your hands and sit at the table," Rachel suggested. "Willie, I'll get fresh clothes for you and then you can have some cookies and milk and tell me all about it."

Christine retold her story in more detail and Mrs. Donovan listened intently, asking a few questions and looking upset. Christine's heart beat faster, fearing she was the target. But Mrs. Donovan reached over and took each child's hand. "Chrissy, thank you, for helping Willie. You were very brave. Willie, I'm sorry that your first day at school was so awful. And I'm so sorry you both got the strap. Neither one of you deserved it. I'll talk this over with Mr. Donovan tonight and we'll see what we can do.

"Now . . . Do you think your parents will be angry with you over this?"

Christine suddenly looked worried. In the urgency of saving Willie, she had given little thought to her parents' reaction but now the prospect of her father's wrath was daunting.

"I guess so," she said. "I'd better be getting home and get my chores done."

"We'll come with you, Chrissy," Mrs. Donovan offered. "We need to talk to your mother about this teacher and figure out what to do."

They set off back up the road toward the Dunning farm. Christine no longer felt like singing but Willie tugged at her arm and showed how smartly he could march.

"Row row row your boat," she began weakly.

And Rachel chimed in. **"Gently down the stream."**

'**Merrily merrily merrily merrily, life is but a dream,"** they sang together, holding hands and marching.

Christine's steps slowed as she neared home. Rachel could see that she was scared. "Don't worry, Chrissy," Rachel encouraged her. "When we explain to your mother what happened, she's sure to be understanding."

But Christine knew better. As Willie had done at his house, she opened the door and walked in, followed by Willie and his mother. "Yer home early," Mrs. Dunning said, wasting no time on a greeting. She glanced up and saw Mrs. Donovan and Willie. "Good day," she said coldly.

"Good day to you, Mrs. Dunning," Rachel Donovan smiled at her. "I'm sorry for this surprise visit but there was some trouble at school today, and I wanted to talk it over with you." Rita Dunning wiped her hands on her apron and gestured to them to sit down at the kitchen table.

"So …?" she asked, staring fiercely at Christine. "Are you in trouble?"

Rachel Donovan didn't wait for Christine to reply. "I think it's that new teacher, Miss Malone, that's in trouble," she commented. And she recounted the chain of events that Chrissy had told her. "From the sound of it, she's very strict – 'way too strict especially with the younger children. And giving two of them the strap on the very first day seems extreme."

"They prolly deserved it," Mrs. Dunning avowed. Without warning she reached across and swatted Christine's face. "What did you do to upset her?"

"I…I wanted to help Willie," Christine was on the verge of tears. "He can't talk but the teacher said he had to."

"Who told you to look after Willie?" her mother scolded. "He has a big sister, doesn't he? You stay away from the likes of Willie Donovan and let his sister look after him."

"Mrs. Dunning, what do you mean by the likes of Willie Donovan?" Rachel enquired.

"I mean it's not smart for her to hang around somebody that's mental," Christine's mother snapped. "Whatever's wrong with your kid is your problem, not Chrissy's and not mine."

At that moment, Old Joe walked into the kitchen and stopped short when he saw the group and heard Rita's sharp rebuke. "What's all this," he growled. Rachel tried to tell him but Rita shouted her down.

"That Willie," she yelled, pointing accusingly at the now-terrified little boy, "got in trouble his first day of school and Chrissy decided to help him out and she got in trouble too. They both got the strap – first day of school."

Joe's response was as swift and sharp as his wife's had been. His blow to Christine's head knocked her off her chair and onto the gritty floor. She was too stunned even to cry.

Rachel was horrified. She rose to her feet and confronted Joe. "What do you think you're doing," she demanded. "Chrissy was not at fault and neither was Willy. Chrissy was very brave to defend Willy against the teacher and very kind to him. She does not deserve to be punished."

Joe's fists clenched as he stared angrily at Rachel. "Mind your own damn business, woman," he shouted. "Ya can just get yerself and yer idiot brat the hell out of here and stay out."

"My son is not an idiot," Rachel replied hotly. "He is in fact a very bright little boy who is unable to speak. And your sweet little daughter was a very kind and helpful girl to try to help him through his first day of school."

Chrissy had picked herself up off the floor and climbed back into her chair but now, Rachel's comment reminded Joe of her presence.

He struck her again but she ducked her head and the blow caught her narrow shoulder. Still it hurt and the tears began. "I'll teach ya to waste yer time with mentals," Joe raged. He slapped her again and again and when she finally fell to the floor, he kicked her in the back.

Rachel couldn't believe what she was seeing. "Stop it," she screamed at him. "Leave her alone this minute. What kind of man beats a tiny girl? You are nothing but a bully." She stood over Christine, blocking her father's rage.

Red faced and breathing hard, Joe advanced on her, towering several inches and many more pounds over her. "Yes, bully," Rachel challenged him. "It's easy to win an argument with your fists and your boots, especially if you're bullying someone smaller than yourself. That's what cowards do. Beat up women and children but run away when they have to face someone their own size. You're a disgusting coward."

Joe stared at her furiously. Then he turned abruptly and headed for the door. "Coward," Rachel shouted after him.

Then she turned to Rita. "I'm sorry you are both so upset, Mrs. Dunning, especially since I firmly believe that Chrissy has told us the truth. I hope that you'll stand up for her now and help me deal with that teacher. And I hope you'll see to her bruises – your husband may have hurt her badly."

She took Willie's hand and headed for the door, filled with misgivings for Chrissy. "Good afternoon, Mrs. Dunning," she said politely. "Please look after your daughter."

As the door shut, Rita Dunning turned on Chrissy. "I'll look after ya all right," she exploded. "Shut up your blubber and get to work or ye'll get more of the same from your pa. Get that wood box filled – and two pails of water from the well. And then ye'll feed the hens and gather the eggs, and mind ya don't crack any. And ye'll empty all the slop pots and clean the lamp chimneys. And after supper ye'll wash the dishes and dry them. That'll teach ya to take up with mentals and upset the teacher." She gave Christine a quick cuff on the head and the little girl winced in pain. Her eyes were already turning black.

She shuddered as she wondered how she would get through the next day.

CHAPTER 5

The Welcome Party

We was all fairly bustin' to lay eyes on the new bride. The party line was never busier what with every woman in the Valley putting in her two cents worth. But we just had to wait a bit.

It seemed an eternity but it was more like two weeks until an invitation came to every single house, a real fancy printed card, inviting every man, woman and child, to a reception in honour of Mrs. Adam Chandler on Saturday, September 18, at four o'clock at the Chandler residence. It was harvest time and we knew that frost was not far off. But the women still found the time, late at night when they should of been in bed, to fuss with their old dresses and add a flower or a ribbon to an old hat to make it fit for such a fine occasion. And although nothing was said about bringing sandwiches and cakes to the table, they set to work whipping up their best treats, because that's how it was done in our Valley.

The great day was sunny and the evening was balmy though a bit cool, perfect for a party. We lived right across the road so we walked over to the Chandler house, but some folks drove their buggies and parked them all down the lane with their shafts lifted like antlers. And they slipped the horses' bits and tethered them to posts along the laneway, where the grass was thick for grazing.

Adam and his missus waited for us at the verandah steps standing in a kind of archway of them purple flowers – yeah, that's it, morning glories. They looked like something out of one of them high-class magazines – two really handsome people in front of their fancy house.

And we could see – well, I sure could – that she was the most beautiful woman I ever clapped eyes on in my life. Her face was as perfect as a picture and her silky dress never tried to hide her figure. Her effect on me was peculiar – me, married twenty years to a fine hard-working woman who was mother of my two sons and two daughters. Me, a solid citizen who had learned young and thoroughly that I must not covet another man's wife. I knew men who would try their luck with any female they encountered, neighbour or not. But such a thing dishonoured the neighbourhood and even more the man who was guilty of it. And yet...

Well, enough said.

Lenny

The neighbours approached shyly. The women in their print dresses, so carefully updated for this occasion, suddenly felt a bit dowdy and the men in their suits and starched shirts that looked too snug and too hot, secretly longed to peel off their jackets and loosen their vests. Later they did just that.

Meanwhile, they had come to meet the exotic Mrs. Chandler at last, and there she was, smiling and waiting for them. She was tall, almost as tall as Adam, and slim as a willow. She wore a silky dress that reached down to her pretty shoes. Its russet colour picked up the colour of her hair – deep golden braids, like burnished bronze, encircling her head like a shining crown. Her eyes held theirs – rich amber flecked with brown – and she spoke to each of them as if they were the only people at the party, enchanting the women and rendering many of the men speechless.

She shook hands with every one of them, including the children, and thanked the women warmly for their gifts of food. "Oh, please call me Julie," she told them, winning their hearts by commenting on every single dish – how beautifully prepared, how tempting the icing, how aromatic the filling, such a lovely plate – and then, the ultimate compliment, might she someday have the recipe to try to make something approaching this perfection.

Julianna and Clara had been busy too, whipping up little meat pies and potato salad, sliced vegetables and devilled eggs, savoury buns and piles of sandwiches, with special emphasis on newly invented peanut butter and on canned salmon, a recently arrived new treat from Canada's west coast. Most farm families could not afford either one.

Clara discreetly added their cakes and cookies and tarts to the neighbours' contributions, ensuring a table that groaned with good food – the stuff that fine parties were made of. There were bowls of apples and pears, and gallons of sweet apple cider. Adam had sent a couple of wagon loads of apples to the cider press at the grist mill in town and back came hefty stoneware jugs, filled to the brim and corked. George and Clara with their two hired helpers took charge of the food and drink, dispensing cups of cider to guests as they arrived. Fogo also joined the party, sauntering casually across the lawn and settling under the table, eager to assume clean-up duties in case of dropped sandwiches or cookies. He did not offer to shake hands with anyone but he turned a sharp eye and a keen nose on all comers.

Lenny Findlay and his wife, Velma, with their four strapping offspring, were the first to arrive. They had known Adam for years although, like everyone else in the Valley, they were somewhat in awe of him. Still, they considered him a friend and Liam, the younger son, worshipped him as a hero, ever since the Donovan fire during which they had together braved the burning barn to save horses. Now he approached with shining eyes, and Adam returned his greeting with pecial warmth.

"Well, ya finally took the plunge," Lenny greeted him. "And I'd venture to say, from viewin' the results, ya done pretty good." Adam pumped his hand and slapped his shoulder. "Julie, this is our nearest neighbour, Lenny Findlay and his wife, Velma. They are great friends and we're lucky to have them living just across the road." Julie took Velma's hand in both of hers and thanked her for coming and marveled over the lofty chocolate cake she'd so carefully carried to the table. And how lucky she was to have this fine family to help her; what were their names again? Their ages? Their grades in school? "Adam has told me what good neighbours you are. Let's have a cup of tea and a good chat one day soon." Velma was an instant conquest.

The Dietrich family walked up the road from their little farm next door. They were dressed in their best – Olga Dietrich and the little girls, Lara and Lotte, in swishing dirndl skirts and brightly embroidered blouses and aprons, with little white caps perched on their blonde hair, Otto Dietrich and their son, Rudi, resplendent in leather lederhosen and knee socks – and carrying a suitcase, for heaven sake. The neighbours had never seen such a sight – these foreigners sure were odd. "They must think they was invited to spend the night," sneered Gertie Biggar, the Valley's gossip-in-chief.

And what was this pastry that Olga humbly offered? "Apple strudel," Julianna crowed. "You made it yourself, of course? Oh Mrs. Dietrich, it's ages since I've tasted real apple strudel and it's my favourite pastry. We developed a taste for it when my father was working in Berlin, but here at home, it's impossible to get anything to match it."

"She lived in Berlin?" whispered one neighbour.

"Where's Berlin?" another asked.

"Way up west of Toronto," came the reply. "Only they changed the name to Kitchener."

Tommy Flaherty came trotting up carrying not just one but two fiddle cases. "Hey Tommy," Hector Hawkins, the blacksmith yelled. "Ya gonna play one fiddle with each hand?" Tommy was a jolly elf of a man, full of jokes and fun, who played at all the parties and dances and house warmings and barn raisings for miles around. He wore his signature hat, a venerable tweed cap, old enough to have come with him from Ireland those many years ago and he gallantly doffed it at the sight of his hosts. Tonight in honour of the occasion, he also sported a fancy brocade vest that didn't quite make it across his tummy.

"Tommy's a bit of a lad," Adam whispered. "But he's one of my favourite people. They say he's a bootlegger, but he's an honest one. And he has a heart of gold. When anybody in the Valley has a problem, Tommy is right there… Tommy on the spot, you might say."

His neighbours often wondered how Tommy got his farm work done, though they had only to take note of his wife, Mabel, following the plough or rounding up the cows while Tommy recuperated from yet another night of musical festivities.

"Here come the Donovans," Adam said. "Their little lad, Willie, can't speak ever since their barn burned and he heard the horses screaming." With introductions over, Adam chatted with John, while Julianna felt an immediate connection with Rachel. Willie stayed near his mother but seemed to follow the conversation closely. His older sister, Betsy, moved off to join other young folk.

The Biggars made a strange couple. The local wags liked to say that Gertie Biggar was a bigger Biggar than her husband, Herb Biggar, the local butcher, whose stocky stature belied his great strength. Indeed she was an imposing figure, towering over her husband and outweighing him by several pounds. "Mrs. Biggar also has a big mouth," Adam had warned Julie. "Lenny calls her Gertie the Gossip."

"I'll win her over," Julie boasted.

"Don't be so sure of that," Adam warned. "She has a tongue like a buggy whip and an overactive imagination."

Gertie was on her best behaviour as she congratulated Adam on his marriage and welcomed Julianna to the neighbourhood. She cast a critical eye over Julie's dress and stared rather too long at the crown of golden hair; before she moved on to join Lizzie Hawkins who had taken up a strategic position close to the feast. "She seems harmless to me," Julie whispered.

"Just you wait," Adam replied.

Annie Walters arrived on foot too, a tiny bird of a woman, her face deeply tanned, her gray hair too curly to be tidy. "Annie's a mystery woman," Adam commented. "Nobody knows her very well. But we do know that she maintains a huge herb garden and makes some kind of an elixir that cures just about anything." And she has such a beautiful smile, Julianna thought.

"Mrs. Walters, what a pleasure to see you," Adam greeted her formally. "Allow me to present my wife, Julianna."

The little woman scarcely reached to her shoulder and her garden-calloused hand felt as tough as leather. But her bearing was stately and her manner almost courtly. Julie longed to quiz her about her herb garden but she sensed shyness and a spirit of isolation so she merely greeted her warmly, thanked her for the jellied sweets she'd brought for the table, and watched her walk away.

Hector Hawkins, the burly blacksmith, his wife, Lizzie and their three children were early arrivals. The bulging muscles that Hector put to such good use pounding iron into horse shoes or shovels or kitchen utensils threatened to burst out of his black suit. In came Dave and Rose Dempsey – he owned the threshing machine that he trundled around to all the farms in the district each fall. Before long they were joined by many more – Harry Ward, the miller, now a widower, Fred Keenan who ran the lumber mill, with his wife, Lily, and Mrs. Viola Brown, president of the Women's Institute, followed meekly by her husband, Alf, who smiled constantly and somewhat apologetically at nothing at all, revealing a spectacular set of badly fitted dentures.

The Wilkins family presented a picture of poverty – Bert and Edna, trailed by four wide-eyed children, each one half a head taller than the last. "They have seven or eight youngsters," Adam commented quietly. "Seems like there's a new one every year. Obviously they left the oldest girl at home to mind the little ones. Which is merciful for us. Poor old Bert took a blast of mustard gas in the war. He's never been the same." They look so desperately poor, Julianna thought. A man whose persistent cough bespoke permanent lung damage. And a woman weary from child-bearing, with nowhere to turn for help.

"Here comes trouble," Adam whispered to Julie as a burly man approached, followed by an equally burly son, and behind them, his wife and daughter. "Afternoon, Mr. Dunning," Adam greeted him. "And here's young Joe. Say, you've grown like a weed." Joe and his strapping offspring shook hands but had nothing to say. They both stared at Julie as if they'd never seen a woman before, and then hurried away to the food table, to graze heartily on everything within reach. Rita Dunning looks tired, Julianna surmised. Dispirited. She thought she saw the shadow of a black eye. She knelt down to speak to Christine and noted angry purple bruises on the little girl's arm. Something is not quite right here, she thought.

"Did you smell the alcohol?" Julie whispered after they'd left. "The father has been drinking."

"As usual," Adam replied. "He's a pretty rough fellow and his son is following in his father's footsteps."

Upfront teetotalers but occasional behind-the-barn tipplers, the local folk were not above surreptitiously fortifying the cider, with liberal assistance from Tommy Flaherty, the Valley's unofficial purveyor of bootleg spirits. But with or without the spike, the entire party grew merrier as the evening wore on and the daunting labour of the harvest was temporarily set aside.

When the feast began to dwindle, Tommy Flaherty tuned up his battered violin, proving that old fiddles can still sing with strong young voices. He beckoned to Otto and the neighbours at last realized what was in the suitcase – not a nightshirt or a change of clothes but a large piano accordion which Otto proceeded to play with as much verve as Tommy applied to his fiddle. Willie Donovan sidled into a spot beside Tommy, the better to observe his flying fingers. The audience clapped their hands or tapped their toes until at last one couple and then two and then more, began to dance – polkas and waltzes and foxtrots, some delightfully graceful, others somewhat awkward variations on a shuffle. Hector Hawkins, grateful for an excuse to shed his jacket and vest, took up a position at the top of the verandah steps and pulled off an energetic step dance that was all about fancy footwork. The McTavishes, born and raised in Canada, took Hector's place on the verandah to dance a stately schottische that honoured their Scottish ancestry. And then couples formed groups of eight for the square dance that everybody had been waiting for. Charlie Austen, the auctioneer, obviously fighting a head cold, nonetheless put his huge voice to work bawling out the calls and the dancers laughed and spun, obeying his commands – allemande left, do-si-dos, promenade, swing your partner, swing and circle, round and round. The lawn, although well manicured, was not the best dance floor but undeterred, they danced on and on, even as Charlie paused periodically for a roaring sneeze.

Julie had never attempted square-dancing so Adam led her into the square and translated the caller's commands for her while other dancers, delighted with her participation, turned her this way and that to enhance her education. In no time she was whirling around the circle, sparkling with enjoyment. Each of the men gave her an extra spin, so by the time she'd made her way back toward Adam, she was slightly dizzy.

One last spin landed her in the arms… not of her husband but of young Joe. Now well fortified from his hip flask and thoroughly drunk, he grabbed Julie and propelled her away from the group, groping her buttocks and grabbing for a breast. In an instant, Adam was beside them and Fogo, sensing trouble, leapt bristling from his station under the table.

"That's enough, Joe. You're drunk. Go home," Adam commanded. Joe was not ready to relinquish his prize. He seized Julie's arm and drunkenly tugged at her. But by now Julie's dizziness had passed. She allowed Joe to pull her toward him, and then she raised her right knee and planted it sharply in his groin.

His howl of pain alerted anyone who had missed the incident and they watched in horror as Old Joe rushed into the fray, knocking Adam to the ground. Teeth bared, Fogo sprang snarling toward Old Joe, ready to protect his people. But three muscular neighbours pinned Joe's arms while several more collected his still-moaning son. Together, with Fogo at their heels and mother and daughter close behind, they marched them out to their rig and stood guard while they hitched up and drove off, still yelling insults.

"Remind me not to get you riled," Adam murmured in Julianna's ear as the couple returned to the party, smiling and calling for more music.

But quiet had descended. Embarrassed by the scene and the insult to the new bride, the guests stood in small groups, shuffling their feet, unable to think of anything to say. Clara and her helpers hastily scooped up trays of sweets and began passing them around while George followed with pitchers of cider.

But it was Annie Walters who revived the party. After a whispered consultation with Tommy, she suddenly burst into song – an old song that almost everyone knew. Tommy knew it well and picked up the tune immediately. Otto tried a few chords and quickly found his way. And bursting with relief, the guests joined in.

'Oh dear, what can the matter be?

Dear, dear, what can the matter be?

Oh dear, what can the matter be?

Johnny's so long at the fair,' they whooped, and Annie added verse after verse detailing the sordid tale of a young man who made many wild promises to his beloved before leaving for the fair and never coming back.

'He promised he'd buy me a basket of posies,

A garland of lilies, a garland of roses;

He promised to buy me a bunch of blue ribbons

To tie up my bonny brown hair.'

Her neighbours were startled. Who'd have guessed that shy, reclusive Annie, who rarely spoke to anyone, would become the life of the party? And she could hold a tune too. They clapped and laughed at this delightful new development, especially since it was clear that Annie was having fun too.

Her performance opened a flood gate of local talent. Rachel Donovan grabbed John's hand and pulled him into the musicians' circle. Once again, Tommy and Otto had to pick up the melody as they sang. John began:

'Rachel, Rachel, I've been thinking

What a strange world this would be

If the ladies were transported

Far beyond the northern sea.'

Laughing, Rachel retorted:

'Reuben, Reuben, I've been thinking

If we went beyond the sea,

All the men would follow after

Like a swarm of bumblebees.'

There were plenty of verses to the old teasing song and they made the most of them. When it ended they were laughing and holding hands and their daughter, Betsy, who had joined the crowd of young folk off to the side, was rolling her eyes in embarrassment.

Adam knew a thing or two about Clara and George and he called them out from their haven behind the food table.

It was another old British song that many people had heard before. They sang with gusto and the crowd clapped enthusiastically, even though few had ever seen the seaside or strolled along the prom:

'Oh I do like to be beside the seaside,

I do like to be beside the sea,

I do like to stroll along the prom, prom, prom,

Where the brass bands play

Tiddley-om-pom-pom!'

When their song supply had run its course, Adam raised his hand for silence. "What ya gonna sing, Adam," yelled Hector Hawkins.

"You'll all be happy to know that I am not planning to sing a single note," Adam replied. "We truly thank you for the pleasure of your company tonight. Thank you for your warm and wonderful welcome to my new bride – your friendship, your music and dancing and of course the wonderful treats you brought to our table. Now I have one more treat for you – something that even my dear bride knows nothing about. It may surprise you to know that we have yet another fine musician in our Valley. And he is here tonight." He paused to heighten the suspense. "His name is Willie Donovan."

A few seconds of surprised silence followed and then some tentative applause. "Mr. Flaherty," Adam called to the fiddler. "Would you mind lending Willie your spare fiddle?" Of course Adam had arranged it in advance and Tommy was ready. He opened up the extra case and handed a small violin to the little boy, who had been standing beside him watching his fingers for most of the night.

Rachel moved protectively closer to Willie but she need not have worried. Tucking the violin under his chin, he closed his eyes and began to play, a piece of music that few of the neighbours had ever heard, a merry mischievous melody that seemed to soar to the treetops and skip across the fields, and tickle the toes of his audience who listened and marveled at the delightful *Humoresque* that Antonin Dvorak had written only a few years earlier. When he finished, he became shy again, placed the fiddle carefully in its case and retreated to his mother's side.

"One more, Willie," called Otto. "Do you know this one?" He one-fingered a phrase and Willie, reclaiming the fiddle, immediately picked up the melody, keeping his eyes intently on Otto's fingers as they shared an unrehearsed duet. As jolly and energetic as the Irish jigs and Scottish reels that had already brightened the party, the music tripped along gaily and hardly anyone knew or cared that it was a *Gigue* by Johann Sebastian Bach.

Now the clapping and cheering went on and on and John Donovan whisked his son up to his shoulders and walked him around the circle so people could shake his hand and pat him on the back.

"Adam, that was a wonderful thing to do," Julie whispered. "How did you know?"

"John Donovan asked me to have a look at one of his horses – it has a nasty spavin. Afterward he invited me in for a cool drink and I heard the violin. I asked if that was Rachel playing but he told me it was Willie and he brought him out to the kitchen to play a tune for me. I was amazed."

"Adam, my love," she replied. "I think that tonight you may have started Willie on the road to a new life."

Little did she know!

CHAPTER 6

Adam Then and Now

I lived across the road from Adam Chandler most of my life. He was just a few years younger than me but we was pretty good friends. But yet I never really knew him, if you follow me. I guess we was all a bit shy of him because he was rich and he had the biggest farm in the Valley. Adam's family was plain folk, just like the rest of us – come from Scotland and Ireland, got crown land and cleared it, built a log cabin and then a big brick house. Then one of their relatives in the Old Country died and left them money so they bought up extra farms, one in the Valley next door to them, and a couple more way over back of beyond on the north concession road. That land was all timber, hardly any of it cleared, so they tapped it for maple syrup and harvested it for lumber and managed to live a bit higher off the hog than the rest of us. But they was never grand nor highfalutin.

Adam was well brought up, always friendly and polite, except when he lost his temper, which nearly always had something to do with a horse that was being mistreated. But most always he was ready to pitch in and help out a neighbour. He seemed stand-offish too, like he was lonesome even in the middle of a big group, smiling and greeting folks but with his mind somewheres else. His folks sent him off to that fancy agricultural college up there in Guelph and he come back with a bunch of new-fangled ideas about farming and what people should eat. He never touched beef or pork after that, and hardly ever chicken. Mostly it was rabbit food: vegetables, beans, nuts, cheese. And rice. Never ate rice in our house. Wouldn't touch the stuff then and I won't now.

Adam's folk was well on in years when he came along so eventually they died and he was alone. He was already past marryin' age – getting on toward thirty, I'd say, so it was time to find himself a bride. And he did.

And that's when life in our Valley got interesting.

Lenny

Adam was truly in love with his new wife and proud of her. But puzzled too. His experience with girls had been limited to the quiet, obedient daughters of his neighbours and nothing had prepared him for a girl with opinions, ambitions and abilities that she seemed determined to realize.

In the three years since their first encounter at the Winter Fair gala banquet in Toronto – just a day before fire destroyed the Donovan barn – they had actually met face to face no more than half a dozen times. But they exchanged dozens of letters, at first gracious and formal, then graduating to warmth, affection and love. But the deepest secrets of their past lives remained hidden.

Next morning after the welcome party, as they lingered over breakfast at the table for two at the dining room window, he teased her about her encounter with Young Joe. "I'm inclined to think our neighbours may step more carefully around you from now on," he suggested. "In fact, maybe in future I'll be minding my manners too. Where did you learn hand-to-hand combat?"

"No hands were involved," Julie quipped. "I used my knee. But the fact is, I have a fairly advanced knowledge of human anatomy and I do know the most vulnerable places to hit.

"But never you mind, my dear. I don't expect I'll ever need to attack you."

"Well, I'm not much of a threat," he observed. "In fact, I can't remember ever threatening anybody." He refilled both their tea cups and added a hefty dollop of honey to his own.

"Well, that's not exactly true. At the Agricultural College, I learned how to snap a bullwhip and one day at the grist mill, I saw young Joe Dunning whipping a horse that had wandered a little way off to eat grass. I was so furious – I threatened to whip him the way he was whipping his horse and I snapped my whip so close to him that he could feel the breeze, just to get the point across. Scared him half to death too. And I'll do it again in a second if I see anyone abusing a horse.

"But I guess not having brothers and sisters to wrestle with and play rough games left me with a shortage of fighting skills. Although I do have some battle scars. I was bullied all through school, partly because I had fancier clothes and toys than the other youngsters, and partly thanks to the stigma of adoption."

"You were adopted?" Julie exclaimed. "Tell me more."

"Not much to tell," Adam replied. "My mother had too many babies and there she was again, in a family way, but very sick and weak with four little ones to care for. So my Uncle Joseph and Aunt Sarah – they were my mother's cousins – offered to take me off her hands. And then they never sent me home again. I was only two years old then, so I have almost no memories of my parents' home and I was never allowed to go for visits, even though I begged."

"Where did your birth parents live?" she asked.

"They were farmers just outside of Andersville – that's a little hamlet out past Paxton Ford, about twenty miles from here. But it might as well have been on the other side of the moon. It was a long journey in those days and my new parents – I called them Auntie and Uncle – warned me that there were vicious black bears and wolves all along the way that would attack us if we tried to drive there. And of course I believed them. I knew they lived somewhere west and north of here – I had no idea of distances of course – and I'd stand at that west kitchen door and imagine myself flying over the fields and forests and past the bears and wolves and landing in my own family's home. But the will is weak," he added ruefully. "I didn't budge. Except once."

"What happened?" Julie prodded. "Did your folks give in?"

"No, I ran away from home," he confessed. "I was about eight or nine. I had a general idea where Andersville was and I figured once I got there, I could ask directions to their farm. So I packed up some peppermints and a piece of bread in a polka dot handkerchief like a bindle stiff – you know what I mean? I figured if it worked for Huckleberry Finn it was good enough for me and there were plenty of red and white dotted handkerchiefs around the place. I tied my bundle to a stick and headed down the road one morning while Auntie and Uncle were at the barn dealing with the milk.

"I walked and walked and walked," he continued. "I passed several neighbours' places but nobody paid any attention. By evening, I made it to Andersville, just a tiny place with a couple of churches, a general store and a blacksmith. I always trusted blacksmiths so I stopped there and asked the smithy for directions to my parents' farm – their name was Salter.

"He stared at me for a bit and asked why I would be wanting to go there. I said: 'They're my parents. I'm going home.'

'What's your name, laddie?' he asked me. He had a strong Scottish brogue. And I told him: 'Adam.' I didn't know whether to say Chandler or Salter. But I guess he was a jump ahead of me.

'Now Adam, you'd best come inside and have a wee bite to eat and drink,' he said and he led me into the house where his wife was getting the supper. 'This bairn is Adam Chandler,' he told her. 'He's walked all the way from beyond Paxton Ford to see his family, away over to the Salter place.'

"So she gave me a long look, but very kind, and invited me to sit down and have some supper. Well, you know, a handful of peppermints and a hunk of dry bread don't go very far so I was starving. I was glad to eat with them. Then I thanked them politely, just as I'd been taught to do, and asked if they'd direct me toward my family's farm.

'Why don't we ride out there together?' the smithy said. 'You've had a right long walk today and it's a bit far to go, especially with dark coming on. In fact, why don't we wait until morning? We'll welcome you to turn in here on the kitchen couch and in the morning, I'll drive you out there to the farm.'

"It didn't take much coaxing. I realized then that I was totally worn out so I tucked under the quilt that the lady gave me and fell asleep.

"Early next day, the smithy told his wife to tell any customers that came by that he'd be back by noon. Then we hopped into his buggy and trotted off.

"It was a good long way and I was glad I wasn't still walking. Finally, we turned in at a lane leading to a farm yard that even at my young age I could tell had seen better days. There was broken machinery scattered around everywhere. The big sliding barn doors on the hay barn were off their hinges and some windows were broken. It was summer so the livestock was out in the fields but what a shock – all skin and bones, horses with their ribs showing through their coats, cows with filthy diarrhea and skin ulcers eating away at them so they'd lost most of their hair. There didn't seem to be any young stock either. Colts and calves – that's how Uncle would judge a herd.

"We drove up to the house and it was just as bad. There was broken furniture thrown out into the yard in a jumble of weeds and no kitchen garden in sight.

'Is this the right place?' I asked the smithy. 'I'm afraid so, laddie,' he said. 'Are you sure you want to go in?'

'But this is my family? The Salter family?'

'It is, laddie. But a world of difference from the family you've just left behind. These folk are very poor and poverty does mean things to people.'

'I'll go in,' I said, and I hopped down from the buggy and headed for the door. By then a couple of the young ones had seen the buggy and me coming up the walk and they yelled for their ma. She came to the door and I stopped in my tracks. Somehow I knew this woman must be my mother but she looked like a witch from hell. Her clothes were dirty; her dress was stained all down the front and torn at the arm pits, her hair straggled down over her face. She was holding a baby and pushing aside a couple of tots that were not more than two or three years old. The two who had spotted me were maybe six and seven. They were all dirty and ragged. Even glancing in the door I could see that the house was shabby and untidy.

"I said: 'I'm Adam, your son.'

"And she said: 'I don't know no Adam. Go back where you come from. We don't want you here.'

"I suppose I stood there staring at them all for a while. Then the smithy came up the walk and put his arm around my shoulders and led me back to the buggy. I tried not to blubber on the way back to his place in Andersville but I guess a few tears fell. When we got there, he took me into the house and told his wife something on the quiet. Then she brought big bowls of hot soup and home-made bread to the table and fed us both. To this day I can't remember a more delicious meal than that one. But I was broken-hearted and finally the tears started to roll in earnest. So then she picked me up like I was a baby and rocked me in her rocking chair and brushed my hair and sang to me. And just like a baby, I fell asleep. I don't recall ever being rocked to sleep, before or after.

"The next morning, the smithy asked me if I'd like to go home now and back we came."

"Was there a search for you," Julianna asked.

"Yes and no. My folks had no telephone, of course, and even if they'd gone to the police, there were no resources for a search – just one policeman covering miles and miles of territory. I think they were terribly embarrassed that I'd run away – it was a reflection on them as parents, I suppose – so they didn't turn to the neighbours as most of us would do in emergency. Uncle rode out along the roads and a couple of neighbours reported seeing me walking by. So they figured out that I was probably trying to get to my birth home. But he never did go to Andersville."

"What did they do when you finally arrived back?"

"It was a bitter-sweet home coming. They were obviously furious with me but I suppose they didn't want to show it to the smithy. So Uncle patted my head and Auntie gave me a little hug. They were not very…how shall I say…physical people. They rarely touched me at all and to be honest, that's the only time I can remember her hugging me. And then they thanked the smithy and tried to give him some money but he refused. 'You'd do the same for me or any neighbour,' he told them. 'I'm glad to bring your laddie safe home.' As soon as he left, they began to rail at me for being so stupid and inconsiderate; after all they'd done for me. That went on for a while and then the silence started."

"Silence? You mean they stopped speaking to you?"

"That was always their way of dealing with a problem. 'Never speak of it again,' was their slogan. It was a potent weapon. When they were unhappy with me, they just gave me the silent treatment. Sometimes for days at a time. Or they sent me upstairs to my room and made me stay there. I'd listen to the creaking of the house and the wind in the chimneys and imagine all kinds of terrors outside my door."

"But they never punished you…physically, I mean? By spanking or whipping?"

"Believe me, Julie, silence and isolation are persuasive punishments. It went on and on. In my memory it seems like weeks or more – plenty of time to feel really guilty. Of course there was plenty of silence in the house anyway. Meals were eaten in complete silence and Auntie and Uncle hardly ever spoke to each other. If I talked too much, Auntie would wag her finger at me and say, 'A babbling fool is the devil's tool.' She had a lot of little warnings like that in her vocabulary."

"They didn't have much understanding of children," Julie observed.

"Nor experience either. They were far past child-rearing age – in their fifties, I guess – when they took me in. Probably visualized a doll, not an active little boy. And they certainly never anticipated either my energy or my homesickness.

"When they broke the silence, Auntie gave me a stern lecture about all they had done for me and how badly I had rewarded them. And then Uncle said he'd buy me a pony if I promised never to do anything like that again.

"And so I stayed. Pony or no pony, I would have stayed. That experience cured me of ever wanting to go back to my family. But I always felt guilty, too."

Julie reached over and took his hand. "You must have been so very lonely."

"Looking back, I realize that I was. Auntie and Uncle were so good to me; they gave me everything they could: good clothes, skates, horses, and finally an education at the Agricultural College and this beautiful farm. I hate to think of what my life would have been if my birth parents had actually taken me back. But at the time, all I could think of was that great big family and all the fun they must've had playing games together and climbing trees and so on. Later I realized that they already had too many mouths to feed and another one would have caused even greater hardship – and not much 'fun'. They probably envied me the life of relative luxury that I was given."

"Well, it is a good life," Julie squeezed his hand. "And we are going to enjoy every bit of it together and have beautiful children of our own. But now that you're an adult and free to do whatever you like, have you ever thought of trying to contact your brothers and sisters again?"

"I've thought of it," Adam acknowledged. "But then I lost my courage. I doubt that they even know about me. It might be better to just let sleeping dogs lie."

"But I'd love to see the place where you were born," she coaxed. "Let's drive out there one day. And maybe visit the smithy who really saved your life."

"Once you catch a glimpse of my past," Adam smiled but his eyes were serious, "you may wish you'd never married me."

"Dear Adam, I've seen poverty at its most extreme," she countered. "In Toronto, working with my father, I've gone into houses so filthy that the smell made me gag, whole neighbourhoods with just a single well in a back alley to supply water to all the houses. No toilets – people just threw their slops out into the street or the back yard. So many sick people with wounds or sores that had become infected because they had no sanitation and no money for medical help. So many exhausted women producing babies year after year, so many undernourished and neglected children with no hope of education or gainful work. The one advantage your birth family may have had was plenty of fresh country air and perhaps a garden with some fresh vegetables in summer. So for at least part of the year, they might have had better food. Poverty destroys souls but in the city it destroys bodies and lives too." She paused for a deep breath, her eyes full of tears.

Adam was taken aback. "I didn't realize that your father's practice extended to the poor parts of the city. I just assumed that as a distinguished city doctor with a comfortable practice, his clientele would be respectable people leading respectable lives."

"Not so. As long as the poor are with us – and at the rate we're going they will be around for a long, long time – doctors who are really committed to their professions will be there in the thick of it, trying to make lives better. That's the first lesson I learned from my father, that those of us who are privileged have a responsibility to help those who have less than we do. If we can end the cycle of bad health, bad schooling, bad jobs – or no jobs at all – we'll all benefit. And women most of all need that help."

Adam was thoughtful. "I envy you, Julie. You have a mission. You've already produced your first book and you have all your medical experience and healing skills from both your father and your Indian friends. You have a purpose in life and I am filled with admiration. I think I've skated though life without any real purpose, no real goal except to look after the farm, and not much enthusiasm even for that. Maybe the time has come to think it through again."

"Let's think it through together," she suggested. "Perhaps we both need to discover some new challenges."

CHAPTER 7

Willie's World

In them days, Valley folks liked to let on they minded their own business. In fact they was as nosy as cats and they liked nothin' better'n a good chewy chunk of gossip. Especially about trouble like what the Donovans was facin' with their lad, Willie.

Ask anybody – well, anybody that lived in the Valley – and they'd tell ya we was all real good friendly people, ready to jump in and help when help was needed. But when I think back to the Donovans, I figger we could of done more. If it hadn't been for his parents and Chrissy Dunning and good old Tommy Flaherty, and of course Doc Julie, Willie probably woulda ended up in some home for backward youngsters. As it was, the school turned against him and most of the neighbours pretty well decided he was mental. Even his grandparents – that was John's folks – was ashamed of him. We all felt sorry for his mother, having to care for such a burden but nobody would ever ask after him for fear she'd be mortified. And after a while, we all kinda forgot about him. At least until the Chandlers' party, when he showed how good he could play the violin. Even so, some folks still figured him for a freak.

I'm ashamed of the way we treated the Donovans and I betcha I'm not the only one. We prided ourselves on how good we was to our neighbours. But we turned our backs on Willie and his folks. And now there's no way on earth to make it up to them.

Lenny

Still aglow from the Chandler party and Willie's triumph, John and Rachel headed for home. "I didn't realize you'd taught him that piece," John Donovan remarked as they trotted up the hill.

"I didn't," she replied. "He must have heard it a couple of times on the gramophone – you know the Bach Suites, that gramophone record with Fritz Kreisler."

"Well, it's a sweet suite," John laughed. "And Willie did it justice."

"And how kind of Mr. Flaherty to bring the violin for him," Rachel enthused.

Rachel's heart sang as she reviewed the evening, Willie's achievement, and the warmth of both Adam and Julianna. "Willie was a hero for one night," she said.

"Let's hope there will be more."

"I just wish my parents had been here to see him," John said wistfully. "Maybe it would have helped them understand that in spite of his speech problem, he's a very special little boy." John's father had passed the farm along to his son after a logging accident put an end to his own farming days. They had moved into Paxton Ford to enjoy the proximity of church, shops and the doctor but their visits to the farm were frequent and fun until Willie's problems began. "They're smart people," John added. "But they still don't seem able to come to terms with Willie."

"They've promised to come for Christmas," Rachel reminded him. "We can stage a little recital for them. Maybe that will help."

She was excited and sleep was slow to descend. She lay awake thinking back over the past two painful years -- especially Willie's eagerness to learn and his first and only day at school when the new teacher revealed herself as the worst bully in the classroom.

She thought back to walking with Willie to school that second morning, arriving well before class time to permit a quiet chat with the teacher. But Miss Malone was neither quiet nor chatty. Masking her lack of experience with arrogant defiance, she assumed an attack mode the moment Rachel and Willie entered her classroom.

"I wanted to talk to you about Willie," Rachel began gently. "Perhaps I was at fault for not coming in yesterday to explain his problem."

"Problem," Miss Malone retorted. "I figgered out his problem all right. He's not right in the head and he never shoulda been sent to school. Shoulda been sent to a home somewhere."

Rachel was shocked and wounded. "He is in a home," she snapped back. "Our home – his family's home."

"Then you shoulda kept him there. He can't learn nothin' anyway, and he wastes my time and bothers the other students. Why, he isn't even toilet-trained. Do you expect me to clean up after him?"

"Absolutely not," Rachel countered. "I expect you to allow him to go to the toilet when he needs to. From what I heard, you forced him to wet himself. Willie cannot speak but he is neither stupid nor as you call it, mental. He is in fact a very bright little boy and I have been hoping that with the stimulation of school, he might regain his ability to speak."

"I never heard of such a thing," Miss Malone countered from the heights of her one-day teaching experience. "They come here to read and write and learn arithmetic.

It ain't my job to toilet train them or teach them to talk." She glared down at Willie, who shrank back behind his mother.

Rachel had had enough. She rose, took Willie's hand and walked out without another word. Miss Malone stared after them, a little less sure of herself than her arrogant speech suggested.

After the children were in bed that night, Rachel talked it over with John. "I don't see any alternative but to keep him at home and teach him myself," she said. "He's already learning to read, and I'm quite sure that he'll be able to write before long. And then there's the music."

"Is there a law about keeping children out of school," John wondered. "I know that older youngsters can be kept home to help with the harvest and so on, but what about little ones."

"I'll find out," Rachel promised. "I'll go and talk to the chairman of the school board. Surely the fact that we were both teachers will carry some weight."

So Willie stayed home. The next day, Rachel hitched up the buggy and drove off to visit Oliver Moore, the school board chairman who lived just up the road beyond the school house. A stocky, red-faced farmer with an everlasting air of self-important irritation, he was not pleased to see Rachel, although she had timed the visit for the noon hour, when he would likely be in from the fields.

"Teacher already told me about this mess," he said brusquely. "It seems your lad ain't toilet trained and refuses to take part in what's going on in the class. She said he was a problem from the minute he got there."

"I don't think that's quite accurate," Rachel countered. "It is true that Willie doesn't speak but he could speak before the fire two years ago. He's already reading books and I have no doubt that he can learn any subject that's explained to him. After all, he is not deaf or blind. And he's very musical. I think he's quite a bright little boy."

"Yeah. I've heard that one before," Moore growled. "If he's so smart, why'd he need the strap on his first day and make a mess on the school floor?"

"The teacher became furious because he could not speak," Rachel replied. "And she refused to let him go to the outhouse until he did speak. It was totally unreasonable."

"Well, madam," the chairman rose to his feet. "I think you're the one that's unreasonable – expecting this teacher to take charge of your half-wit brat. He belongs in a home somewhere, not in a public school. Good day to you."

Rachel was so angry and confused that she wept as she left the house. At home, John was waiting. "That teacher is a disaster," Rachel told him. "She bullies the whole school and relies on the strap to enforce discipline. And Mr. Moore won't admit she's anything but perfect because he's the one who hired her."

"I wonder what the school inspector would make of it all," John pondered. "It's his job to review the schools and the teachers."

Rachel stared at him. "Why didn't I think of that? Mr. Drew. I wonder if he's still the inspector for this county. He was appointed school inspector back when I was teaching and he actually made one inspection of my school, just before we got married. I was terrified when he walked in the door – I don't know a teacher who isn't in awe of the inspector. But he was really inspiring. He was so courteous and he gave me so much good advice and encouragement.

"I don't suppose he'll remember me," she added thoughtfully. "But what matters is that I know that he's conscientious and he cares about children and good schooling."

Appointed by the department of education, school inspectors visited each school in their district regularly and reported back on everything from the hygiene of the toilets to the state of the library to the deportment of the students to the techniques of the teacher. And the inspector had the power to recommend that government funding be withheld from a school that earned a failing grade.

Next day, Rachel crafted a carefully worded letter, devoid of anger or accusations but laying out both the treatment that Willie received and the teacher's apparent bullying of Christine. She reminded him that he had inspected her school just before she retired from teaching and thanked him for his time.

She received a brief note back within days. "Dear Mrs. Donovan," Mr. Drew wrote. "Thank you for your report on Bass River School. Please be assured that I shall give the matter my full attention." She did not hear directly from him again.

She did hear from Chrissy, however, when she dropped in one day after school. "I can't stay long," Chrissy explained. "My parents don't know I'm here."

"And I imagine you don't want them to know," Rachel said. "How has school been for you these last few days?"

"Well, Miss Malone has it in for me," Chrissy reported. "She keeps glaring at me and she always asks me the hardest questions so she has an excuse to get mad at me. And the other kids are really mean. They yell things at me and won't let me play in their games."

"I'm so sorry, Chrissy," Rachel felt genuine regret. "You should not have to suffer because of that teacher and her attitude toward Willie. But if the teacher won't take steps to stop bullying, I don't know any way to do it. I wish I could just keep you here and give you lessons along with Willie."

"My parents wouldn't like that," Chrissy remarked. "They are still mad at me for being friends with Willie. And likely they'll stay mad for quite a while.

"But today was kinda fun," she added. "The school inspector came. He stayed the whole day. He did math and arithmetic with us and reading and he asked what books we liked and he played some games with us – word games, I think he called them where he'd say a word and we had to tell him another word that meant the same thing. Or he'd give us a word and we had to say one that rhymed. It sounds hard but it was fun. He said I should be a poet because he said 'apple' and I was the only one that found words to rhyme with it – chapel, grapple, dapple. And we sang some songs – or at least a few of us did. We don't do music this year so most of the others don't know the songs.

"And then he talked about being good students and working hard and paying attention to the teacher and he asked how many of us had got the strap. And everybody in the whole school has had the strap.

"I don't think Miss Malone liked him. She frowned a lot – when he wasn't looking."

'And so she should,' Rachel thought to herself.

Willie was already tugging at Chrissy's arm, showing her a colourful book that Rachel had found for him. "You want to read, Willie," she asked. "Let's take a look at this book."

She opened it to the first page which showed pictures of various farm animals, and asked him to point to an animal and then to its name. He identified horse, cow, sheep, pig, hen. And so it went. Willie knew the printed word for every picture in the book.

Another day when she arrived she found Willie with his nose in a book, tracing the lines of words with one finger. "Let's try some writing, Willie," she suggested. He raced off for a slate and chalk and she wrote his name. "See this? W I L L I E. Do you know what it spells?"

To her amazement, Willie pointed to himself. "That's good, Willie. What about this?" She wrote M U M M Y and he pointed to his mother.

"Can you try to write them, Willie," Chrissy encouraged him. "Here. Hold the chalk like this…" She placed it in his right hand and arranged his fingers and thumb to hold it. But Willie transferred it to his left hand, angled the slate accordingly and set to work to copy the letters.

"Look, Mrs. Donovan," Chrissy called. "Willie knows all his letters and he's writing them real well. But he's using the wrong hand."

"He's left-handed," Rachel explained. "It's not the wrong hand – let's say that left is right for him."

Proudly they surveyed Willie's work, realizing how quickly he absorbed his lessons. Then Chrissy raced for home, before her parents missed her.

Eventually Willie tired of copying the letters and wandered into the kitchen. An old alarm clock was sitting on the bureau, waiting for John to find time to repair it. As Rachel busied herself with preparing supper, Willie carried the clock into the dining room and began taking it apart. Glancing in, Rachel was horrified to see the clock in pieces and Willie picking up each piece, turning it over and over and staring at it, before moving on to the next.

"Oh Willie," she chided him. "What are you doing to that clock? I'm sure Daddy could have repaired it if you'd left it alone."

Willie began systemically to reassemble the clock. He seemed to know intuitively where each part belonged. Finally, he picked up a tiny spring that had escaped Rachel's notice and slipped it into place. He set the hands to match the big clock on the dining room wall and wound the key. The clock ticked happily and Willie proudly handed it over to his mother.

"I'm amazed, Willie. This is wonderful," she applauded. "Now if you could just fix my sewing machine. But I think it's more challenging than a clock."

Willie grinned and raced to the sewing machine, sitting idle in its cabinet by the kitchen window, hopelessly jammed up with thread.

"No, no, Willie, I was just joking," Rachel intercepted him. "You mustn't play with the sewing machine. You don't know a thing about it and anyway you could hurt yourself badly."

Willie looked crestfallen. He pointed to the sewing machine and to the clock that she still carried in her hand, to tell her that he could do the job.

Just then John came in from the barn. "Look John. Willie fixed the alarm clock," she reported. "At least it seems that he did. And now he wants to fix the sewing machine."

John examined the clock carefully and determined that Willie had not only reconnected the tiny spring that had slipped off the ratchet, but that he had reassembled the whole mechanism correctly.

"Let's look at the sewing machine together," he invited Willie. "Maybe we can figure it out. Two heads are better than one."

John opened the cabinet and flipped the machine up to its sewing position. Willie immediately opened the tiny door to the bobbin and pulled out the roll of thread. Then he slid back the metal plate that covered the whole sewing mechanism. "Better pull out that needle before you stick your fingers in there," his father suggested. Willie ferreted the minuscule screwdriver out of the tool kit and deftly loosened the needle. John had not yet moved a muscle. He watched as Willie dug deep into the cavity where the needle connected with the bobbin, his tiny fingers just the perfect size for the job. He pulled out a bit of thread and then a hefty tangle that had jammed the machine, showing John a solid knot in the thread that had probably caused the obstruction in the first place.

"Another triumph," John called to Rachel. "Your sewing machine is now in working order and I didn't do a thing. This young man has a knack for fixing."

"Well, we have lots of things to fix," Rachel smiled. "Let's see, that door latch, the water pump, the front door bell..."

Willie dashed to the door but Rachel headed him off. "Willie, I was just joking. That latch has been faulty for years. It can wait until after supper." Barely suppressing his excitement, Willie sat at the table, fidgeting as he waited for the family to assemble for supper. Over the next few days, he fixed the latch and the front door bell but the water pump temporarily defeated him – it needed a leather valve. John drew the line at allowing Willie to cut the new flap himself but the little boy watched closely as his father laid a thick piece of hide on his work bench and using the old valve as a template, cut a new one. Together they screwed it into place, primed the pump and called Rachel to admire their handiwork.

And admire she did, while Willie beamed and preened a bit. John scooped up his son and set him on a chair, giving him a hug that soon turned into a playful wrestling match.

Along with his school lessons, Rachel began to teach him music, especially piano. He was fascinated by her violin but his hands were too small to reach the positions. Fearful that he would develop incorrect habits that would later be harmful, Rachel actively discouraged him from the violin but she often found him toiling over it anyway, stretching his small hands to reach the strings.

Tommy Flaherty recognized the problem. "Another fiddler in the Valley," he crowed next day as he arrived for an unexpected visit. "But he needs a fiddle that fits him..." Reaching under his buggy seat, he hauled out the small violin that

Willie had played at the party and handed it over.

Willie opened the case and patted the glowing wood as if it were a cat. "Go on, pick it up." Tommy urged. "You know how to play it. You proved that at the Chandlers' party. It's just the right size for you so you should be able to fiddle to your heart's content."

Willie took it in his hands as if it were a sacred relic. Tommy had tuned the instrument and tightened the bow before leaving home, so Willie had only to tuck it under his chin and play. And that's precisely what he did, a smile spreading across his face and never disappearing until he placed the violin back in its velvet wrap, closed the case and handed it back to Tommy. "No, no, Willie. It's yours." Tommy said. "I found it years ago at an auction and I held on to it all this time, waiting for someone to come along that was just the right size for it. And you already showed that you're the man." He opened the case again and reminded Willie to loosen the bow before packing the violin away.

"Tommy, this is wonderful," John enthused. "Rachel's violin is really too big for him yet but he's been trying to play it anyway. Just tell me what it's worth and I'll gladly pay you for it."

"Well now, John," Tommy replied, adopting his old Irish persona. "This here fiddle is worth more than money. I'd say it's worth at least one fine tune and that merry smile of his every time Willie and I meet up. And maybe one of these days, we'll play together again."

Willie's eyes shone. He stood before Tommy, gazing up into his face and then climbed onto his lap and hugged him. Rachel could have sworn she saw a tear in each of Tommy's eyes.

Willie tackled both violin and piano with zeal and his playing flourished. In time, he worked his way through the Toronto Conservatory of Music books of scales, arpeggios and simple melodies, the same Frederick Harris books that instructed, frustrated and challenged most music students across Canada for decades. Within weeks he had mastered the beginner book and embarked upon Grade One, effortlessly absorbing both the notation and the rhythms of the music. In a few weeks, he graduated to Grade Two, then Grade Four. He loved to doodle with both instruments, improvising little melodies or playing chords or riffs that pleased his ear. Rachel often stopped her work in the kitchen to listen to his musical experiments and marvel at his progress while grieving that her teaching skills were limited.

The Chandler party and Willie's small but significant triumph had shown the world, or at least the neighbourhood, that in spite of his silence, he could make beautiful sounds. Rachel and John were elated, Tommy was triumphant and Willie seemed to sense the significance of the event. Only his grandparents and his older sister, Betsy, failed to share their enthusiasm. Ever since the barn fire that robbed Willie of his speech, Betsy had been jealous of the attention their parents paid to him and missed no opportunity to bully him or blame him for mishaps. And John's parents still viewed him as defective.

But Willie sailed on past these challenges, forging ahead, mastering both instruments and reveling in both the music and his newly discovered fix-it skills.

One day as he tinkled little melodies at the piano, Rachel heard a new sound that stopped her in her tracks. She listened carefully, unable to believe what she was hearing. Shaking with excitement, she pulled on a jacket and ran to the barn to find John. "You won't believe this, John. You must come and hear Willie."

"Can't it wait until I've finished the milking?"

"NO! Come now. This is too important to wait. You've got to come now."

Giving his cow a friendly farewell pat, John set aside his milking stool and bucket and patiently trailed after her as she ran up to the house. He couldn't imagine what could have caused such excitement.

At the back door, she laid her fingers to her lips and tip-toed into the kitchen. Willie was still at the piano and Rachel signaled to John that he should listen. It sounded just the same to John as it had yesterday and the day before and he grimaced at Rachel in confusion. "Ssshhh," she commanded. "Listen closely."

And there it was – the soft, sweet sound of Willie humming along with the melodies that he was playing.

John reached out to her and wrapped his arms around her. Silently weeping for joy, they held one another and listened to the first language their son had vocalized since the fire – the sound of his music.

It seemed that the new life that Julianna had predicted had indeed begun.

When the new school term rolled around in January, Miss Malone was nowhere to be found. The new teacher, Chrissy reported joyfully, was a really nice lady "nothing at all like Miss Malone." But watching Willie's progress in school subjects, in music and in mechanical skills, Rachel and John decided together that their school-at-home was the place where he belonged.

CHAPTER 8

Annie's New Friend

I guess the oddest nut in our Valley was Annie Walters. She lived just down the road from us and even though she wasn't very friendly, she was a neighbour so me and Velma, we kept an eye on her.

Annie came to the Valley 'way years back with her old man, Oscar. He was a foreigner but he was friendly and he spoke real good English. He said once that he could speak seven languages and he rhymed off a whole string of 'em. Didn't mean nuthin' to me – they all sounded foreign. He said you're as many times a person as the languages ya speak, whatever that means. I guess he had to be a lot of persons to remember all them words – it don't seem possible for one man to keep them all in one head.

Oscar always carried a little knife and he was forever whittlin'. His favourite whittle was little cups that he said they was called something like jinchicha in his language, that the shepherds used to drink fresh whey. Sometimes they had people's faces carved on them, sometimes animals. He especially liked cat faces so I often seen him drinking out of his cat's ear if ya follow me.

But his fence, now, that was the most peculiar. Right up and down his laneway from house to road, Oscar carved people and animals into his fence posts, just about life size so they gave ya a start first time ya seen them. Last I heard they was still there but this Dr. Butters that's collecting stories about country life says they're valuable folk art and should go to a museum. Oscar sure woulda had a good laugh over that.

Now Annie, she always seemed stand-offish but Velma said she was shy. She worked like a horse in her garden – all kinds of green stuff that nobody never heard of. And potatoes. She had so many potatoes that me and Velma wondered if she ate nuthin' but spuds. And all winter she kept on brewin' up this here tonic that she and Oscar made. She never told us what was in it but it sure was effective – cleared up colds and even pneumonia, set women back on their feet after birthin', and anybody else that was sick. It burned the tongue like blazes, but it sure did fire the blood. We even gave it to horses that had a cough and it seemed to work for them too.

But it didn't do nuthin for Oscar.

When he got sick and knew he was dyin', he asked me if I'd work his farm and let Annie stay on in their house. So that's what I did. I rented the land, not for money but for enough hay, straw and oats for her horse, and enough firewood for heating and cooking year-round. Every fall, she'd give us a few bottles of her tonic to last us through the winter. She never invited us into her house – when she wanted to talk to me, she'd come out on her porch even in the bitter cold.

Me and Velma, we took a look down to her place each morning to make sure there was smoke comin' out the chimney. Sometimes we saw her heading out to feed her hens or drivin' off in her little buggy. Once in a while she'd leave real early in the morning – off to visit a distant cousin down Morganston way, so she once told me, and then she'd be gone til past dark.

The neighbour youngsters was scared of them fence post faces and they called her a witch – all but Willie.

Lenny

Annie Walters gathered up the six brown eggs in a little basket. She paused at the door and looked back at her plump red hens, settled on their roosts. "Thank you, my dears," she said. "Your eggs are beautiful." Then she moved into the cozy stable that housed her one horse and stopped to pat his head and lean her forehead against his velvet nose. She reached into her pocket for an apple and allowed him to slurp it up off her flattened palm. "Thank you, sweet Dobbin," she told him. "You worked hard today."

Annie talked to her garden too – to the rows of herbs and flowers that she tended so faithfully, to the potatoes and carrots that would see her through the winter, to the apple and cherry and plum trees, the raspberry and currant bushes, even the broad maple where she rested briefly on scorching days and the bright red geraniums in her kitchen window. It was something she'd learned from Oscar.

"The animals serve us well. They deserve appreciation and your voice tells them that they matter to us. And the plants and trees. Who knows whether they hear us? But thanking them reminds us of their value to us…of how much we need them.

"Anyway," he added, "talking to plants and animals does no harm and it makes us feel good."

At first she thought Oscar's obsession was a bit silly. But in time she came to realize his sincerity and the wisdom of recognizing how much animals and nature contributed to their lives. And he thanked her too, warmly and often. Now she recalled sadly his gratitude for all she did for him – for his oatmeal porridge, that most mundane of breakfasts, for his dinner and his supper and his darned socks and for the joyful lovemaking that they shared. It was all long ago, yet the memories remained poignantly sweet.

"Dearest Oscar," she said aloud. "Why did you leave me so soon?"

Annie's days were busy, rain or shine so, forcing herself to set aside her melancholy, she got to work. In summer, it was the garden. In winter, it was the tincture that Oscar had entrusted to her, the secret potions that he had taught her to brew in their beautiful cellar.

Like all farm women, she rose with the sun, stoked up the cook stove and set the oatmeal to cook. Then she tended her livestock – first feed the hens and gather the eggs. Then see to her horse, a bucket of water and a forkful of hay or in summer, out to pasture in the little meadow next to the garden. Later she'd clean out his stall and the chicken coop and throw in fresh straw. Then to the garden to plant, weed or harvest, as crops and seasons dictated. "Savoury, sage, rosemary and thyme," she'd sing to herself as she harvested the mints, the marigolds, the yarrow, the echinacea, and hung them to dry in the sun or in bunches from her woodshed beams. And inspected the orchard where trees needed pruning in winter and crops needed harvesting in summer. Once a week she'd hitch Dobbin up to the buggy and drive into town for groceries, coal oil, matches, fly papers or feed for her livestock.

Occasionally she'd meet people she knew on the street or on the road. They nodded or wished her an icy good day but she was accustomed to her loneliness. After Oscar died, she was consumed with grief and fear and an unspeakable sense of loss. Already shy, she found herself unable to speak with her neighbours without breaking down in tears, which she – and they – considered a sign of weakness. So she kept her head down and turned away. Before long, they left her alone. Even Oscar's 'cousin' down Morganston way, the one she visited every few weeks, could not be called a friend. But she told herself it didn't matter; stopping to gossip about the weather or the neighbours' health would simply deflect her from her goal. Oscar would understand.

Yet two visitors, new to the neighbourhood, penetrated her solitude. First it was Julianna. Annie had a busy day ahead and she was none too pleased to be interrupted. "I won't stay," Julianna promised. "I'm just on my way to town. But I wanted to compliment you on your garden and especially the herbs. My father and I make several different medications using various herbs and I'm always eager to learn more."

Some of Annie's irritation vanished. No one else in the Valley was interested in herbs, except to reap the benefits of her mysterious tonic. Their idea of seasoning was salt and an occasional onion. "I need to tackle these weeds right now before the rain," Annie explained. "But you'd be welcome to stop in on your way home from town." And Julie did just that.

"Could we stroll through your herbs first?" Julie asked eagerly. "I think the healing power of herbs is terribly underrated." She commented enthusiastically on the cooking herbs but paused in wonder at the rows of medicinal herbs that stretched beyond. "Agrimony," she exclaimed. "Surely that herb has more health benefits than any other I can think of."

"My husband called it repichek," Annie replied. "It grows wild in Europe and parts of Canada too. This crop actually started with some plants that he dug up by the roadside years ago."

"The Cree have many uses for this plant," Julie said. "They make a tea that's good for internal problems. And poultices for wounds and burns. And they make a salve that heals wounds and helps with rheumatism and muscle problems."

"Yes, Oscar taught me to use it for all those things," Annie agreed. "I'll send some of my salve home with you and you can compare it to the one you got from the Cree."

As they exchanged facts and lore about the herbs they loved, their friendship warmed. But Julianna was not invited inside Annie's house and even when she asked about the remarkable tonic that Adam had mentioned, Annie was not forthcoming. Julie blamed herself for overstaying her visit and soon hurried off home. She was eager for the day when she and Annie could truly become friends.

One morning, as Annie knelt between two rows of marigolds, delicately removing weeds that were crowding their roots, she looked up to see a small boy watching her. "Mind you don't step on the plants," she warned him. He nodded and checked his feet to be sure they were on safe ground. "Well, what's your name?" she asked. "Where do you live?"

His small body tensed but he did not speak. Instead he pointed up the road to the top of the hill. 'Ah yes,' Annie thought to herself. 'The Donovan boy. The boy who can't speak.'

Aloud she said more kindly: "Willie Donovan – the fiddle player. Come to learn to garden, have you?"

He nodded. Then he knelt down and grasped a plant, looking to her for approval before uprooting it. "That's right," she encouraged. "That's called pig weed and if we don't get rid of them, they'll crowd out the plants we want to keep. Can you find another? Mind you pull very gently or you could pull out flowers at the same time."

He stepped over the row of flowers and knelt across from her in the next row. Side by side, they worked their way along the row, Annie keeping a close eye on his work. He was careful and thorough – obviously he helps in the garden at home, Annie decided.

"You've been a big help," she told him. "Would you like a cool drink now?"

He looked toward home and shook his head. "Time to go home?" she suggested. He nodded and turned to go. Then he turned back and took her hand in both of his, holding it softly and looking up into her face, before turning to go. She thought she'd never before seen such a beautiful child. "Come again," she called after him, to her own amazement.

As Willie turned to go, Annie made two sharp clicks with her tongue and he turned back, curious. But she was not calling him. From beneath a broad-leafed rhubarb plant, an apparition emerged – a huge white cat that stretched luxuriously before strolling over to Annie and winding itself around her ankles. Willie stood still and stared. "This is Araby," Annie announced.

Willie loved cats. He reached his hand down toward Araby, awaiting approval. The cat sniffed his fingers carefully before deciding in Willie's favour, pushing its nose into his hand, proposing a between-the-ears scratch. It stared up at him with huge eyes, one of them bright blue, the other amber, and he knelt down to dispense an expert set of scratches and tickles, allowing Araby to give his fingers a few licks in thanks. He ran his hands down the cat's back from the head to the tip of its lavish tail. The fur was so thick and deep that he could scarcely feel the spine.

"Araby is a Van cat," Annie replied to his unspoken enquiry. "He is Turkish. My husband bought him for me at the Winter Fair in Toronto. He was just a tiny kitten but he has grown into a very big cat." Willie could see that for himself.

From then on, Willie was a frequent visitor. He would arrive silently and stand by patiently, waiting for Annie to greet him and then give him a job to do. Weeding and watering were the never-ending summer challenges. She kept an eye on the sky for rain and if it failed to come, they would tirelessly march back and forth from the well to the garden carrying water to every plant. And then he would touch her hand briefly and hurry home.

Araby was seldom in evidence when he arrived but Annie's clicks would woo him from the shade of some bush or plant for a bit of petting or even a romp with a piece of string. He stays close to her, Willie thought. More like a dog than a cat.

Annie's garden flourished. Maybe it was Dobbin's manure, left to ripen for a year and dug in each fall. Or maybe it was another elixir – an aromatic brew that she carried down from the house and carefully dumped, dipper by dipper, at the roots of each plant. That was one job that Willie was never permitted to help with, nor did she give him any details about the pungent fertilizer. But by June her plants were knee-high and by harvest time, they were glorious.

Willie was fascinated as Annie and Dobbin maneuvered the scuffler between garden rows and he signaled that he wanted to drive. But there, Annie drew the line. Instead, she helped him clamber up the harness onto the horse's broad back where he could ride the rows, king of the garden, master of all he surveyed.

He learned to harvest the herbs and the root vegetables and he could scamper up a fruit tree like a squirrel to collect the ripest cherries or plums from the topmost branches that Annie could never reach. She worried about him and admonished him to be careful but his response was a smile and a dismissive wave of the hand.

Rachel dropped by occasionally to check up on her son, but she had decided early on that this was Willie's special friendship and she would not interfere. She was touched by Annie's kindness, by her instinctive awareness of Willie's needs and her willingness to adapt to him. With so many neighbours branding him as a mental defective, here was a hidden treasure she had not anticipated.

"He is a fine boy," Annie told her. "He likes the garden and he's a big help. But if you need him in your own garden, I can send him home." There was an edge of regret in her tone.

"This is a wonderful experience for him," Rachel replied. "He's learning about plants that we don't cultivate and he enjoys your company. Send him home only if you get tired of him."

"Not likely to happen," Annie muttered. She was afraid she'd cry, but this time for joy.

So the summer wore on and Annie's workload never lightened – raspberries, red currants, black currants, blackberries, the cherry tree gleaming with sweet red fruit, the deep blue plum tree following suit. Four varieties of apples ripened in her orchard next door to two types of pears, all awaiting harvest between late summer and fall. Come September, Dobbin was back on the job with the scuffler, carefully negotiating his path between the rows, loosening the earth around the potatoes. She harvested them herself, fork in hand to winkle out any that lay hidden in the soil, and Willie helped wheel them to the cellar, down the wooden chute and into the bin, along with parsnips, onions, carrots. The little boy's strength and staying power amazed her.

Willie was especially fascinated by the herbs and he spent many happy hours sniffing the plants in the garden and later as they dried in bunches on her clothes line or hanging from the woodshed beams if rain threatened. She told him the name of every herb and showed him how some were preserved in oil for cooking and baking.

On one oppressively hot summer day, she suggested they embark on an expedition. Clicking for Araby, she led him down through the orchard and into the lower meadow to a small pond. When Araby dashed ahead and plunged into the water, Willie ran after him, terrified that he would drown.

"Don't worry, Willie. He's perfectly safe," Annie called. "Van cats like to swim and there's nothing he loves more than a good paddle in the pond. Come on, let's sit down and have some cookies and tea and enjoy his escapade." Araby swam sedately, back and forth, back and forth, with his nose barely above water and his vast tail floating out behind him. Willie couldn't resist wading into the water and finally dropped down, clothes and all, to cool off and paddle along beside the cat. He emerged, dripping but refreshed. When Annie finally called, Araby came willingly, his girth considerably reduced thanks to the wet fur clinging to his body.

Willie had ventured as far as the stable and the woodshed but he had never been inside Annie's house. He seemed to accept her reluctance to invite him inside but his curiosity never diminished. When they gathered the dried herbs from the clothes line, he would carry them as far as the door but always she stopped him and took delivery of them there.

But one frigid day, he made it inside. He had helped her pull out the last of the dead plants in the garden and lay them between the rows to be returned to the earth in the spring when Lenny applied plough and harrow to her garden plot. Now he was shivering and his hands were raw from the coarse plants. "Come up to the house, Willie. We'll have a warm drink."

He followed her eagerly.

Her kitchen smelled of all the herbs she had ever grown, many of them hanging in bunches from the ceiling beams. The stove was warm and a substantial pot of something aromatic simmered on the back of it. He stretched his hands out to the heat gratefully. "Let's have some soup, Willie," she suggested, and he nodded vigorously.

She spooned tiny dumplings into two bowls and from the pot on the stove; she ladled out steaming soup loaded with vegetables. Willie loved his mother's cooking but he thought he'd never tasted anything as good as this. He pointed to the dry herbs overhead and back to his bowl, mutely asking what it contained. "Oh yes, I understand," Annie replied. "Well, onions and garlic to start, and then marjoram and thyme, some rosemary, and of course all those good vegetables from the garden like the carrots, and peas and parsnips you've helped to weed, and then some barley and plenty of beans. It makes a good meal, doesn't it?"

He nodded his agreement and held out his bowl for more.

Finally warm and well fed, he looked around the kitchen. It was very plain but very clean, not much furniture except for the cook stove, the kitchen table where they sat, a bureau for dishes and a couple of high-back rocking chairs facing the window. And beside them, shelves of books stretching from floor to ceiling.

Araby unwound himself from one of the rockers and sauntered over in search of attention. Annie picked up a tough-bristled brush and gave the cat a few strokes, showing Willie the wad of white hair that she had harvested. "This hair is so long that some people spin it into yarn and knit it," she told him.

Long after Willie had trotted off homeward, carrying a bouquet of cookery herbs for his mother, Annie continued her work – processing her fruits and vegetables and herbs, sorting, chopping, grinding, boiling, until they were just right.

And as she laboured, Annie thought about Oscar and about Willie and about the children she had never had. She had come to love Willie and to look forward to his visits, although she wondered whether it had been a mistake to let him into the house. But he can't speak, she told herself, so there's no danger of him gossiping about what he sees.

But first among her memories was Oscar – at her side, encouraging her, applauding her, inspiring her. She thought back to their first meeting, twenty years ago, soon after Oscar, then called Oskar Walter, arrived in Canada from Moravia. He discovered Anna working as a waitress in a Montreal restaurant, already developing a hard shell against a world that seemed intent on finding ways to wound her. But he cracked that shell. She helped Oscar with his English; he helped her with her self-esteem. They didn't wait long to marry and she began to experience the first happiness she'd ever known in her young life. He changed his name to Oscar Walters and she changed hers to Annie, although Oscar's private name for her was Andulka.

They came to the Valley because they perceived farm life to be one of freedom and fulfillment. But Oscar's foreign accent and Annie's shyness were hefty obstacles to forging friendships in that Irish/Scottish enclave. So they retreated to their own company, and they dreamed a dream.

Their house was built on the site of an earlier one that had burned to the ground. The previous owners could not afford to rebuild it entirely, so they had built only over the old cellar, leaving a large stone foundation at ground level.

"That's a good solid base," Oscar observed one day. "Why don't we build on it? It would make a fine stable."

"A stable? Next to the house?" Annie countered.

"In my country, the stable and the house are often one building. The animals are warmer in winter and easier to care for." And so they set to work, hauling stones from all across the farm and painstakingly fitting them atop the old foundation, mixing lime mortar to hold them in place. It took a full summer of rock hauling and stone masonry before the walls were high enough. Then they added a peaked roof, with a ladder for access from inside. To separate house from stable, they built a storage space next to the house for grain and machinery and Oscar devised a pulley system to haul the cutter up to the ceiling in summer and the buggy in winter. Adjacent to it, the stable contained two box stalls with mangers. They filled the upper level with hay and straw and finally introduced two horses, one cow and ten chickens to their new home.

Next they turned their attention to the cellar, building bins for winter vegetables and shelves for processed foods. They built partitions and split stones, crafting handsome flagstones to pave the floor of the largest room. plastering its walls and covering the ceiling with elaborate pressed tin. Then they added the equipment they needed to make their dream take shape and began to brew the elixirs that Oscar remembered from his own family home in Bohemia. Once a month, he would stock the back of the buggy with the stoneware bottles they had filled in the cellar and make the two-hour trek to Morganston to visit Ralph Peters, another Moravian immigrant he had met on arrival in Montreal, and called his cousin. He would return late that night with a wad of cash and a buggy full of empty stoneware jugs.

But Oscar's energy began to wane. Over a period of almost a year, he became weaker. And the weakness turned to pain. He tried to ward off the ailment with tonics that he created himself but their effects were short-lived. "We must make plans for you," he said one day. "We must be sure that you can manage after I am gone." Annie refused to listen to him. "Gone? You are not going anywhere, Oscar. There must be something we can do to get you well again." But Oscar persisted and finally she listened. And when he died, she forced herself to rally from her grief and pursue the plan they had mapped out together. Hard work helped to dull the pain.

Annie clung to the dream she had nurtured with Oscar but she never shared it. Not even with Willie who continued to visit, helping with the garden, tending Dobbin or the chickens, clearing the snow that sometimes threatened to swallow the house, and spending more and more time with Annie.

But that day, in the warm winter kitchen, she succumbed to an impulse.

"Willie, do you know where Spain is," she asked. A well thumbed atlas lay on the bureau and he retrieved it, turning immediately to Europe and planting his finger on Spain. "That's right," she conceded. "Spain. That's where we were planning to live."

Willie looked baffled. He extended his arms to encompass the house and farm and shook his head. "Oh yes, we love this place," she replied. "But we always wanted to go to Spain and own an orange grove. It was our dream – our secret dream."

Never before had she uttered a word about their vision to another human being, except Oscar. But she knew her secret was safe with Willie. After all, he was mute.

CHAPTER 9

Hearing Voices

In them days, there weren't no such thing as women doctors. Ask anybody and they'd agree that women wasn't cut out for doctorin' – too weak and inclined to be hysterical or downright foolish. Of course Velma was quick to point out that a woman who could run a house, cook three square meals a day, care for youngsters, separate the milk, tend the garden and fill the cellar with food each fall and even milk the cows and follow a plough if need be, was plenty strong and also pretty good at doing a lot of things at one time. They also delivered babies and bandaged up bleeding cuts and broken arms if no doctor was around. So I had to agree, a few of them could be nurses, but not doctors. They could be teachers but not school inspectors. They could be store clerks but nuthin more. "Why not?" Velma yelled at me. "Because they're women," I said, "and that's my last word." But it wasn't.

When we heard Julianna had wanted to be a doctor after learning all sorts of medical stuff from her pa, we wasn't surprised. Count on her to want to kick over the traces and do somethin' that women wasn't allowed.

She was a caution, that woman.

Lenny

❧

Julianna was eager to get better acquainted with the neighbours. But first, she pumped Clara for details, especially about those who seemed most interesting – the Donovans, Annie and the Dietrichs on the plus side, Joe Dunning and his shy wife and daughter, the sole contenders so far, on the negative team. She was curious too about Clara and George with their impeccable English accents and courtly bearing and she asked Clara how they came to be in Canada and on this farm in this Valley.

"We escaped servitude," Clara responded with a smile. "We were in service to the Sheridan household, a very old and aristocratic family in England. We were both sixteen, newly arrived from the countryside and very intimidated by the grandness of it all, and by all the other servants who looked down on us because we were country bumpkins and the lowest in the servant pecking order. So that helped to draw us together.

"Lord and Lady Sheridan had houses in Sussex and in London but George worked with the horses so he lived mostly in Sussex. And as a kitchen maid I moved back and forth with the family between Sussex and London. We were in love from the first day we met but we needed Lord Sheridan's permission to marry and he was not in favour of it."

She explained the rigid hierarchy of the British class system, from the highest aristocracy right down to the lowliest servant. And she told Julianna about the deterioration of the British upper class, accustomed for centuries to great wealth and power, now facing 20th century financial problems that forced them to sell off their land and in some cases their ancestral homes.

"So was that the situation with your employers?" Julianna enquired.

"We heard whispers that Lord and Lady Sheridan were facing some financial problems," Clara confided. "Of course financial hardship is relative, isn't it? I mean, when you're incredibly rich, you have resources – you can sell one home or a few thoroughbreds or a painting or two. Or marry your daughter off to the rich Earl of Whatever in the next county. These people had no concept of the hardships that poor people in the country faced, even on their own estate." Her face hardened as she thought of the ever-widening gap between rich and poor.

"But to be honest, we were tired of being servants for a group of people whose entire life seemed to be about clothing, hunting, parties and making profitable marriages. So we saved every penny and when we had enough for a passage to Canada, we resigned our positions and . . . here we are."

"But how did you come here, to this farm?" Julianna prodded.

"The Sheridans' butler, Mr. Barton, had taken a shine to George. He had already emigrated to Canada and he urged us to do the same. We landed in Montreal and then moved on to Toronto," Clara continued. "Mr. Barton was very formal and icy when we knew him in England, but he turned out to be the best friend we could have had when we got here.

"He and Adam met at a dinner in Toronto and Mr. Barton learned that he was looking for someone to manage the farm so we were introduced. And when Adam offered, we jumped at the chance of coming to work here. We could not possibly have afforded a farm of our own but here we have a wonderful employer, enjoyable work, a beautiful place to live. Adam doesn't treat us as servants, he treats us as friends. Neither one of us can imagine any other life now."

"Have you been able to make friends with any of the neighbours?" Julie asked.

"Not really. They seem somewhat shy. Perhaps our accents confuse them and they're not sure of our relationship with Adam. I do like Rachel Donovan though and I'm fascinated by Annie Walters, even though she's something of a tough nut. There's more going on in that grizzled head of hers than she wants to admit to."

"I'm not so sure they'll trust me either," Julie admitted ruefully. "I want to fit in but I don't know where to begin. I agree with you about Annie. And I liked what I saw of Rachel Donovan.

"What's the story about Willie? Has he never talked or has he had some illness that affected his vocal abilities?"

When Clara recounted the story of the barn fire and Willie's stricken reaction to the brutal death of the horses, Julianna's eyes filled with tears. "I wonder…" she murmured and Clara turned to her expectantly. "I wonder if I could help."

"Whatever do you mean?"

"Well, it's likely that his vocal chords and larynx were not damaged," Julie surmised. "If he'd met with an accident, a blow to the throat for example, or suffocation from the smoke, then the damage might be physical and permanent. But I believe it's his nervous system reacting to the horror of it all that prevents him from talking. And there may be ways to overcome that problem."

Clara smiled but said no more. Her new friend had already exhibited some extraordinary skills. "Please take these sugar cookies to Rachel when you go," she said simply.

Julianna walked the mile or so to the Donovans, revelling in the brisk fall air and the still-glorious colours of trees and fields along the way. Rachel greeted her warmly and immediately pushed the tea kettle to the front of the stove in readiness for the ever-mandatory cup of tea. At his mother's invitation, Willie shyly emerged from the sitting room and obediently shook Julie's hand. He stood before her, gazing intently into her face as if trying to read her mind and she looked back at him, smiling. What beautiful eyes, she thought. A small boy, but not frail. Shining eyes, silky hair. His face was tanned by the summer sun and many hours of outdoor work and play had built sturdy legs and arms. But it was the extraordinary perception and intelligence of his gaze that caught at her heart and rekindled her longing for a son of her own.

"Wonderful cookies," Rachel beamed. "Willie, Mrs. Cooper sent us a batch of your favourite sugar cookies. Here – let me give you some cookies and milk to take into the sitting room and you can keep on with your puzzle while Mrs. Chandler and I get acquainted."

Willie happily scooped up his snack and disappeared.

"What a lovely boy," Julianna ventured. "Is he your only child? Oh no, I remember – you brought your daughter to the party. Betsy, isn't it? I didn't get much opportunity to talk to her."

"Yes, Betsy is five years older than Willie. She's a bit moody – I suppose it's her age, but I also think she's jealous of Willie and all the attention he gets from us. We try to maintain a balance but inevitably, because Willie is home with me all day and I'm teaching him his school work as well as music, she feels left out. I wish I could find some way to overcome that problem."

"Is she helpful with Willie's school lessons?" Julie asked. "Might she feel more positive if you were to emphasize her more advanced schooling?"

Rachel hesitated. "I've tried in the past to involve her in the teaching, but she tends to bully and hector him so he ends up in tears and then he tries to avoid her. I haven't decided how to handle that. She says she hates teaching and wants to be a nurse."

"May I make a suggestion?" Julie asked. "How do you think she would feel about learning some simple massage techniques that might release Willie's vocal chords and help him to speak?"

Rachel's eyes widened and her hands trembled as she sipped her tea. "I don't understand what you're suggesting," she gasped. "What is this procedure? How do you know about it?"

"My father is a doctor in Toronto," Julie revealed. "I worked alongside him for several years and he taught me many of his techniques and ideas. He practices a gentle massage of the throat, using a salve that's made by the Indian people up north of Toronto. He is on very good terms with the shaman there who is both a graduated medical doctor and an Indian medicine man. They spend hours and hours exchanging ideas and healing methods and the good Indian doctor – his English name is Dr. Rankin – he keeps my father supplied with this remarkable salve that relaxes seized muscles and stimulates blood circulation. And I have some of that salve in my pharmacopeia. Would you consider allowing me to try it, with very gentle massage, on Willie's throat? And possibly involving Betsy in the work as well?"

Rachel stared into her tea cup as if searching for the future in the leaves. "I'll need to talk to my husband about it first," she said. "But something has happened recently that makes the timing of this idea especially appealing. Willie often plays violin or piano for his own amusement and since your party, I was shocked to hear him humming along with the melodies he was playing. It's the first vocalization I've heard from him since the fire, except when he cries in pain."

Julie was so excited that she jumped up and paced around the table. "That is amazing, Rachel. No guarantees but this could be a breakthrough. Do talk to your husband about this. I'll gladly come back and tell both of you all I know and about the success my father has had with it. It's a harmless procedure – there is no surgery, no drugs to swallow and the ingredients of the salve are all herbs that the Indians gather from the fields and forests. I hope you'll both decide to give it a try."

And they did. Within days, Julie began twice weekly visits to the Donovan house, coaching Willie in deep breathing to help him relax, patiently massaging his back, his shoulders, his neck, applying her salve to his throat and wrapping it in flannel to ensure that its heat penetrated. She set out to teach Betsy the techniques as well and the girl showed surprising skill at massage, though she still bullied Willie. "Sit up straight, stupid," she would snarl at him. "Do you think I like touching your dirty neck? Why does my brother have to be such an idiot?"

Willie had no choice but to endure his sister's verbal abuse but Julie knew it was counter-productive. She decided to tackle the problem obliquely.

"Nursing is such demanding work," she mentioned one day, keeping her tone casual. "I often think that nurses actually suffer some of the pain that their patients feel – as I'm sure you share Willie's frustration while he struggles to find his voice again." Betsy listened intently; proud that Julianna was sharing her insights into the medical profession and singling her out for special attention.

"And I think that nurses – and doctors, too – can become annoyed with their patients because they are not recovering fast enough. Even though you know the healing process is long and difficult, you want your patient to make faster progress." She paused as she checked Willie's shoulder and throat muscles for tension. "You have excellent hands, Betsy. You've learned the massage techniques perfectly. I think we're almost ready for the salve now."

Betsy beamed and applied herself to the task at hand.

"There's still some tension there and of course we know that what we are trying to do is to release all the tensions that may be blocking Willie's vocal chords. Along with the massage, I've found that patients respond very well to positive thoughts and words reminding them of how well they are doing but never venting frustration or exhaustion. Negative words have negative consequences in the healing process."

Did Betsy understand the lesson, Julie wondered. After all she was just a child, albeit on the cusp of womanhood. Without comment, Betsy continued her work. But for now, the insults and bullying seemed to diminish. Julie sincerely hoped the message had hit home.

Julianna involved Willie in his own therapy too, explaining every step and process to him, delighted to see his face light up and his eyes shine when he understood. She urged him to practice deep breathing at every opportunity, to massage his own throat, and above all to try to make sounds. It was hard work and he worked hard.

They played noise games. They hummed melodies together and she showed him how to click his tongue, make slurping sounds and blow rude-sounding raspberries which always elicited gales of laughter. She encouraged him to imitate animal and bird sounds, challenging him to be a dog, a cat, a chicken, a crow and any other critter he could think of and the house echoed with her barks and meows, and his valiant attempts to replicate them. And besides his incredible will to learn and to conquer his disability, Willie revealed another side of his character - a sense of humour.

"Let's pretend we're dogs," Julie suggested one day, several weeks after the therapy had begun. She expected a bark but instead Willie snuffled and then growled, as he'd seen dogs do when they tackled a woodchuck den. The cat's meow was a little beyond him so he tried purring instead. Julianna patted his head and scratched behind his ears, calling him a good kitty and offering to catch a mouse for him as a reward. He smacked his lips and produced his slurping sound.

Betsy watched the games sourly but her participation in the hands-on therapy was enthusiastic and skilled. Julianna leapt at every opportunity to praise her and give her credit for each new step that Willie was able to manage. "You have a real aptitude for nursing, Betsy," she remarked. "I'm really impressed with the way you've mastered the massage techniques. Have you thought about becoming a trained nurse when you grow up?" She was gratified to see Betsy's smile. From that moment, she was Julie's acolyte and willing slave.

Chrissy continued to visit whenever she could slip away from her parents. She longed to help with the massage therapy and Julianna welcomed her assistance but Betsy now became territorial.

"You have to do it just right," she warned Chrissy. "If you start doing it wrong, you'll make it worse, not better. Mrs. Chandler taught me all the right techniques and I think it's better if it's done by a trained person. See, I'm going to be a nurse when I grow up. In fact, I'm almost a nurse now," she bragged. "And this is nurse's work." So while Julie and Betsy worked on Willie, Chrissy read to him, working her way through all the books that arrived at school each month in the big wooden crate from the travelling library.

"Don't let yourself be discouraged, Willie." Julie sensed one day that Willie's spirits were low and she assumed it was the slow progress they seemed to be making. "After all, it's been…how long? Two years at least since your voice took leave of absence? An overnight cure would be lovely but that's not reasonable, is it? Your voice needs time to get back on its feet, so to speak. You're doing wonderfully well so what we must do now is work, work, work. And you're just the lad to do it." He watched her intently and smiled, seeming to read more into her words than she actually said.

Julianna looked forward to the time when the therapy session was finished and she settled in for a cup of tea with Rachel. They enjoyed one another's company and were becoming fast friends. "Are you enjoying country life?" Rachel asked one day. "You must find it a big change from your life in the city. I know I did and I still do." Rachel and John had both been teachers and decided together to go back to farming when their first child arrived and John's parents moved into town.

"Well, the neighbours are somewhat stand-offish," Julie replied. "I'm so glad to have made your acquaintance. And Clara Cooper is delightful too."

"The neighbours will warm to you in time," Rachel reassured her. "But let me share a badly kept secret with you. When Adam came home from his wedding and you weren't with him – and didn't arrive for…what was it…two weeks or so, the gossip mongers in the Valley went wild. They surmised that you'd had a big argument on your wedding day and you changed your mind. Or that you were one of those modern women who didn't really live with their husbands. Or any number of other fanciful stories. And you know you were wearing black the day you arrived? So the story spread that someone had died at your wedding and you were in mourning. Everybody had a different theory and it's been a hot topic of conversation ever since."

Julianna was amazed. "To think that I've been on everyone's lips and never been kissed," she laughed. "How disappointed they'll be to hear the truth. First of all, I prefer black for travelling. And as to the delay, I've been working on a book about women's health and the printing was behind schedule. I needed to stay in Toronto to oversee its completion. Simple as that." She reached into her satchel and extracted a slim volume, passing it to Rachel. "It's a modest little book but you'd be amazed at how complicated the printers can make it."

Rachel took her time to examine the book, before handing it back. "No, please keep it," Julie urged. "I'm already looking ahead to a bigger, new edition so before long this one will be out of print.

"But what can I do about the gossips," she asked. "I had no idea."

"Well, it would be fun to tweak their noses, don't you think?" Rachel smiled wickedly. "There are one or two – Gertie Biggar is the worst – who dream up vague ideas that they soon convert into God's truth. And she has a few cronies who are ready to believe every silly story she spouts. Gertie has already announced that Adam realized he'd married a fallen woman and refused to bring you home. Her earlier version was that you were simply too grand for country life and refused to associate with the likes of us."

"I wonder why Adam didn't tell someone why I was delayed," Julie commented. "Maybe he was enjoying their suspense. I have half a notion to keep it that way."

"Let's do that," Rachel responded enthusiastically. "I'll keep your naughty secret. A book! Outrageous! Shocking! I won't breathe a word of it." Julianna was still chuckling as she headed up the road for home.

The therapy continued without much apparent progress, but Julianna was patient. Then, a few weeks later, Willie startled his mother by clearly meowing like a cat. Rachel thought it was his own cat, Droplet, but she was curled into a sleepy fur ball on the couch. Then he meowed again, more insistently, holding out his empty cup for milk, and when she looked at him, he chuckled. The pitcher shook in her hands but she was laughing. "You come with me, young man," she ordered. She grabbed his hand and marched him out to the barn where John was finishing up the milking. "All right, Willie," using her cross voice as she secretly winked at him, "this is something that your father had better hear about." John glanced up at her stern tone but immediately noticed Willie's merry smirk. "What mischief has this young man been up to," he growled.

Willie moved closer to his father and hunkered down to a near-sitting position, resting his hands on the floor in a cat pose. And he meowed. Then he rocked back on his heels, lifted his 'paws' and opened his mouth wide. John stared for a moment and then he got the message. He grasped the cow's hind teat and carefully aiming toward his son, shot a long stream of warm milk straight into his open mouth, just as he sometimes did for the cats.

"Prrrrr," said Willie, when he finally finished swallowing, choking and wiping the spills off his chin.

"You're prrrrrfectly welcome," John replied.

And their joyous laughter rang throughout the stables.

Fear of Farming

Adam liked horses, honey bees and apple trees in that order. Leastwise, they seemed to be his main concerns. Of course he had a big farm but he could afford hired help to pitch in with the ploughin' and mowin' and barn chores. So that left him plenty of time for other stuff – like goin' to the auction and buyin' broken down horses that he'd nurse back to health. By times I'd look out the window and see him drivin' real slow with a poor sad critter draggin' its tail behind his buggy or once or twice a wild thing rearin' and frothin' as he led it home. And then a few weeks later, there's the sick old nag sleek as an apple and full of pep, right alongside the bronco, all meek and mild. More than once I wondered how he managed to stay out of the way of the kicks and bites that a horse like that can give a man. What he did to calm it down and make it trust him. But all's he'd say was: "Talk kindly to it. Be gentle. Never use a whip. Give it lots of treats. And give it lots of time." Seemed to work for him. As for bees, the dang things sting so I always stayed well away when Adam was tendin' his hives. Though I was happy enough to sample the honey. And the apples – well, he liked to collect odd kinds of apples and then graft one branch onto another tree and mix 'em all up. Never did understand what enjoyment he got from it but then, there's a lot I didn't understand about Adam.

Lenny

"I have a surprise for you," Adam told Julie at breakfast. He was looking very pleased with himself. "We're going for a drive so wear something warm."

Together they walked down to the stables. Julie loved the sounds and scents of the stables – the unmistakable smell of horses, their little nickering greetings, their eagerness for the apples or carrots that Adam always carried in his pockets. He handed her a bright red apple and led her along to a spacious stall near the back. "Come 'round the front," he suggested. "This one doesn't know you yet so she might be a bit skittish. I don't want you to get kicked."

The horse that peered out at them over the manger was certainly a gem – a slim, sleek black beauty with a white star on her forehead, matching the three white socks that Julie had noticed when she entered the stable. "Well, Cleo – meet your new owner," Adam said. "Julianna, this is your very own horse."

The horse was tossing its head and shifting its weight noisily from foot to foot. "Offer her your apple," Adam suggested. "And talk to her."

Julianna extended her hand with the apple but she jumped back when Cleo tried to snatch it. "Hold the apple on the flat of your hand so she can pick it up without any risk to your fingers," Adam advised her. Those huge teeth and the animal's apparent disregard for her ten digits were daunting but Julie finally mustered her nerve, served the apple as Adam had instructed, and was gratified to see the horse munching it down and then snuffling for more.

"Talk to her," Adam urged. "She needs to get acquainted with you." Julie was still a novice in conversational skills involving animals and briefly wondered what subject the horse might be interested in. The idea was so silly that she laughed aloud. "Hello, Cleo," she said. "My name is Julianna but you may call me Julie. How are you today?"

Cleo fixed her with an intent gaze and extended her neck over the manger. "It's fine to pat her forehead and scratch her behind the ears," Adam said.

Julie extended her hand again but the horse bared its teeth, looking for another apple. "Just reach up and pat her forehead," Adam instructed. With some trepidation, Julie did as she was told and Cleo bowed her head regally to receive the caresses.

"First lesson successful," Adam chuckled. "Want to take her for a drive?"

Julie wanted to shout an adamant 'NO' but she couldn't dampen Adam's enthusiasm. She managed a rather weak "What fun!" instead. But she was already thinking back to the black horse that Adam had brought home from the auction just a few weeks back. It was tethered to the back of his buggy on a very short lead but not short enough to control its constant bucking, kicking, rearing and throwing its head from side to side, showing the whites of its frantic eyes and flicking foam from its mouth.

"That's some wild horse you got today," she had remarked at supper.

"Oh she's not so bad," Adam had responded. "She was just nervous about the trip home. The auction is a very upsetting experience for a horse, especially a high-strung one like her. And then she smelled my horses and me and the countryside and everything was strange. So she needs time to unwind. She's already calmer and she'll be fine in a few days."

"What do you have in mind for her," Julie asked, without much caring. Horses were Adam's world, not her own.

"Time will tell," he replied. "But she's a fine little horse. After she's settled in, we'll see what she can do."

Now he walked round to the back of the stall and talking quietly, moved in beside the horse, laying his hand on her haunch and sliding it along her back all the way to her head. Cleo shivered a little but she turned her head and nudged Adam's shoulder. "Is Cleo the horse you brought home a few weeks ago?" Julie asked in a weak voice.

"Yes indeed. Isn't she coming along beautifully? A bit of kindness, a carrot or two – they work wonders."

He grasped Cleo's bridle and backed the horse out of its stall, its shod hooves ringing on the stone floor. "So first we get her out of her stall and into harness," he told Julie. "Why don't you hold her while I get the harness?"

"I'm not good with horses," Julie responded timidly. "Until I came here, I'd never ever touched a horse in my life. I'm happier with those quiet ones you use on the wagonette."

"Well, no time like the present, m'dear. Come round to Cleo's head, talk nicely to her and hold on to the bridle. You'll get the hang of it in no time."

No I won't, Julie thought to herself. But again, spurred by Adam's enthusiasm, she initiated another one-sided chat with Cleo and held her bridle while Adam took down the harness and dropped it across her back. Cleo shied and tossed her head, and Julie's stomach lurched, but Adam spoke to the horse and she settled immediately.

Adam led Cleo – and Julie as well – out of the stable and over to the drive shed. Julie had only been inside it once – a vast chilly space full of farm machinery, wagons and buggies, with sleighs and cutters pulled up to the ceiling, waiting for winter, and upstairs a workshop for repairs, construction and supplies. There by the door was a charming little buggy, gleaming black with scrolls and whorls of gold-coloured trim, its dashboard lavishly painted with flowers and birds. "This is the rest of your surprise," Adam announced proudly.

Julie couldn't help loving the buggy and loving Adam for buying it. "Thank you, Adam," she exclaimed, holding both his hands and planting a kiss on his cheek. "It's simply beautiful. With all that decoration, it should be in the parlour."

Adam backed the horse between the shafts and hitched up the traces. Then with a courtly bow, he invited Julie to climb into her chariot for a ride. And off they went, out the long laneway and down the dusty road, with Cleo covering the miles as if she were on a dance floor, her white-stockinged feet lifting high, her neck proudly arched, her fine black tail and mane flying in the breeze. "Why don't you drive now," Adam suggested, offering the reins to Julie. The idea struck terror to her heart. "I'll wait for another time," she demurred. "I'm not sure Cleo is ready for me yet. Nor I for her."

"Well, my dearest, Cleo and this buggy are yours, exclusively for your use. You need your own rig to get around."

Visualizing all the buggies and carriages she had seen since coming to the farm, Julie was tempted to argue that another one wasn't needed. But she kept her peace. She even managed to hide her relief when finally they arrived back at the farm, returned the buggy to the drive shed and led Cleo down to the stable, with a stop at the water trough for a noisy drink. Adam pulled off the harness and the horse immediately headed into her stall, snuffling about in the oat box in case some grain had magically materialized while she was on the road. Minutes later, it did materialize as Adam handed Julie a bucket of oats to pour into the box while he pitched a bit of hay into the manger. Cleo settled down for lunch.

Adam's stable was constantly in flux thanks to his weakness for the horse auction, where he bought frequently and sold occasionally. Most of his horses were workers essential to a large farm – a three-horse team of huge black Percherons for hauling the double plough or dragging logs or boulders, an extra pair of heavy horses for busy seasons, a team of hardy Canadian horses for lighter jobs like harrowing or disking the fields, and now three frisky thoroughbreds for riding or carriage work. Julie's favourites were the Canadian horses, descendents, Adam told her, of an equine gift sent by Louis XIV to Canada's earliest settlers three centuries ago. Gentle, intelligent and hardworking, they were the unsung heroes of many farms.

But Adam had a particular weakness and that was abused animals, especially horses. They almost invariably came home with him for special care and cosseting before being re-sold or more often given away to a needy family that he knew would treat them well.

He was also proud of his cattle – a herd of soft brown Jersey cows whose milk, copious and rich in butterfat, was the envy of many Valley farmers, who depended upon the ubiquitous black and white Holsteins for meat and milk.

Adam's cows were never slaughtered for beef. Instead he bought beef from Herbert Hawkins, the local butcher, but to Julie's surprise, he never ate it himself. "Blame it on the Agricultural College," Adam explained. "I learned to respect animals there and I don't want to kill them. And I also learned that we don't need a lot of meat.

"And apple trees. That's something else I learned at the Agricultural College too –

how to grow apples and how to graft them." He showed Julia how he would cut a branch from one tree, then slash the bark of another, slip the graft into it, and seal it up with bees wax.

"Why not just buy a new tree?" Julianna enquired reasonably.

"Grafting is more interesting," Adam replied. "And some trees, like this golden spy, just aren't available here. This one for example." He showed Julie a branch that looked remarkably like every other branch on every other tree. "I ordered this from Scotland and it took three months to get here. It was packed in a pot of honey but it travelled beautifully and last year it finally produced fruit. And that fruit winters very well. We'll still be able to eat these apples in February."

That apple tree, on which he had grafted three different varieties of spies, was his pride and joy. "There was an amazing teacher at the college, an elderly British horticulturist named Dr. Theodore Manley," he explained to Julia. "His ideas about horticulture were brilliant and quite radical and I spent as much time with him as he'd permit, picking up nuggets of information about everything from tree grafting to bee keeping to the job that swamps and forests do to keep the soil from eroding and keep the air and water clean.

"He was vegetarian and when he talked about it – the cruelty to animals but also the health benefits – it made so much sense that I decided to stop eating meat. Auntie and Uncle were appalled when I got home and refused the Sunday roast."

Honey was another of his passions. Though Julia dreaded bees and their propensity for entangling themselves in her hair and stinging her, Adam was completely at ease with them.

At the edge of the orchard below the house sat a dozen or more white hives and the bees were hard at work in the fruit trees and in the clover that grew beneath them, all summer long. Soon after her arrival, Julie had an encounter with a bee in which both she and the bee lost. It swooped down out of nowhere and invaded her hair. In a frenzy, it stung her scalp. Julie ran up to the house and Clara removed the bee and then the stinger, which would have continued to seep its poison into the wound long after the bee was dead. After that, Julie covered her hair with a hat or a scarf before venturing into bee territory.

But Adam was fearless. His only defense was a straw hat and a 'smoker', a metal container fitted with bellows and stuffed with smouldering cedar bark, that subdued the bees long enough for him to raid their hives. With an empty box beside the hive, he'd lift out the frames of honey, brush the bees off them with a goose feather and slip the frame into the empty box. Then he'd gently refill the hive with empties and carry the loaded frames into the summer kitchen to extract the honey.

Julie was wonderstruck one day when she watched him deal with a huge swarm of bees. Adam explained that there was room in the hive for only one queen bee so if a second queen emerged, she would leave the hive with an army of acolytes and lead them to a nearby tree or perhaps a corner of the house. The angry buzzing and the writhing mass of bees, sometimes as big as a milk bucket, sent shivers down her back. But Adam calmly carried an empty beehive to a spot just below the swarm and stood quietly peering into the cluster until he spied the queen. Reaching into that great tangle of bees bare-handed he gently lifted out the queen and deposited her in her hive. And immediately, the swarm began to follow her, settling happily into their new quarters. "Now we just have to wait for them to quiet down and by tomorrow they'll be ready to start work in their own honey factory," Adam explained. At dusk when all was quiet, he picked up the hive and carried it gently to where it belonged. If he ever got stung, Julie was never aware of it. "Bees smell fear," he explained. "So I just will myself to stay calm."

Easy for you to say, Julie thought, as she imagined a bee in her hair, in her shoe, in her pocket, in her bed. "Will myself to stay calm," she told herself. "Stay calm. Stay calm. Leave the bees to Adam and stay calm."

Then she remembered her new horse with its sharp hooves and wild eyes, and panic struck again. She had already determined that she would never venture forth alone with Cleo. Now the challenge was to manage it without offending Adam.

"Stay calm," she repeated. "Stay calm." She almost succeeded.

CHAPTER 11

Eaton's for Overalls

That woman sure brought about some changes to our Valley and I'm not sure they was all to the good. Before she turned up here, life was simple. Our wives and daughters did what they was told, made do with what they had and did all their grumblin' to other women on the party line.

But Mrs. Chandler changed all that. For one thing, they all wanted to look like her so you started to see them more and more with their hair braided and twisted up over their heads – though they couldn't match the gold colour of her hair nor the thickness of her braid. They all wanted to dress like her too but even if they owned some of them fancy city togs that she brought with her, they'd never look like her.

But I do believe it was the trousers that gave our Valley such a shake-up, things was never the same again.

Lenny

❦

Julie's skirt was her enemy. Determined to share the hefty workload of the household, she followed Clara into the garden to help with the end-of-season harvest. There were still potatoes to gather from the scuffled rows, beets and carrots to pull, turnips and cabbages and a few late apples to collect. But she continued to trip over her skirt and she knew that before long, the already mud-stained hem would begin to tatter. She tried hitching her skirt up higher at her waist but it continually slipped down. Unlike some of her city sisters who were cropping both their hair and their hemlines, Julie preferred longer dresses.

Clara seemed to have a remedy. She had taken an old dress and simply chopped a few inches off the skirt. "It's my garden dress," she explained. "Better than spraining an ankle or skinning my knees. And the part I cut off will find new employment as a duster or maybe an apron."

"I don't have a dress that I'm willing to sacrifice to the cause," Julie replied.

Just then they saw the mailman clopping by, his well-trained horse criss-crossing the road to deposit mail in all the tin mailboxes along the way. So together they strolled out the laneway to collect it.

"It's here at last," exclaimed Clara. She was waving a plump book. "Eaton's catalogue," she explained. "The fall and winter edition. Time for some new boots.

Oh yes, and a roast pan to replace that one that I scorched."

Julie peered curiously at the illustrated book. She had been a regular customer at the Eaton department store in Toronto – like just about everyone else in the city – but the mail order catalogue was a new experience for her. Clara opened the catalogue on the kitchen table and quickly leafed through its glossy pages while Julie peeked over her shoulder. Sure enough, the book seemed to be packed with every single thing anyone could ever want – patent medicines and plough shares, boots and buttons, perambulators and preserving jars, hats and harnesses and – what's this? "Houses? Barns?" she gasped. "You can buy a house from Eaton's?"

"You can indeed," Clara replied. "And a very nice house too." She ceased her meditation upon pots and kettles to return to the page. "It comes as a kind of kit, you see, all ready to assemble. With instructions too. And the same for barns."

"Well, I never," Julie stared in amazement. "But how do they get it to customers? A house is…well…big."

"You're right. And a barn's even bigger," Clara chuckled. "It's all packaged up and shipped by train to the nearest order office. There's one just here in Paxton Ford. The customer has to arrange to collect it there and take it home. Several strong men and a hay wagon and there we are! Bob's your uncle."

Julie continued to stare at this new discovery. "It's really pretty,' she exclaimed. "Look at the verandah. And the windows. Good heavens, Clara, look. It has four bedrooms. It's wonderful."

"I'm told that out west, in the Prairies, there are plenty of these houses," Clara said. "They've saved people's lives, especially if they've gone homesteading and can't get a house built in time for winter. Eaton's to the rescue."

Timothy Eaton's big department stores were front and centre in several Canadian cities, especially in Toronto where his business began. Hard-working immigrants from Ireland, the Eatons had been shunned by the city's hoi-polloi as mere 'trade' but his business acumen and generosity had earned them a loyal following and in due course, admittance into the inner circles of the rich and influential. Everyone knew and admired the company's decision to maintain the salaries of their enlisted employees throughout the war while regularly sending them generous packages of goods straight from Eaton's shelves. Only recently, the company had celebrated its fiftieth anniversary by unveiling a fine bronze statue of the founder near its main doors. Everyone in Toronto, including Julie, had made a pilgrimage to the store to admire the statue and rub Sir Timothy's left toe for luck.

And most people knew about the famous Eaton mansion on leafy Lowther Avenue. With its formal gardens, its turrets and towers and exotic Eastern ornamentation and, according to those elite who had penetrated the interior, magnificent furniture and carpets imported from every corner of the world, it was one of the city's finest homes.

Eaton's was Julie's favourite store, one she could depend upon for good quality and fair prices. And best of all was Sir Timothy's famous guarantee, the first such ever offered by a retail store – Goods Satisfactory or Money Refunded. But she was surprised to learn that both Eaton's and its money-back guarantee had won the hearts of people here in the Valley and across the country.

So when Clara set the catalogue aside to see to dinner, it was Julie's turn for a leisurely browse. She leafed through the fashions, noting the slightly shorter dresses that were gaining favour now, the dropped waist lines, even bare arms that no decent woman would consider only a few years ago. The models with their bobbed hair and bow lips all looked alike. She fingered her own thick braid, determined never to be shorn.

She turned to the back and worked her way forward -- an old idiosyncrasy of hers -- studying cream separators, seeders, bridles, hen feeding stations. Much to learn here.

There were fabrics and linens, couches and bedroom sets, cabinets and wagons and push chairs for invalids. She encountered cameras and pianos, candle sticks and flower pots, teddy bears and horseshoe nails – pages and pages and then more pages of merchandise, some of it totally new to her, each item carefully sketched and described.

Then she came to the men's wear.

She studied the drawings and read the descriptions – finest wool worsted from England, men's suit – jacket, vest, two pairs of trousers – for $19. Boy's wool suit with knickerbocker trousers just $9. Still more money than most Valley people would see in a year.

She couldn't help lingering over baby clothes, dreaming of the children she and Adam hoped for.

Then riffling idly through a few pages, she saw them: the overalls.

All the men in the Valley, including Adam, wore overalls for farm work – tough denim pants with bibs over the chest, broad suspenders over the shoulders, fastened with sturdy metal clips, and fitted with deep pockets that held everything from hammers and nails to tobacco to red polka dotted handkerchiefs and occasionally, from Julie to Adam, a tiny bouquet of buttercups or clover.

Overalls, she thought. That's what I need. Ugly, shapeless, heavy. But practical and safer than skirts.

"Clara," she called. "I think I'll buy a pair of overalls."

"Certainly. You can order them by telephone and they'll come to the order office in Paxton Ford. Or you can send the cash and they'll be in our mailbox in just three or four days. You'll just have to check Adam's size."

"Not for Adam. For me."

Clara paused over the stew she was stirring. "For you? That might cause something of a sensation in the neighbourhood."

"Oh, I wasn't planning to wear them to parties," Julie replied. "I'm just tired of tripping over my skirt in the garden and hitching it up to scandalous heights when I try to ride a horse. Overalls just seem to be really practical."

"They are that," Clara conceded. "Why don't you borrow an old pair of Adam's first and see how it goes?"

"I'm sure his breeches would be far too big for me," Julie countered. "I think I need my own."

She checked the catalogue and found youth sizes. "That's for me," she decided. And she sent off her order.

So it was that Gertie Biggar, the undisputed gossip queen of the Valley, got the shock of her life a few days later when she glanced into the Chandler's garden on her way to town. At first she thought they had a new hired hand – another of them orphans from England that the government kept bringing into the country. Never worked a day in their lives, she grumbled to herself. Hands as soft as a baby's backside. Useless as tits on a hen, she sometimes added for good measure.

But then the new hired hand removed a broad straw hat and revealed Julie's golden hair. No mistaking it. It was the new Mrs. Chandler and she was wearing trousers.

Gertie was delighted with her discovery and lost no time in spreading the word. She started in town, telling the grocer and the hardware man, both equally disinterested, and she stopped three acquaintances on the street to share the stunning news.

Trotting home from town in her little buggy, she decided to share her insights. She turned in at Tommy Flaherty's laneway and spotted Mabel picking red currants. "Mabel," she yelled, long before she reached her. "You won't believe what I just saw." She proceeded to recount her story, complete with embellishments, and enjoyed the way the other woman's eyes widened and her face formed a scowl. "What's the world coming to," Mabel exclaimed rhetorically, relieved when Gertie shook her head and drove off. Valley folk tended to humour Gertie, fearing that they themselves might become the next target for her imaginative gossip.

On up the road, she thought of Lizzie Hawkins, whose husband Hector was the Valley's blacksmith. Neither of them had ever distinguished themselves as deep thinkers but in this instance, Hector showed some common sense.

Gertie told the same tale again, with a few additional frills, and Lizzie, who always followed Gertie's lead, was suitably aghast. But Hector happened on the scene, heard the last bit of the conversation and sneered. "What kind of hogwash is this?" he growled. "Ya know nothing' about the woman. Ya thought she was good enough when you was swillin' back her food and drink and enjoyin' her party. What do you think Adam is, if he was to marry a woman like that?"

"You can't never tell about them rich guys," Gertie argued. "They go off to the city and they get bad habits. What kind of a woman would wear overalls like she was a man?"

"A smart one," Heck retorted. "A woman that has dirty work to do, like I do when I'm bangin' out horse shoes or pot handles. Ya don't see me wearin' silk and frills."

He laughed heartily at his own wit. Silk and frills. No sirree. Not his usual get-up.

Gertie glared at Hector and then nodded to Lizzie, before trotting off home. But the image of Julianna clad in her overalls haunted her.

At home, she rushed to the telephone to alert the party line, that dependable conduit to almost every home in the Valley, to the details of Julianna Chandler's new outfit. Of course she told her husband, Herb, who made it abundantly clear that he had no interest in the peculiarities of women's clothing.

"I never saw such a thing," she raged. "Adam Chandler's new wife out in the vegetable patch, wearin' pants. Overalls. Prolly stole them from her husband. Well…now we know who wears the pants in that family."

Gertie's imagination rushed into overdrive and her story expanded. Before long she had convinced herself that Mrs. Chandler probably had a whole wardrobe of men's clothing and the pale silk she had worn for her welcome party was her only dress. She probably only wore skirts to impress the neighbours. Gertie figured that up there in Toronto, where all manner of evil flourished, Julianna hobnobbed with fast women who liked to dress in trousers and top hats and smoke cigars and drink hard whiskey. Eventually, she convinced herself that the new bride undoubtedly refused to sleep in her husband's bed and that she locked him out of her room every night. She could almost hear the click of the lock.

But that night as she readied herself for bed, she gave in to a whim. Foraging in the old wooden trunk in the spare bedroom, she hauled out a pair of overalls that had been the right fit for Herb before the delights of the table had done wonders for his girth. It must be 15 years since he wore these, Gertie thought. Now wasn't I clever not to throw them away. Gertie was no starving waif herself but she managed to ease herself into the overalls and swagger a bit in front of the dresser mirror. Too short, she decided, so she loosened the shoulder straps as far as they'd go. She shoved her hands deep into the pockets and extracted a polka dot handkerchief that she tied round her head.

She surveyed the result. There in the mirror was a whole new Gertie – a modern Gertie, a daring Gertie, exotic as a Gypsy, wild as a movie star, wearing trousers.

But was this Gertie daring enough to share her new-found persona with the world? She admired her mirror image for a good long time, turning from side to side, peeking over a shoulder and arranging her legs one way or the other. Then she carefully removed the scarf and the overalls and tucked them back into the trunk from whence they came. Maybe one day…

The subject of Julianna's wardrobe was now closed. But several of the younger women followed her lead.

Overalls were there to stay. And Gertie kept her peace – for now.

CHAPTER 12

Educating the W.I.

That Julianna Chandler – it sure didn't take her long to get into trouble. And of all places – the Women's Institute. Mostly them women just set around talking about how to beat eggs or grow geraniums. But it sounds like Julianna shook them up a bit. Velma wouldn't tell me much about it – she said it was women's talk – but from what I hear from some of the other lads, I shoulda been a fly on the wall that day. I mighta learned something useful myself. Y'see in them days, nobody talked about where babies come from or why. The mothers might whisper a few words to their daughters: old tales like that they was cursed once a month so cakes wouldn't rise or preserves would spoil if they touched them during their monthlies. The men knew more than the women, what with breedin' their livestock and helping with the birthin'. But women didn't know nuthin' about the subject. And everybody thought it was dirty to talk about it so they stayed ignorant. And we all figured that's the way it should be. Until Julianna came along.

Lenny

In no time at all, Julianna found herself plunging feet first into Valley life. At the Chandlers' welcome party, Viola Brown, the bustling president of the Women's Institute, invited her to join the newly organized group. She proceeded to explain in great detail how the W.I. came into being and the role that Adelaide Hoodless, who had envisioned it a couple of decades earlier, had played.

Julie listened politely although she needed no introduction to the W.I. – Adelaide Hoodless was one of her heroines. Back in Toronto, she and her Aunt Margaret had attended lectures by the visionary Canadian farm woman and crusading educator whose dream of creating a social and educational forum for farm women was materializing swiftly across the country and around the world.'

Women on isolated farms looked forward each month to W.I. meetings in neighbours' homes, listening to a speaker on a domestic subject such as food poisoning or first aid and then enjoying a song or a poem, a tasty lunch made tastier because someone else had prepared it, and a chance to gossip to their hearts' content or at least 'til milking time.

Julie had been inspired by Mrs. Hoodless' vision of educating women to take better control of their lives. But she said nothing of that. She listened carefully to

Mrs. Brown, realizing that here was a place where she might make a contribution to her new country life.

"Perhaps you would consider being the speaker at our next meeting," Mrs. Brown suggested. "You could tell us how your life has changed since you moved away from the city."

"Well, I'm very interested in women's health," Julie countered. "Women tend to neglect their own health in favour of their families. And that puts the whole family at risk."

"Of course," the president replied vaguely. "No doubt you could mention that."

The educational possibilities appealed to Julie. Even in the crush of the party she noticed how many women looked unwell: exhausted, she thought to herself, and undernourished despite the bounty of their gardens and barns. Many of them looked bloated and old beyond their years – too many babies, Julianna surmised, and not enough attention to their own health.

But sober second thought suggested that she approach the W.I. gently before embarking on her real mission.

And so it was that within a few weeks, Julianna stood before a group of curious women, each one analyzing her hair, her dress, her shoes and even occasionally her speech.

"Thank you so much, Mrs. Brown, for inviting me today," she began. "I'm honoured to be here.

"This is my very first W.I. meeting but over the past few years, I've followed the growth of the W.I. with amazement and delight. As women, we truly need to connect with one another and the Women's Institute does just that. We need to exchange our ideas and talk about our problems and help one another to deal with them. As we rush to take care of our husbands and children and household duties, we tend to neglect ourselves – both our health and our minds. Thanks to the W.I., we can learn about health, including our own, and take steps to protect the health of our families and ourselves. After all, without women, where would the family be? We are the nurturers, the caregivers – the ones who bring children into the world, and by and large, raise them and take care of them, as well as our husbands." She paused for breath.

"Women who neglect their own health are, in a sense, neglecting their whole family. Because what can be more tragic than a family without a mother. Yet women tend to sacrifice themselves. If food is in short supply, they feed the rest of the family and starve themselves. If medicine or a doctor is needed, they'll do their best to find the money for their little ones or their husband. But they refuse to get help for themselves.

"I want to talk to you about the woman responsible for founding the W.I.," she continued. "I had the great honour of hearing Mrs. Hoodless speak on two separate occasions in Toronto. She inspired me to try to work with women, to deal with their health issues and help them take better care of themselves.

"Many of us tend to think that we have no influence," she added. "We feel we're not strong enough or not well enough educated to play any part in concerns outside our own home.

"But women are strong and Adelaide Hoodless is a perfect example of that strength. She lost her little son because of impure milk so she set about educating men, women and the government in the importance of sanitation in food preparation. The W.I. is just one amazing result of her energy and there are many more.

"I'd like to think that each one of us can be inspired by Mrs. Hoodless to take better care of ourselves and our families, to pay attention to our health and to try to influence other women to do the same."

Her talk was politely received. She had said all the right things about the W.I. and its esteemed founder and the fact that she spoke from the heart may have registered with a few of the more alert in her audience when they could wrench their attention away from the way she braided her hair.

The lunch break brought many compliments, including effusive thanks from the president. But as she headed for home, Julie was far from satisfied with her contribution. Next time, she thought. I have to arrange a next time.

The opportunity came sooner than she expected from a worried Mrs. Brown. "We were supposed to have a speaker from the city for the next meeting," she explained. "She was going to talk about the history of quilting. But I just had a letter saying she's sick and can't come. You made such a lovely speech last month," she added. "Do you think you might be able to come up with another nice talk for the next meeting?"

"I'll do my best," Julie replied ambiguously. "Let me give it some thought and I'm sure I can think of something." She already knew what she would tell them.

Most speakers stood awkwardly behind a little table. This time, Julie moved an armchair close to her audience and encouraged the women to pull their chairs up in a circle around her. "Let's talk about life," she began. "Your life. And mine. We are women and without us, there would be no life, no families, no homes, no children. And yet, we are in danger."

She paused for effect. They were listening politely but…danger? What danger?

"We put ourselves in danger every day of our lives by neglecting our own health in favour of the health of our family. In fact, I'd venture to say that on some farms, the cows get far better care than the wives do."

A gasp and a few muted giggles reflected their startled acknowledgement.

"You know firsthand that women – especially women here in the country – work very very hard. You probably handle all the housework, the cooking, the washing, the cleaning, the garden, the child care. And then many of you pitch in to help with the milking – even the haying and the harvest – because you know the jobs have to get done.

"When the men come in from the barn, they pull off their boots and sit down and wait for supper. When supper is over they fall asleep on the couch. And the women are still washing the dishes, cleaning up the kitchen, putting the children to bed and then, likely as not, settling down to do the mending or knit new socks before they can fall into bed exhausted. And then, exhausted or not, they are subject to their husbands' appetites."

Some of the women looked embarrassed but she knew she had their full attention.

"And so, women have babies," Julia continued. "Too many babies in some cases. Some women have a baby just about every year and some of those babies die at birth because their mothers are too tired or too undernourished. Or the children grow up weak and sickly because a baby needs nourishment while it's still in the womb and after it's born – and it can only get that nourishment from a healthy mother.

"And we all know that some women die in childbirth – agonizing heart-wrenching deaths that usually leave small children motherless. These are tragedies that we, as women, need to know about and try to prevent."

Several women stirred uncomfortably and Julia knew she had touched on a sore point for them – the unspeakable personal tragedy of a baby's death.

"Many women think they have no choice except to continue having babies every year. But that's not the case. As women we can take control of our bodies. We can decide whether and when we want to have children. And we should have a right to do that."

Julianna paused. Her audience was turned toward her, waiting for what was to come. She glanced at Viola Brown whose face registered both shock and surprise. She ploughed on.

"I'm talking about birth control," Julie continued. "And it is still considered an obscene subject. But for many of us, all that is required is to pay attention to our monthly cycle. Your periods. Your monthlies. Most of us have periods as regular as the cycles of the moon. Every 28 days or maybe 29 or 30 days, our periods begin – and you can keep track of that on a calendar. Well, at the half-way point, the 14th or 15th day, you ovulate. That means that you produce an egg that moves from your ovaries down toward your uterus, ready to be fertilized. It stays fertile for about ten days which means that during those ten days, women can become pregnant. During the rest of the cycle, they do not. It's as simple as that."

Julie opened a slim medical book to a detailed illustration of women's reproductive organs. "This," she pointed, "is what is inside each of our bodies. These are the parts of you where babies are made."

Several women blushed bright red and intently examined their hands. This subject was strictly taboo. They had no idea what happened inside their bodies and the sparse information that was shared was passed along in whispers by women whose knowledge was equally inadequate and distorted. Misinformation and superstition prevailed and women were constantly scolded that any interest in their bodies was sinful and evil. Words like uterus, ovaries and sperm were not in their vocabularies. Most had never heard them before. Yet in spite of their inhibitions, they found themselves intensely curious.

"These are the ovaries," Julia pointed them out in the drawing and then patted her abdomen. "They are just about here in your body, one on each side, and they produce the tiny eggs from which babies grow." She continued through the diagram – the fallopian tubes, the uterus or womb, the vagina. "So your infertile times – when you are not so likely to become pregnant – are just before and just after your periods.

"Unfortunately," she emphasized, "this type of birth control does NOT work for everyone. That's bad news for some of you and I'm sorry. If your monthly periods are irregular, if you can't chart them precisely every month, then your risk of pregnancy is much higher. Lots of women get minor cramps around the time of ovulation so that is a sign to watch for, but it is not foolproof.

"In fact, this entire method is not foolproof. But it's worth the effort to try to control the number of pregnancies you experience. And on the other hand, if you're like me – hoping for babies but not yet successful – the same calendar method can help you choose the right time of the month to invite your husband in from the woodshed."

Her little joke broke the tension and the group burst into laughter – embarrassed, shocked but delighted that so much of the mythology and mystery of their own bodies had been dispelled in a single short meeting.

But the president could tolerate it no longer. "Really, Mrs. Chandler," she interrupted angrily. "This subject is not suitable for a public meeting. Even married women don't discuss such things."

"Well, they certainly should," Julie retorted. "And they should discuss them with their daughters too so that young women understand their bodies and have some control over when and how many children they have."

"Women have to give in to their husbands," Viola argued. "The Bible tells us that. Right there in Genesis, God says that women will belong to men…be ruled by men."

"Mrs. Brown, I'm sure that God didn't intend women to kill themselves and their children in order to satisfy their husbands' lust," Julie replied. "If women are here to be the helpmeets of men, as that same book of Genesis suggests, then they need to stay alive and healthy and take care of themselves at least as well as their husband takes care of his young heifers in the barn."

The exchange was interrupted by young Lily Keenan, already pregnant with her third child in three years, who shyly raised her hand, as if she were in school. "How can I tell my husband all this?" she enquired timidly.

"Good question," Julianna conceded. "In an ideal world, you would be able to sit down with your husband and explain your fears and your needs, and plan your family together. But you're the only one who knows your husband well enough to know how he would react.

"I don't like to counsel people to lie," she continued, "but if your husband is the type who demands total obedience from you, then you need to develop a serious stomach upset or headache or back ache and tell him you need to sleep separately for those few days."

Another hand rose. "What is abortion?" Rosie Ward asked boldly. "I heard some women had abortions to get rid of babies."

Julianna hesitated. The very thought of some of the abortions she had witnessed in the city set her heart to pounding and her mind to spinning. But, she thought, they need to know. She took a deep breath and faced her audience again.

"Abortion does get rid of babies," she said. "But all too often, it kills the mother or injures her so badly that she can never have any more children. That's because abortion is illegal in this country and qualified doctors are not allowed to perform the procedure, even though many of them believe it can save lives. That leaves the field wide open to quacks and criminals who are not trained and in most cases, care not a whit whether the woman they are working on lives or dies, as long as she pays them their fee and keeps her mouth shut about it.

"There are some safer methods that Canadian Indian women have used for centuries – herbs that are made into teas and help induce a miscarriage. And some that prevent pregnancy in the first place. But sadly, those methods too are not available to most women."

She paused, noting the president's glares as she whispered in the ear of her friend, Gertie the Gossip. But I've started this, Julianna thought, and I'd best finish it.

"We women really need to take charge of ourselves and our lives," she challenged them. "We need education and knowledge and the courage to insist on our rights. Superstition and religious beliefs hold us back but so does the law, in many cases. Why did we have to fight so long for the right to vote or run for political office? Why are our legal decisions still decided by our fathers or husbands or brothers? Why must women lose their jobs when they marry? Why do the universities still discourage women from studying? It's considered ladylike to study art or literature but it's a man's world in medicine and law.

"My father is a doctor and I've worked as his assistant for several years. I've delivered babies, set broken bones, treated stomach problems, infections, fevers – all manner of ailments. But when I applied to medical school, I was refused – in Toronto and in Montreal – because women are still not considered suitable for the medical profession. I was accepted at Harvard but then the war started and my mother died, and my father needed me even more. And so I stayed.

"Men like to say that women are too weak and foolish to take on the stress of medicine or law or business. Well, anyone who has ever had a baby or attended at a birth knows perfectly well just how strong women are. And anyone who's ever raised children, and kept a tidy home, and cooked and cleaned and scrubbed and laundered and gardened and helped at the barn – is this weakness? If you manage all those jobs at once, and still have time to bake the delicious treats we're about to enjoy here today, are you foolish or weak? I would say a resounding NO. Wouldn't you?" Her questions stirred a flurry of whispers, the older women's sullen expressions signaling silent disapproval while the younger ones, still somewhat embarrassed, nonetheless gave these revelations their full attention.

"Women did not make the laws but many of us suffer as a result of them," Julie continued. She spoke gently, gazing into each listener's rapt face. "What we all need to do is to support those crusading women – and a few enlightened men – who want to change the laws and give women the right to make decisions about their own lives."

The president, her mind in turmoil, knew she had to put a stop to it. She rose staunchly to her feet. "Thank you Mrs. Chandler for your time today," she announced sourly. "The meeting is now adjourned."

Adjourned perhaps, but not over. The lunch table awaited and the questions continued. While some of the older women feigned shock, many of them wanted to know more. "Why is an abortion dangerous? How is it done? What's the right way? What are those herbs you mentioned? Where can I get them? My mother says that any form of birth control is a sin against God. What do you think? My periods are not regular. What can I do about that? I get terrible cramps with my monthlies and again at the middle of the month. There's so much blood. Could I bleed to death? No wonder it's called the curse."

Aware of the president's disapproval, Julianna answered some of them and suggested that the subject be placed on the program for future W.I. meetings. Dipping into her satchel, she unearthed copies of her little book, Protecting Women's Health by J.M. Brightson, and handed one to each of the member of her audience. They received them eagerly.

Viola Brown was upset and confused. While some women might whisper about such subjects, she knew that they were not acceptable in polite society. And to advise women to deny their husbands in order to avoid having babies was advocating sin, although, she thought guiltily, she herself had often feigned illness to stave off her husband's heated demands. But she was intimidated by Julie and amazed at the way the women crowded round her with questions that became more and more frank.

"What should I be telling my daughters," Mary Gormley asked. "Surely it's normal to want children and be a good wife and housekeeper."

"Of course," Julie agreed. "I certainly want children and lots of them. But I also want control of my life. Being a wife and housekeeper and a mother – those are important jobs – three jobs in one – but it's not the only road open to us. The world really is changing and women like Adelaide Hoodless, a loving mother and a fine housekeeper who also founded the W.I., are helping to make it change. If girls stay in school and study hard, they can be anything they choose to be. Let's help them to look at the world before they limit themselves to a life of household drudgery."

No one had ever called farm life drudgery and the term shocked them all. Especially Viola Brown. Household drudgery indeed.

At home that night, she leafed through the Women's Health book that Julianna had given her, never realizing that the author, J.M. Brightson, was Julianna Margaret Brightson, now Chandler. She stared at the illustrations and tried to imagine that scenario inside her own body. And she could not stop reviewing Julie's comments. She thought about her good friend, Lucy Everett, who died, along with her baby, giving birth to her ninth child and left eight, all under the age of 12, to be cared for by their father. The oldest girl, Rosie, still just a child herself, was kept home from school to care for the younger ones and as the years slipped by, her resentment at the burdens she was forced to carry turned into bitterness and rebellion. Finally her father married a younger woman who took charge of the children with a heavy hand. Before long she too was pregnant and her step-children were neglected. So the cycle began again with Rosie acting as mother to her seven siblings whilst her step-mother nurtured her own.

But what became of women who rebelled. She heard tell of the Reverend Josiah Whitman's wife Sara. She wasn't cut out to be a preacher's wife, that's for sure – they said she wore a bright red dress to church and refused to attend Ladies Aid meetings. She up and stole the reverend's horse and buggy and drove away one day and was never heard from again. And good riddance to her.

But then there was Herbert Lowery's daughter. She wasn't yet twenty when she went off to the city and everyone assumed she'd got herself into trouble with some neighbour boy until she came home for Christmas, slim as a willow and no baby in sight. Still, everybody figured her for a whore. Her parents were tight-lipped about their daughter, taking their own sweet time to reveal that they had once tucked away a small inheritance and decided to dip into it to send her to university – the first girl – in fact, the first person – in their family to continue past grade school. And, Viola had to concede, she seemed to have done pretty well for herself. Started teaching in a high school and then moved to a smart private school in Toronto where she was assistant to the head mistress. But all the same, she had no husband and no children and surely that's what most women were meant to have.

Women were meant to do women's work. That's what Viola had been brought up to believe – she and all the other women in the Valley. Silly girls might dream of going off the city and living free. But nice girls knew their place – to find a husband and take care of him. And their fathers were quick with the willow whip if they tried to step out of line.

Viola Brown conjectured that Julianna was destined to corrupt every girl in the Valley with her prattle about having an education and a profession and the 'maybe you'll have a family and maybe you won't' advice.

But even with Gertie Biggar's well-honed gossip skills, the campaign against Julianna was destined to fail. Many of the women who had heard her talk were already at their calendars, marking the good days and the bad days. And they were leafing hungrily through J.M. Brightson's book, devouring the drawings and the previously unheard-of details they revealed, unaware that the writer was none other than Julianna Chandler, their neighbour and speaker.

Change was in the air.

CHAPTER 13

The Tide Turns

That Gertie Biggar, she had the meanest mouth of any woman I ever laid eyes on. She could sour a can of milk just sayin' g'day.

Gertie the Gossip, I used to call her. Nuthin' she liked better'n a good story, true or not. And the party line was her best friend. She listened to every call, even if it was just one of us talkin' to the miller about bringin' in a wagonload of oats to be ground. And if she had a juicy story to tell, she'd plop herself down in her rocking chair and crank the phone, knowin' that nearly everybody on the line would pick up and listen in.

Gertie was a big woman, taller than her husband, Herb, who was the butcher, built like an ox and just about as smart. They'd lived in the Valley for years, so everybody knew her and she knew everybody else and their business.

Along with gossip, Gertie liked to preach. She was a raging teetotaler, forever preaching temperance to anybody who'd listen. Or even to us who wouldn't. "Lips that touch liquor shall never touch mine," she liked to say. And I often wondered why any lips, with or without liquor, would ever go near her, even Herb Biggar. I never had the nerve to ask him though.

"The devil makes work for idle hands," she once yelled at Julianna, who was sitting on her verandah reading a book. "Sound and fury, signifying nothing," Julie called back to her. I wasn't quite sure what that meant and I betcha Gert didn't neither. But it shut her up for a while. But only for a while. After a bit, Julie became her number one target.

Lenny

Gertie had been a faithful member of the local Women's Institute ever since it was founded. Not that she approved of the programs – useless twaddle, she called them. "No city slicker woman gonna come down here and tell me how to boil eggs," she growled. She detested the giggles of the young women and scorned the eager chatter of their mothers who were delighted to meet a kindred soul, if only once a month. She ranted against spendthrifts, though they were mighty scarce in the Valley and so was the actual cash that they supposedly wasted on frills and furbelows. But she singled out Adam Chandler and his new wife for special vitriol.

"Fancy horses, fancy buggies, fancy harness," she railed. "And now a fancy wife that's too grand for a horse and buggy so he needs a fancy automobile to drive her around." Adam's acquisition of a gleaming 1921 McLaughlin Buick triggered that declaration.

"More money than brains," she liked to add.

She took umbrage at the new fashions pictured in Eaton's catalogue, calling the short-haired, short-skirted models whores and warning young women of the evils that would befall them if they cropped their hair or their skirts.

She welcomed opportunities to regale both her neighbours and W.I. members from beyond the Valley with cautionary tales about the evils of drink and idleness. And like every other member, she found much solace in the cookies and cakes that other W.I. members shared at the monthly meetings, often hovering over her favourite sweets to discourage interlopers.

"She's not a happy woman," Julie remarked to Clara. "She can't seem to say a single positive word about anything."

"She's one to watch out for," Clara warned. "She seems to love making trouble and spreading lies about people is her favourite pastime.

"She certainly nipped at our heels when we first arrived from England. Of course everybody hated 'the English' in those days. Remember those signs on factories in Toronto – **'NO ENGLISH NEED APPLY'**. I'm not sure where they originated or why but they certainly were widespread.

"So as if being English wasn't bad enough, Gertie decided that we must be criminals, running from the law. By the time her over-active imagination had finished with us, we had probably robbed banks, stolen horses, cheated old ladies out of their last penny and lived lives of loose moral decadence. It all sounded rather exciting, but alas, it wasn't true."

"Did you take any action?" Julia was incredulous. "Is there any way to stop her?"

"Adam saved the day, really. He had a reception for us, a bit like the welcome party when you arrived, but he invited only about a dozen families to come for tea on a Sunday afternoon, including Mr. and Mrs. Biggar. He introduced us to all of them, and then he made a funny little speech about how the Valley really needed more excitement and he had gone to great trouble to provide it and here we were. But sadly, we had disappointed him because we were law-abiding and hardworking. He said our crime was that we had abandoned one of England's most prominent families, living like royalty in huge manor houses, in order to come to Canada and live in this Valley."

"I'd love to have been there," Julie chuckled.

"He was brilliant," Clara said. "He went on to say something like: 'I've been hearing some of the stories that has been circulating about Mr. And Mrs. Cooper and I know you've heard it too. It's exciting – lies are often more exciting than the truth – but I'm happy to tell you that your new neighbours are salt of the earth people, highly regarded by their employers in England and in my opinion, a great asset to our Valley.' Then we plied them with plenty of cakes and tea to seal the deal."

"Did it work?" Julie asked.

"It seemed successful," Clara conceded. "Gertie ignored us after that and looked for other targets. And I have a feeling," she added ominously, "that you could be the next one."

Gertie rarely missed a W.I. meeting but many a member devoutly wished she would. Of course she was on hand for the meeting at which Julie spoke about babies and birth control and quickly allied herself with Viola Brown in condemning both message and messenger.

They had retired to a spot behind the lunch table to share their distress. "Who does she think she is," Gertie fumed, "coming here from the city and corrupting the minds of our young women? That kind of talk is wicked. It's a sin against God."

"Awful!" Viola agreed. "I thought she was going to talk about what it's like moving from the city to the country but instead she started right into this dirty talk and upset every woman in the room."

They chose to ignore the obvious enthusiasm of the young women who now surrounded Julie, eager for more information about a subject that until then had been strictly taboo. Though some had witnessed farm animals' breeding and birthing, none of them understood their own bodies or how they functioned, or even the proper names of the organs that produced babies. They had been taught to be ashamed of their private parts, ashamed of their menstrual periods which, according to superstitious older women, contaminated their bodies. And most of all they were impressed by the simple calculation that Julie had described to control conception by the rhythm method.

But the mood of the group meant nothing to Gertie and Viola. Nurturing their rage and disgust, they stalked out of the meeting and headed for home where Gertie swiftly turned to her old friend, the party line, delighted that both those who had attended the meeting and those who hadn't would be listening intently. She started by ringing up Lizzie Hawkins, the blacksmith's wife, and describing in as many euphemisms as she could muster the gist of Julie's talk. Lizzie never disagreed with Gertie, perhaps on the grounds that she might become the next target, and today, she outdid herself, expressing her dismay and disgust as eloquently as her limited linguistic powers would permit.

"Oh dear," she exclaimed. "Oh my. Just awful."

The party line listened and learned. Gertie had indeed found a new victim.

Yet some of those listeners were the same young women who had clustered around Julie begging for more information.

"That old bat is crazy," Emma Foster raged. "And that's the kindest thing I can say about her. It's time those women came into the twentieth century and got in step with the times."

"I want to have a family but I don't want a baby every year like some women have," her friend Wilma replied.

"I think we should have a meeting of all us younger women and see what they think of Mrs. Chandler," Emma suggested. "I think I already know what they think of Mrs. Biggar."

Julie was aware of the fuss but unconcerned. However, Adam wasn't so sure.

"Looks like you stirred up a hornet's nest with your Women's Institute talk," he said one evening. "Lots of people are upset about it. And that book of yours – I hadn't realized how graphic it is. A lot of folks are shocked."

"Yes. New ideas are always difficult to accept. But this message is one that every woman, and man, should hear."

"Well, the men are hearing it all right, from their wives. How they should retire to the woodshed every so often to save their wives from becoming pregnant."

"Over-simplified," Julie chuckled. "But that's the basic message. So many women – and men too, I'm sure, have no idea how their bodies work or why. They are kept in ignorance and as a result, they don't take proper care of themselves. And those women who are producing a baby every year or so are the most at risk. They become weaker, more tired, more susceptible to illness. After too many pregnancies, many of them die in childbirth and they may leave a big family of children that can't look after themselves. So it's a multiple tragedy."

"I accept your logic," Adam commented, "but you're dealing here with long-established beliefs, many of them based on religion and superstition – rightly or wrongly. Some of the neighbours have declared your book filth and they've actually burned it. People think it's a sin to control pregnancy and a sin to even speak about their own bodies."

"The greatest sin is forced ignorance," Julie replied hotly. "Are you advocating that we maintain a system that rewards men for their lust and lets women die as a result?"

"Whoa now. I'm not advocating anything. But are you blaming men for this state of affairs?"

"More or less," Julie conceded. "You either condone the situation or you fight it. If men continue to insist on their marital right, which is another word for lust, then women will continue to suffer. Surely a man can control his impulses for a few days each month. The result will be healthier and happier wives, smaller families and for poorer families, fewer mouths to feed."

"Big families are important here in the country," Adam argued. "A farmer wants sons to help with the work and take over the farm when the time comes. And daughters are less useful, but still, marrying them off to neighbour lads helps establish 'the ties that bind', so to speak."

"Less useful," Julie repeated, her voice shaking with rage. "Like brood mares or heifers you put out for breeding. Is that your view of women?"

"Simply being realistic, Julie. Farm work demands plenty of muscle so strong sons are important. Women have their place too but in the country, that place is always at a man's side."

"Adam, I can't believe what I'm hearing. Are you telling me that women are here simply to be used by men? That in spite of the multitude of jobs that they do, they have no value? Is that what you think?"

"Julie, this is not the city," Adam reminded her. "Our people tend to follow the same patterns as their parents. It's not a question of right or wrong. It's the way lives are lived and you have no right to come here and start upsetting the applecart with your radical new ideas.

"I know you believe in your convictions. But I wish you'd back away from this subject. It's starting to be an embarrassment to me, with men haranguing me about your bad influence on their wives and daughters. Let's just put it to rest and let the Valley get back to normal."

Julie was furious. "Normal is not acceptable, Adam. And neither is ignorance.

Keeping women ignorant about their bodies and their health is certainly a sin against them. And it's just one of a whole long list of sins – denying them their legal rights, refusing them university educations, pulling young girls out of school to look after even younger children while their mothers produce even more unwanted babies – those are sins, Adam – sins against women.

"Knowledge is NOT a sin," she raged. "Knowledge is freedom and freedom is what women deserve. And I will never back away from helping them achieve it."

Adam stared at her in amazement. He had never before seen her angry – in fact they had never had a notable disagreement about anything. After she stormed out of the room, he was left to think it over. And try as he might, he could not find any valid argument to counter her ideas. He decided to drop the subject then and there and let complaining neighbours prattle on. They've always enjoyed gossiping about us, he thought to himself. Why spoil their fun?

The next W.I. meeting saw a substantial influx of younger members, eager to meet Julie. The mood had swung. Frustrated and furious, Viola and Gertie realized that, at least for the moment, they had been bested.

Women's rights, however fragile and fragmented, were tip-toeing cautiously into the Valley.

CHAPTER 14

Otto's Accident

We never seen too many foreigners in the Valley so when the Dietrich family arrived, we didn't know what to make of them. First off, they didn't speak no English and worse still, they was German and thanks to the War, we all hated Germans. And yet, as time went by, we kinda got used to them. When the Donovan's barn burned, they was right there helping, from start to finish. In fact that Mrs. Dietrich – she's a big sturdy woman – she pumped water for hours at a stretch for the bucket brigade. And Otto Dietrich, he not only pitched in with carrying the buckets but he also went right into the burning barn and helped round up the sheep and get them outside. Well then, after a while, the youngsters went to school and they got pretty good at talking English and they helped their parents learn some too. So we never forgot they was foreigners and we never forgave them for being Germans but they was neighbours and we couldn't turn our backs on them.

Lenny

Otto hitched up his team to the harrow and headed out to the back ten acres. The land had already been broken up with plough and disk and spread with redolent manure. Now it needed raking to smooth out the clods of earth and prepare the field for seeding. He planned to plant fall wheat here, a verdant crop that would germinate before frost, then nurture the earth and rise again to mature in the spring.

A lonely business, this farming, Otto thought to himself. But still. They had made it this far. Life was good. And getting better. They were paying off the farm debt, managing to put food on the table and shoes on their feet. Not as well off as they'd been in Germany but far safer and hopeful for the future. And he was grateful to Canada that they had escaped the horrors of the war.

He climbed up on the metal seat of the harrow, dropped the lever to lower the long row of prongs into the pungent earth and clucked up the horses. The weather was good. Perhaps with luck he'd finish this field today.

Flies buzzed around his head and around the horses. They swished their thick tails and swung their heads to ward them off. They aren't the best horses in the Valley, Otto told himself. But they're hard working and strong. I'm glad to have them.

He pulled up under a maple tree beside the rail fence to rest the team. Suddenly conscious of a far-off buzz steadily growing louder, he glanced all around to identify it and then looking into the sky, he spotted a small aircraft approaching from the south, flying low over the fields. It dipped and roared overhead, startling the horses. They tossed their heads and stamped their feet, unaccustomed to motors and nervous of this noisy intruder in the sky. And then suddenly, as the plane swooped even lower, they shied and plunged forward. Otto grabbed for the reins to restrain them but they launched into a full gallop, running wildly across the field. The harrow lurched over a rock and Otto fell forward from his seat, where the prongs of the harrow scooped up his body like a bag of potatoes and tumbled it along under the machine. The horses were in full runaway mode. The reins slipped from his hands and his shouted commands meant nothing.

A massive boulder that Otto had been unable to remove slowed their progress only slightly. The team separated just enough to get round the rock on either side but the harrow struck it dead on and broke apart. And Otto lost consciousness.

Back at the house, Olga prepared his dinner, glancing out occasionally to see if he was on his way. And then she saw the team dragging the harrow's drive shaft and whiffle trees into the barn yard, gleaming with sweat, foaming at the mouth. Trouble. She knew there was bad trouble.

The Dietrichs had no telephone but Olga knew one communications method that worked. Like most Valley houses, theirs had a large brass bell at the back door, for calling the family in to meals – or to announce emergencies. Olga grabbed the rope and clanged the bell desperately. It was the prolonged ringing that alerted Julie and she hurried to the door, calling out to Olga across the two fields that separated them.

"Bitte helfen Sie," Olga shouted back. "Bitte. Otto." She waved wildly toward the back field.

Julianna's childhood memory of German was shakey but she got the message. An accident, she guessed. She called for Clara to go and find Adam and rushing to the cupboard behind her pantry door, she seized her black doctor's bag, stuffing bandages, bottles and tins of medications into it. By then, Adam was at the door. "Wait for me," he called. "I'll bring the wagonette."

"Blankets too," Julianna called after him.

At a gallop, they covered the quarter mile to the Dietrich laneway. They could see Olga already running up the hill beyond the barn, headed for the north field. They overtook her and urged the horses on until they spotted the broken harrow, wedged crazily against the boulder. Beneath it, Otto's motionless body was already staining the ground with fresh blood.

"Must roll it back," Julianna gasped as together they seized the wheels to push the harrow away and release Otto's inert form. Julianna's heart sank. He was covered in blood, earth and manure that seemed to protrude from myriad cuts, gashes and scrapes. If he is alive, she thought, he could have infection in every one of those wounds. And almost certainly some broken bones.

But she found a pulse, though weak, and knew he was still alive. His skin was clammy and pale and his breath was shallow. No time to waste.

They lifted him as gently as they could onto the blanket and up onto the wagon. "Olga, help me here," Julianna commanded. "Waschen hus Gesicht. Vorsichtig. . . Wash his face. Gently, gently." She handed over a jug of water and a wad of bandage. Olga knelt beside her husband and set to work, murmuring his name while Adam drove as gently as the terrain allowed back to the Dietrich house. Again they lifted him, carrying him into the house and tenderly placing him in the kitchen bedroom, handy to Olga and the warmth of the family.

Julianna unrolled her blood pressure cuff and measured his blood pressure. Low. And his damp skin and shallow breath indicated deep shock. Suddenly, her courage wavered.

"A doctor," she decided. "If only Daddy were here." She turned to Adam. "This is so serious. Do you think we could get that doctor from Paxton Ford out here? Would you be able to drive your automobile into town and bring him so he gets here faster?"

Adam was off like a shot and Julianna bent again over Otto's wounds, probing his arms and legs for broken bones. Indeed his left fibula was broken but to her relief, she was able to set it readily. With Olga's help, she cut away the rest of his tattered clothing and Olga continued to bathe his injuries, stopping only to put kettles of water to boil on the stove. Dipping into her black bag, Julie found a flat tin of a strong-smelling salve that she immediately applied to Otto's temples, his throat, his wrists and the soles of his feet. She massaged it gently into the skin and watched his eyelids for any response. There was none.

From a small bottle she used a medicine dropper to extract a stinking brown tincture that she applied to each of the cuts and gashes that dotted his body, even squeezing it deep into each wound. Otto still did not stir.

One ear had been badly torn. She threaded a surgical needle with silk thread and began to stitch the ear. She was half way through her task when the door opened and Adam entered, followed by the doctor.

He was a self-important little man in a pinstriped suit, with a gold watch chain across his paunch. He was obviously not pleased with what he saw.

Without greeting or introduction, he strode to the bed. "And just what do you think you're doing?" he demanded.

"I'm stitching a torn ear," Julie replied mildly. "While he's still unconscious he doesn't feel the pain."

"And who gave you the authority to conduct medical practice?"

She continued with her delicate stitching. "I have no authority. I am simply helping a badly hurt man. It seems to me that saving a life should take priority over protocol. But I'm glad you're here because I've detected a break in the left fibula that will need a cast."

The doctor's eyes bulged in rage. "I'll be the judge of what this patient needs. You can go and make yourself useful boiling some water and finding bandages."

"I'll finish this ear first," Julianna said firmly. "Olga...Ist das Warmwasser bereit? Is the hot water ready?"

Olga pointed toward the stove where several kettles were already steaming. Julianna tied off her thread neatly and applied more of the brown medication to the ear.

"What exactly is that?" snarled the doctor. "It stinks like some witch doctor's brew."

"Yes, you might call it that," Julie responded. "My father is a doctor in Toronto and he often goes to visit the good Indian people up north and learn about their medicines. The shaman there showed us how to make this from herbs that they collect in the fields and woods. It helps prevent infection in open wounds. We call it swamp eucalyptus but I don't know the proper name."

The doctor was aghast. "This is absurd," he shouted. "A woman talkin' foreign gibberish while applying Indian slop to an injured man. That's the problem with women — you're all superstitious. You think anything you hear from an itinerant pedlar or an Indian savage is God's truth. This man needs proper medicine and proper care."

Julie stepped back. "Then let's provide it, Doctor," she responded. "The patient is all yours."

With Olga's help, she brought a small table to the bedside with space for the doctor to spread out his wares, along with hot water, strong soap and a small basin. "No doubt you'll want to wash before handling the patient," she suggested quietly. The doctor's expression suggested that he had thought of no such thing but he sluiced his hands briefly and then turned to Otto.

"Plaster of Paris," he snapped. "He needs a cast."

"I have some," Julie replied quickly. "I'll be back in just a few minutes." She paused only long enough to enjoy his look of amazement.

Her pantry shelf pharmacopeia stocked plaster of Paris and with Adam driving, she rushed back with it. She checked Otto's pulse again and reported it to the doctor. Then she began again to apply the salve to his temples, wrists and throat.

"Now what?" the doctor roared. "Another witch doctor remedy?"

"No, doctor," Julie replied patiently. "It's a very effective medication from a very skilled doctor who happens to be Indian. It stimulates the blood and raises the blood pressure. His blood pressure is low, his pulse is still weak and his eyes are not responding. This may help him to regain consciousness. But I suggest we deal with that broken bone as fast as possible.'

"I'm perfectly capable of making that decision," he snapped. "I don't need a woman telling me how to practice medicine."

"Shall I prepare the plaster?" she asked politely.

"Go ahead if you know how," he grunted. "I'll set the bone."

"I believe I set it already, Doctor," Julianna commented. "While I was waiting for you to arrive with my husband."

The doctor checked and double-checked Otto's leg. "Alright. It seems firm enough. Prepare the plaster," he snapped.

And she did – quickly, efficiently and correctly.

Julie was deeply worried about Otto but she was enjoying the doctor's discomfort.

They dipped strips of cloth into the liquid plaster, smoothing them up and down the leg well past the break, a great sloppy welt that would soon dry to rock solid. "Elevate the leg," the doctor ordered and the women produced pillows to raise Otto's foot.

The doctor stood back and wiped his hands on a towel. Then he glanced over at Julie's black bag and his eyes widened. 'Julianna Brightson' was embossed in gold letters across its leather surface. "Brightson?" he queried. "Any connection to Anthony Brightson, the TB man?'

"TB and venereal diseases," Julianna replied. "He's my father."

The doctor was speechless. Briefly. Then he spluttered back to life. "Obviously he was able to teach you some of the basics; though I'm sure he'd agree with me that women have no place in the medical field. Except as nurses, of course."

"On the contrary, Doctor," Julia retorted. "He very much wanted me to study medicine and join him in his practice. Unfortunately the stupid blind prejudices that still riddle most of the medical profession make it almost impossible for Canadian women to enter medical school. I applied at both major Canadian universities and they turned me down. They have a quota for women – one per year – no matter how impressive one's credentials or previous experience. And then the war came along and with my brother off to the war, my father needed me in his practice. So here I am – a doctor in training but not in practice."

He seemed ready to offer another argument but she stood proudly, her head high, and fixed him with her disquieting amber gaze. Since his squat height brought him only to her shoulder, the triumph was an easy one.

"Humph," he finally grumbled. "See that you keep the leg elevated and the patient well hydrated. Mind you keep him still and you can apply this iodine to his wounds instead of that witch doctor potion you are using. And you'd better change this bedding too." He paused, still hoping to deliver a final salvo for misogyny. But no words came.

"I'll be on my way," the doctor said, snapping his bag shut. He ignored Olga totally, nodded to Adam that he was ready and headed for the door.

"Whew! Glad to be rid of him," Julie remarked. She realized that he had performed no useful function during his visit that she could not have achieved on her own.

Julie showed Olga how to massage the stimulant salve into Otto's nerve points. As she glanced up she saw his eyelids flutter.

"He's awake," she exclaimed. "Oh, Olga, look. His eyes are open. He's awake."

They both stared in wonder and Olga wept from relief.

Julie produced an invalid cup from her bag – a tiny china cup with a handle and side spout that allowed her to inject a few drops of water into Otto's mouth without lifting his head. She foraged for glycerin and gently applied it to his lips which were already dry and cracking. She and Olga returned to the task of massaging his pressure points and checking on his wounds in case of excess bleeding. Together they folded back the bloodied blanket and eased his body onto clean sheets.

"I'll make tea, Olga. You stay with Otto." They needed time together.

The day wore on and the three Dietrich children came in from school, wide-eyed and frightened. Julie left Olga with her husband and escaped to the kitchen where after just four hours, she found the table half filled with stews and casseroles, cakes and cookies, as neighbours rallied to neighbours in the time-honoured tradition of all country folk.

"What about the milking and the livestock?" she asked Adam as he came in the door.

"Nothing to worry about," he assured her. "Five of the neighbour lads are out there milking at this very moment and they've already sluiced down the horses and given them a good brushing. Lenny Findlay and his lads are bringing the harrow down from the back field and by the end of the week, Bert Wilkins will have it repaired and then someone will finish that field. Otto's job is to get well."

When Olga entered the kitchen and saw the array of contributions from her neighbours, she wept again. "I not understand," she sobbed. "So kind."

Julie hugged her gently. "We're neighbours, Olga, and your neighbours love you and Otto and want to help when you have trouble, just as you help every time any of your neighbours are in trouble. You and Otto are part of this Valley. We all belong to one another." She was far from sure that Olga had understood all of her words, but certainly she grasped their intent. She laid her head on Julie's shoulder and wept away the fear and stress of the afternoon and some of the uncertainty of the past few years.

"I'm going to stay the night, Olga," Julie announced. "I want you to put the children to bed and then go to bed yourself. I'll stay here with Otto and if there is any change, I'll come and wake you up." Olga hesitated to leave but with an arm around her shoulder, Julie led her up the stairs to the children's room and left her there, reassuring them that their father would recover. Then she moved a rocking chair into the bedroom where she could keep a close eye on her patient and as her father had trained her, settled in for a long night of healing.

Adam popped in again to check up on her. "I think all is well," she told him. "But I'm staying the night so Olga can get some rest. She's worn out."

"You had quite a day yourself," he chuckled, "parrying the thrusts of that woman-hating doctor. And I have just one thing to say about that." He paused and assumed a stern look. "Mrs. Brightson Chandler...will you be my doctor...forever?"

CHAPTER 15

Chrissy in Crisis

I mind me seein' Christine when she was maybe thirteen – a real pretty little miss, quiet and shy like a young lady should be. But being the daughter of Old Joe and his mousy wife Rita musta been a tough row to hoe. Everybody in the Valley knew that Joe hit the bottle and then beat up his wife and daughter pretty regular. And young Joe was thick as a plank and a brute from an early age. I mind catchin' him once whippin' a tied-up horse with a harness strap and buckle and the animal's back and flanks was runnin' with blood. When I yelled at him, he turned on me and threatened to whip me with the same strap. He was a lad that kicked a dog for no reason at all and once when his little sister was about four years old, he threw a stone at her and laughed when it killed the kitten she was holding in her arms.

Joe raised his son hisself from an early age. I heard tell that his first wife died of some strange illness that many a neighbour suspected had came of being beaten too often and too hard. But nobody knew for sure. Husband and wife problems belonged in the family – it was an unwritten law that no neighbour ever interfered. So the women gossiped, but nobody done nuthin' about it.

Joe needed a housekeeper but we felt sorry for his new wife, Rita. She was none too pretty and no longer a maid so of course she couldn't be too fussy about who she married. But I bet she hadn't reckoned on two brutes like Joe and his son. Christine was her only child but Rita was no more able to protect her than she could save herself.

My lad, Liam, he was just turned sixteen, and he was kinda sweet on Christine but he knew she was too young to step out with him. So when she went away, his heart was broke.

It was tragedy and heartache all round.

Lenny

Young Joe had an instinct for bullying and Liam Findlay, who was smaller and showed no inclination toward fighting, was as good a target as any. It was obvious from the way he looked at Christine and teased her, that Liam had a soft spot in his heart for her. So Joe jumped at the chance to taunt him.

It started in town one Saturday night with Joe and his cronies smoking and passing around a bottle in the laneway beside Kirby's general store.

"Hey there Liam," Joe shouted, as Liam walked by."I got my sister ready for ya. Broke her in, saddled her up and rode her for ya." He thought he was hilarious and he laughed heartily, along with his pals, who slapped him on the back and begged for more details.

"What are you on about?" Liam responded.

"Thought you was hot for Christine," Joe roared."Well I got her ready for ya, last week in the barn. She was real juicy too. Almost as good as one of the sheep."

Liam ducked his head down and hurried away. He wanted to be sick but he was too proud to let Joe see him.

Later on the way home, he told the story to his father and asked what Joe could have meant.

"Well now, Liam," Lenny stumbled and stammered, reluctant to talk about such a taboo subject. "Ya know…that Joe has a big mouth and a small brain. He likes to bully. He's just tryin'to get ya all riled up, like he does everybody. Ya done right to walk away."

"But pa," Liam argued. "It sounded as if he…well . . . as if he was…well, y'know, doing like the bulls do to the cows."

"Now Liam," Lenny told him. "That lad is a fool and a loudmouth. Pay him no mind."

They were quiet then for the rest of the ride home, both realizing the truth but not daring to express it in words. Her own stepbrother, a brute twice her size and ten years older, had cornered his sister in the barn when she came down to gather the eggs and taken her by force. And he thought it was a joke.

The pain was searing and she was bleeding profusely. Joe had thrown her against the back wall of a stall, slapped and punched her, torn at her clothes and raped her furiously and viciously."Ya keep yer yap shut about this or ye'll get worse," he threatened as he rose, landing fierce kicks in her ribs and back for emphasis.

He left her lying there in the straw, afraid to move, afraid she would have to meet him, afraid he would grab her again. At last she tidied her clothing as best she could and scurried out of the barn. Then she remembered the eggs and knew the storm that would blow up if she failed to bring them. Shaking, she crept back into the barn, picked up her egg basket and ran for the house, escaping to her room before her mother noticed her. Her monthly periods had begun that summer so she had a stock of rag pads. She pinned a couple of them inside her bloomers and hurried back downstairs to complete her chores before her absence was noted.

The days that followed were agonizing. Her cracked ribs made breathing a torture. Her dresses hid her bruises but her fear of Joe and the shock of his violation invaded her dreams and interrupted her sleep. And then the morning sickness began.

Christine was tired. The long walk from school and then the nightly chores – gathering the eggs, filling the wood box, hauling the water and doing the dishes – seemed endless and by supper time she was too tired to eat more than a few bites. And then each morning, she was sick. Rita, too engrossed in her own problems, paid little attention to Christine until she saw her throwing up outside the house. When it happened again, she cornered Christine in the kitchen and demanded to know what made her sick.

Christine burst into tears. In spite of her youth – she had only recently reached puberty – she had heard about morning sickness and already suspected what was wrong. And she was scared. When her mother immediately flew into a rage, demanding to know who was responsible, Christine finally blurted out the truth: "Joe."

"Not yer brother," her mother gasped.

"It is," said Christine, and she told her about Joe's attack in the barn.

Now it was Rita's turn to weep – for her daughter but also for herself, and for her fear of her husband when she relayed the story to him. And her terror was justified. She waited until evening when Joe came up from the barn for supper.

"Joe, we gotta talk," she began, her voice trembling. He eyed her coldly, his cheeks bulging.

"Chrissy's in trouble," she blurted out. "And Joe did it to her."

He stared at her for a long moment and then his face reddened as he realized what she had said. He was livid.

"Dirty little slut," he roared. "Blamin'my son, is she? Who's she really messin' with? That Liam Findlay, I'll bet. Or somebody up there at the Donovan's where she spends so much time. And what the hell were ya doin', lettin' her run wild? Where the hell are ya every afternoon? Wouldn't s'prise me if ya was out ruttin' with one of the neighbours too. Ya never seem to be around the house."

Rita dared not look at him or respond. Her afternoons were her private time and until now she believed no one had noted her absence. He stood over her shouting, fists clenched, breathing fumes of the cheap rum he kept at the barn for his regular sustenance, and she felt utterly powerless in the face of his uncontrolled rage. He had hit her so many times; she knew that any word of protest would elicit another beating.

"Where the hell is she?" Joe raged. "I'm gonna teach that little slut a big lesson. Where is she? Git her in here right now."

Rigid with anxiety, Rita walked to the foot of the stairs and called to Chrissy. She waited for her to come down and looking up at her, marvelled at how small and helpless she seemed, as she slowly descended to face a tyrant three times her weight and twice her height. "Yer pa is real mad," Rita whispered. "Don't say nuthin' or he'll get even worse."

And he did. Without a word, he attacked her with fists and feet, knocking her to the floor where she curled up into a ball, covering her head with her arms in a futile effort to protect herself. When she struggled to stand, he slapped her head and shoulders until she reeled back and fell again. With his heavy boots, he kicked her tiny body again and again until she lay still and quiet.

Rita was terrified but she could tolerate it no more. "Stop it, Joe. Stop it now," she screamed. "Leave her alone. It ain't her fault." Joe turned on her like a bear, striking a blow to her head that sent her hurtling across the room. Then, leaving both of them semi-conscious, he stomped off to find Young Joe, who was sitting comfortably in the kitchen, listening to the uproar as he helped himself to the final slice of last night's suppertime chocolate cake.

"What's this about Christine?" Joe demanded.

His son stopped chewing for a bit, watching his father warily for signs of attack.

"Don't ya have enough sense to leave yer sister alone?" his father shouted."If ya have to have a woman ya know damn well there's plenty in town that'll have ya fer half a dollar. Takin' yer sister like that is just plain stupid."

Young Joe was stupid, but he didn't like being reminded of it. He jumped up ready to fight but his father knocked him down with a fistful of muscle to the jaw. He sat up but stayed on the floor, waiting for whatever was to come next.

They eyed each other for a bit and then Old Joe gave a sour laugh."From now on, sow yer wild oats somewheres else than home."

Young Joe figured the laugh was a sign of peace."Well, she was handy and I was horny. A lot better'n that dirty slut Myrtle in town. "Ya should a knowed better," his father snarled. And that completed Joe's punishment. But for Christine, it had just begun.

Every bone in her body ached from the force of her father's fists and feet. And she knew there would be more – the ill will of both father and step-brother had now found a focus. She had suffered many blows from both of them in her young life and witnessed the beatings that her father inflicted on Rita, sometimes for no reason. Now the situation seemed hopeless – there was nowhere to turn.

She knew that her parents – mostly her father – had discussed her 'situation'; from her room overhead, she heard him bellowing. There were just two options to consider – she could stay home and have the baby and face the scorn and shame and the neighbourhood. Or go to a home for wayward girls to have the baby and then leave it there for adoption. And still come back to the scorn and shame of the neighbourhood. And in both cases, the brutality of her family.

Her tears turned to desperation. Frantic and frightened, she tried to think it through. Should she run away? Should she kill herself? Where could she turn?

And then she thought of Julianna. Julie would know what to do.

"Chrissy, what's the matter?" Julie opened the door to the desperate girl. "What on earth is wrong? Is someone hurt?" By now, Julianna was accustomed to being on call when any mishap occurred in the Valley.

Christine was sobbing so violently that she could hardly speak. Julianna sat her down on the sitting room couch, wiped away her tears and brushed back her hair, hugging her until she calmed down. It was embarrassing to tell Julianna her story but once she began, it flooded out and Julianna's gentle questions clarified the details. She was furious. Her amber eyes snapped and her hands shook as she listened to the outrageous story and she wept herself at the injustices that Chrissy was suffering.

"I don't know what to do," Christine sobbed. "I'm scared of all of them. I'm scared to go home but I need to go now or they'll beat me up even more."

"No, stay a while longer," Julianna urged. "Let's have some tea and we'll talk some more."

And so the inevitable pot of tea appeared and under Julianna's subtle probing, Christine revealed a brief life full of pain, blows, kicks, threats and bullying. Rachel had told here about the beating that Joe had administered when Chrissy tried to champion Willie's cause. And she shuddered to recall young Joe's attempts to attack her only a fortnight after her arrival in the Valley. But she was horrified by the systematic abuse that Chrissy and her mother were facing day after day.

'Oh what I would give,' Julie thought to herself, 'to have a bright lovely daughter like this. Those brutes don't deserve her.' The injustice of it all brought tears to her eyes.

"Chrissy, I want you to go home now and just try to keep your head down and get your chores done. But I want you to come back tomorrow afternoon – sooner if you need to – and we'll put together a plan."

With fear dragging at her feet, Christine walked home, ready to start her chores. But she was met at the door by her father, beet-faced with rage. "Where the hell were ya, ya stupid slut? Down the road there talkin' to that Chandler bitch, wasn't ya. What did ya tell her?" he roared. "I'll teach ya to tattle about our family. Ya better learn to keep yer fat yap shut." His fist knocked her down and his kicks were so painful that she screamed. She tried to roll away from him but the next kick caught her in the stomach. At last he backed away, and she escaped bleeding and sobbing, to her room. Within minutes, the door slammed open and her father was there again, dragging her up from the bed where she had fallen and hauling her back downstairs.

"I've made up my mind," he roared. "I've had enough of ya and yer runnin' around all over the neighbourhood. There ain't no place for ya in this house. If that bitch Chandler is so quick with her charity, let her take ya in. Get outta this house and stay out."

Christine was stunned. She stood staring at him, trying to process what he had said. He simply grabbed her by the neck and propelled her to the door. "Ya heard me. Get the hell out and don't come back."

And so, terrified and sobbing, her spirit broken, her dress bloodied and torn, her face and body slowly discolouring from a new set of bruises, she returned to Julianna. And Julianna had already formulated a plan.

"Your father has done us all a favour," Julianna assured Chrissy. "I want you to stay here with me for a while. I can treat your bruises and help you build up your strength again. Then I'll go with you to the city and we'll make sure that you get the very best medical care." Chrissy shivered with fear and wept again but Julie reassured her. "Don't forget, my father is a doctor and he can take really good care of you. He has an excellent clinic and his sister, my Aunt Margaret, lives just across the street from him and has a big comfortable house where you can have a room of your own." Unwilling to entrust her request to the party line, where everyone listened in, Julianna had not yet made those arrangements but she felt confident that her family would back her up.

CHAPTER 16

Three Good Things

We never heard nuthin' more about Chrissy. When Julie come home, she never talked about her and we was too polite to ask. The Dunnings was as miserable as ever and just about everybody was happy to stay away from them. So it was like a stone got throwed into a pond and after a bit, the ripples died down and people forgot about it.

Lookin' back, I'll bet the one that suffered the most was Willie Donovan. He and Chrissy was pals ever since he was five. She stood up for him against the bullies at school and helped with his lessons at home. Now she was gone and nobody wanted to say why. But life went on in the Valley and most of us put Chrissy out of our minds.

Lenny.

A week later, Adam drove Julie and Chrissy to the train station and they were on their way to Toronto. Chrissy was scared but excited. It was her first train ride and her first visit to the city. The magnificence of Union Station was stunning and Julie walked her across Front Street and into the lobby of the Queen's Hotel where the opulent decor and furnishings took her breath away.

They took a cab to Dr. Brightson's house and Chrissy was in for more discoveries – indoor plumbing, for a start, but also the warmth with which they were greeted, the doctor's unabashed joy at seeing his daughter, Aunt Margaret's loving welcome and her new room at Aunt Margaret's place just across the street. She was less thrilled with the physical examination that Dr. Brightson performed in his clinic, but Julie stayed beside her, holding her hand and reassuring her that all was well. In fact, Julie stayed with her for a week, helping her to settle into her new home, showing her the city, and setting out a healthy regimen of food and exercise for the next six months as she waited for the baby.

Finally, Julie said goodbye, hugging Chrissy and promising to write and send news from home. "Tell Rachel and Willie that I miss them," Chrissy implored. "But no, I don't want Willie to know what happened to me. Please don't tell them anything about me. I'm so ashamed."

"Dear Chrissy, you have nothing to be ashamed of," said Julie, wrapping Chrissy in her arms. "Your father and your brother are the villains here and you are the innocent victim.

"Sadly we live in a society that puts all the blame on women and lets men go scot-free. But think about it. How can you possibly be at fault? Don't let those dark feelings take hold of you. Every day, I want you to tell yourself over and over again 'I am a good person. I am going to have a good life.' Make yourself healthy and strong and start making plans for the future."

"I can't imagine any kind of future," Chrissy replied sadly. "My life is ruined."

"Take it one day at a time, my dear. Try to dwell every day on the good things and try to let the bad things fade," Julie urged gently. "Look, here's a little booklet I want you to use. Every evening I want you to sit down and write at least three good things that you remember from that day. Whether it's a bird in a tree or the first dandelion of spring or a piece of Auntie Margaret's amazing apple pie or whatever good thing you can think of, write it down and think about it. You may be amazed at how much good there is in your world.

"Now I must catch that train. Please write to me often – every day if you can – and tell me all the news. And I'll be back to visit you in just a few weeks." Another hug, a light kiss on the cheek and she was gone.

That night, Chrissy opened the little notebook and wrote her name on the first page. Pondering for a bit, she finally wrote her first three 'good things'.

1. Julianna is my friend.
2. Auntie Margaret is my friend.
3. Dr. Brightson is my friend.

A good beginning, she thought to herself.

And a few days later…

1. I am safe here.
2. Trip to the library - my own card.
3. Rode the elevator at Caton's.

So Christine's new life began under the gentle guidance of Aunt Margaret and the careful surveillance of Dr. Brightson, with occasional visits from Julianna. Her bruises faded, the cracked ribs mended and her nightmares became less frequent and less fearsome. Still more child than woman, Chrissy delighted in discovering the city with Aunt Margaret, in poking through the library's vast wealth of books – more books than she ever imagined could exist – and choosing the ones she wanted to read. Within weeks, she was back at 'school' – Aunt Margaret called upon her former teaching colleagues to provide lesson plans and books for Chrissy's home schooling and supervised her daily lessons. A skilled and patient teacher, a quick and conscientious learner – before long they became a two-person mutual admiration society.

Somewhat removed from their day-to-day activities, Dr. Brightson nonetheless kept tabs on Christine. "How does she seem?" he grilled his sister. "Is she active and energetic? Is she eating well? Does she seem to have any pain? Is she sleeping well? Any nightmares?"

"She's a healthy young girl," Aunt Margaret replied. "She seems to have rallied very well."

"What about the pregnancy? Does she understand what is happening to her body and what will happen during the birthing and afterward?"

"She has no intention of keeping the baby," Aunt Margaret replied. "With all that she has suffered, I think that she would have difficulty loving this child, and besides, she's far too young to take on motherhood. She's a very bright girl and she needs to complete her education. But her figure is changing and we went shopping last week for roomier clothing. As to the birth itself, we haven't really discussed it. As the time gets closer, we certainly will. She's a very small girl so I worry about her. "

Sensitive to Christine's shyness, Dr. Brightson had not attempted another pelvic examination after the initial one when the girl arrived. Still traumatized by her parents' rage and the beatings they had inflicted, she had been sore in body and soul and he deferred to her pain and her shyness. He had detected the enlarged uterus and scar tissue in the vagina, no doubt the result of the brutal rape she had endured, but otherwise decided to let nurture take its course.

"We'll keep a close eye on her," he told his sister. "There's not much to be done about the pregnancy itself, as long as she continues to eat and sleep and feel well."

The months rolled by...

1. Ballet at the Royal Alexandra Theatre. So beautiful.
2. Julianna's book about women's health. Learned so much.
3. Lovely white swans at High Park.

Chrissy willed herself to be happy, grateful for her reprieve from the violence of her family and for the kindness of her benefactors but lonely too, for Willie and Rachel. She longed to write to Willie but she still felt deep shame for her situation and she could not explain her absence to him. She noted the expansion of her belly but now, thanks to Julianna's book, she understood it, and looked forward to the day when she would be free of this encumbrance. Her back and legs often ached, especially at night, but she bore it stoically, rather than worry Auntie Margaret.

They walked everywhere – to nearby shops, to the library, to huge High Park with its lake of swans and its zoo. Mornings belonged to school, while afternoons were for outings or learning needlework and cookery with Julianna's aunt. Sometimes Auntie Margaret would attend to IODE business. The Independent Order, Daughters of the Empire had recently formed in Toronto and Margaret Brightson was its president. Chrissy would spend those solitary days in the garden or in her room, reading a good book. The days slid by and she waited.

It happened suddenly, in her seventh month. They were walking home from the park and her back was aching miserably, shooting knife-like pains down both her legs. Suddenly a violent cramp encircled her entire lower body. She doubled over in pain and fell to her knees on the sidewalk, wrapping her arms around herself and moaning. The pain passed and she was able to stand again. Sensing what lay ahead, Auntie Margaret hailed a cab for the short ride home.

"We'll go straight to the doctor's office," she told Chrissy. "I want him to have a look at you." As they waited for Dr. Brightson, another vicious wave of pain wracked her body. She was gasping when he reached her and her body was rigid.

"Margaret, would you please help Christine to change into a gown? We'll take her into the clinic and keep an eye on her there." They exchanged glances that said it all: 'the time has come.'

Dr. Brightson avoided anesthetics in childbirth. He believed that they had a negative effect on the baby. But he was able to control some of Chrissy's pain, thanks to native medications that he had received from his shaman friend. And mercifully, the labour was short, though violent.

The twisted little creature that slipped into his hands just a few hours later had no hope of hanging onto life. In fact, he was dead at birth, his tiny deformed body reflecting his grandfather's legacy – the damage of multiple kicks and blows. Semi-conscious, Christine was unaware that he had already emerged or that the doctor had wrapped him in a sheet and carried him away immediately to the clinic's cold room.

A telephone call from Auntie Margaret, short on words to thwart the inevitable party line audience, was all that Julianna needed to bring her rushing to Toronto. "Hello Julianna," Margaret said. "We're looking forward to your visit this afternoon."

Julianna put two and two together. "I'll see you soon," she replied. "Please tell Daddy that I'm on my way." And they hung up.

Looking very young and very pale, Chrissy was sitting up in bed when Julie arrived. She had obviously been crying but she greeted Julianna with a joyful smile. They held one another in silence for a while.

"Dear Chrissy, it's over at last," Julie whispered. "Now your great new life can begin."

CHAPTER 17

Bullying the Hun

Them little German youngsters got the worst of it. They didn't talk much English at first but they sure got the message when the other youngsters started pickin' on them. Young Percy Hawkins, he was the worst – he was about twelve then, a big strong lad with muscles he'd built up from helping his Pa hammer horseshoes. Considering his size, he didn't have no need to bully people, but for some reason, he did. And those three Germans, two little girls and a wee boy, they was handy targets.

Lenny

Julianna was peering out the sitting room window that morning watching the neighbour children trudge up the road toward school. She'd noticed them a week or more ago and had been watching them off and on. She was worried about what she saw. The students fell into two groups – up ahead, a larger contingent led by Percy Hawkins, the blacksmith's son, and far back, the three Dietrich children, two little girls and an even smaller boy, heads down, feet dragging, obviously scared. Percy and some of his allies were looking back balefully and yelling insults and Julie had seen them sometimes take menacing runs at the little group, push them or even throw pebbles in their direction. Bullies must be confronted, she said to herself.

Adam had already supervised the barn chores and now, with the carriage team and wagonette pulled up at the door, he was upstairs changing into town clothes, ready to head out for supplies.

"Adam," Julianna called up the stairs. "I'm borrowing the rig for a few minutes." She gave him no time to object. She was out the door and up on the high driver's seat in a flash and overcoming her aversion to driving, urged the gentle team out the lane to intercept the children.

"Good morning, children," Julianna greeted them formally, sounding for all the world like a regular school marm. "I hope you're all well today?"

The children dutifully mumbled "good morning, miss", just as they would at school but they looked puzzled. Why was the beautiful Mrs. Chandler out here at the road with a team and wagon, asking after their health?

Julianna hopped down from the wagon and looped the horses' reins firmly round her arm. "Percy," she called. "Can I have a word with you?" She motioned to him to join her beside the wagon, out of earshot of the group. "I'm puzzled, Percy," she continued. "You seem upset with the Dietrich children. Can you tell me what the problem is?"

Percy hesitated, examining his feet, but she waited expectantly. Finally he looked up defiantly. "I hate them," he replied.

"But why?" Julianna persisted. "Have you had some problems with them?"

He looked sulky and kept his head down.

"Tell me, Percy. What's the real problem?"

He looked up angrily. "They're Huns," he said. "We hate Huns."

The other children edged closer, hoping to listen in. The Dietrich children still hung back.

"Why do you hate them, Percy?"

"They're Huns. They killed my uncle Ted."

Julianna was quiet for a moment. Then she turned the full force of her golden gaze on him and he was forced to look up into her eyes. "Percy, I'm so very sorry that you lost your uncle," she said. "I've been told that he was a fine person and a very good soldier. You must miss him a lot."

"Uncle Ted was the best uncle," Percy responded. "And them Germans killed him."

Julie took a deep breath. "I understand completely, Percy. You see, I lost my older brother in the war. He was a doctor, tending to the wounded in a medical tent right at the front lines. The shells that hit that tent killed everyone in it, all the wounded soldiers, two doctors and three nurses. I miss my brother so much that I still cry at night thinking of him."

She had his attention now. His gaze never left hers but he was still confused. Why was she telling him all this personal stuff that grown-ups never told youngsters?

"The worst part of it is," Julianna continued, "we haven't got anyone to blame. No one knows whether it was our own side or the enemy that hit that medical tent. We can't say the Hun killed our Philip because there's strong suspicion that it was a wild shot from one of our own."

She paused to let her words sink in. "Oh, we can blame the war, of course. War is cruel and stupid and wasteful. Just think about how many of our young men, all the bravest and the best, just like your Uncle Ted or my brother, Phil, were killed – over 60,000 dead and twice that many wounded. They were looking forward to coming home and living good lives right here in Canada. Coming home to their families, getting back to work, enjoying life again.

"But Percy, about the Dietrich family. They didn't kill my brother or your uncle. In Germany, a lot of people knew that war was going to come. So long before the war started, they decided to leave Germany and settle here. People like the Dietrichs are called conscientious objectors. That means that they hate war and refuse to take part in it. If they had stayed in Germany, they would have been arrested and sent to jail and their children would have been sent to orphanages. So they packed up and left and came to Canada – before the war ever began.

"I think they were very brave, don't you? Just think about leaving your home and friends and family, coming to a strange country where you don't speak the language or understand it, finding work, making a living, giving your children a chance in life. And the great thing is – they're succeeding. They've been able to buy their farm and send their children to school. They are incredibly hard-working and they never waste anything. They're a lesson to all of us, really."

Percy shuffled his feet and kept his gaze fixed on the ground. Finally, he replied: "Well they talk funny too."

"Yes, they speak with an accent. You would too if you were learning a new language. It's really hard to get your tongue around all the new words and the right way to say them. And then too, they all speak German at home so those children never heard a word of English until they started school. And already they're doing very well at it. In a few more months, you won't hear a trace of an accent."

Percy still looked doubtful. "Percy," Julianna said gently. "I want you to do me a favour. I want you to be as strong as the Dietrichs were when they gave up everything to come to Canada. I want you to stop bullying them. Maybe even think of ways to help them get along. You might be able to teach them things they need to know – like the English names of animals or trees. You're the biggest boy in this group, Percy, and you can be a leader.

"Will you try that?"

Percy straightened his shoulders and gazed up at her. "Maybe," he replied at last.

"Well that's a good beginning," she smiled at him. "Now I've kept you all late for school so hop in and I'll drive you there." The first group clambered aboard but the three Dietrich children still held back.

"Percy, would you please go back and ask the Dietrich children to come along for the ride to school? That's your first job as leader."

He hesitated, but the power of her persuasion won out. He jumped down and trudged back to the three stragglers. They shrank back from his approach, expecting insults or kicks.

"She's givin' us a ride to school," he announced. "Come on. You can ride too." Then he turned swiftly and headed back to the wagon. Julianna waved to them to come along and slowly they approached, clustering at the back of the wagon, unsure that they should climb up.

"Jump in, my dears. I'm driving you to school," Julianna called out cheerily. "I don't want you to be late."

The littlest one, Rudi, had to be lifted into the wagon and then his twin sisters, Lotte and Lara, climbed aboard. They still huddled together near the back, heads down but keeping a wary eye on the others.

Julie clucked up the horses and off they trotted, the wagonette with its comfortable springs skimming over the bumps with ease. When they reached the school, the children clambered down and dutifully came round to say 'thank you' to Mrs. Chandler. She smiled her radiant smile at each of them and wished them a good day. Laying her hand on Percy's arm, she detained him for just a moment. "Thank you, Percy," she said quietly. "That was admirable."

Percy nodded. And tucked 'admirable' away in his vocabulary, determined to look it up in the dictionary as soon as he got into the school, to see what it meant. He felt sure he'd like it.

CHAPTER 18

The Iron Rose

That Dr. Butters from Toronto wants to know about art and music and so forth. In them days, there weren't much call for useless work like that. Closest we ever come to it was the women makin' crocheted tablecloths or knitting baby clothes and socks. Sure, they stitched quilts from worn-out scraps of cloth or old sugar bags but they was made to be used around the house, and when they got too wore out for that, they ended up in the dog's bed under the woodshed steps.

Old Andrew McTavish, he always had a chunk of basswood in his overalls, and a sharp little knife in its own little wooden holster that he'd carved himself, and he was forever chippin' away. He liked to make spoons – real pretty spoons they was, with flowers or animals or little angels carved into the handles. He made bowls too and he'd give a set of bowls and spoons to anybody that got married in the Valley. He said in the Old Country they was for eatin' oatmeal porridge.

He showed me how to handle that little knife and I got to whittlin too. Mostly I made toys for the youngsters – little wood dolls for my daughters and Velma dressed them up in fancy clothes made out of scraps. They loved them dolls. Fact is, they both have them still and give them to their own kiddies to play with – with new clothes, of course. The old ones wore out. And I whittled out a farm for my older boy, Bernie, when he was little – cows, pigs, sheep, even a dog. And some little horses for my boy, Liam. And a wagon. Made a little harness and hitched up the team and wagon. I'll never forget how Liam's face shone when he found that horse and cart under the tree the Christmas he was maybe six.

But I mean to say, that was just whittlin'. It ain't art. Men was far too busy to waste their time with art. All spring, summer, fall, we slaved in the fields and in winter, we had to harvest timber and cut it and chop it for the stoves. The livestock still had to be tended, cows milked, horses exercised, and in spring, sheep sheared. And there was always harness and machinery to mend, and maybe a chair or two that needed a new rung.

And music? Well, Tommy Flaherty made a lot of music and so did Willie Donovan. Rachel Donovan had a fine voice and loved to sing. But nobody could make a livin' playin' the fiddle or whittlin' bits of wood. And if there was some, like Otto Dietrich, that kept on puttering in their workshops long after they should of finished their work and settled in their rockers beside the fire, well, we never thought much of it.

Now this here Doc Butters is tellin' us diff'rent. She's been goin' round collecting up some of the old toys and spoons and takin' pictures of Oscar's fence posts and Percy's flowers and she's calling it all 'folk art'. Now she wants to put it all in a book. What will that woman think of next!

Lenny

On the last day of school before Christmas holidays, the Dietrich children took their teacher a gift. It was tightly wrapped in cloth and Lotte, the eldest, cradled it close to her chest. Percy, who had not fully abandoned his bullyboy tendencies, was tempted to snatch it from her and wave it about for all to see or pitch it into a snow bank but instead he merely watched suspiciously as Lotte handed it over to her sister, Lara, in the cloak room.

While the students marched and shuffled toward their desks, the three children approached the teacher's desk and placed their gift before her. Then they hurried back to their own desks without a word.

Teacher gifts usually ran to tins of cookies or jars of jam so Miss Arnold couldn't imagine what the lumpy package contained. It was swaddled in a cloth that, when she unwrapped it, revealed itself as an exquisite table cover, richly embroidered in the time-honoured motifs of central Europe – bright flowers, hearts and twining vines. And inside – she gasped. It was a black rose in its own vase, a perfectly formed half-open rose bud, made of iron that had been worked and hammered to the thinness of china. She draped the table cover over the front of her desk to display its colourful stitchery to the students, and placed the wrought iron flower on top of it. Then she arranged her other gifts around it.

Percy gulped and stared. Working in iron was nothing new to him. In the family blacksmith shop, his father had long ago taught him to make perfectly fitted horse shoes that coddled the hard working hooves of the Valley's draught horses. He had tried his hand at garden tools, crowbars, pokers for the fire, and dippers for the water pail. None of them ever measured up to his father's expectations and he had come to hate working at the forge because of the constant stream of criticism. But now he stared at the wrought iron rose and he felt envy, admiration and a kind of hunger to learn to make something as beautiful as this. He longed to pick it up and examine it, petal by petal, to figure out how the iron could be hammered to such a delicate textured depth and shaped subtly as rose petals are, how it was assembled, how he could create such beauty himself. He could almost hear his father's scornful dismissal of such tomfoolery, but his yearning persisted.

"Lara, Lotte, Rudi. Please thank your parents for this beautiful gift," Miss Arnold interrupted his thoughts. "Do they do this kind of work themselves?"

Lotte stood beside her desk. "Yes, Miss," she replied respectfully. "They helped us to make it for you."

"You made this?" Miss Arnold gasped. "But this is iron. Surely working with iron is too difficult for children."

"Our poppa learned from his poppa when he was our age," Lotte replied. "And he teaches us."

"What about the beautiful embroidery," Miss Arnold persisted. "Surely you didn't do that as well."

"Yes, Miss," Lotte said modestly. "Momma helped us and we all worked on it for you."

Miss Arnold felt tears prick her eyes but she forced them back. The beauty of the gifts and the image of the three children diligently crafting such fine workmanship touched her heart. But to ensure that the other students did not feel that their modest gifts of jam and cookies fell short of her approval, she knew she had to contain her enthusiasm and her emotions.

"Thank you, all of you, for your very sweet gifts," Miss Arnold gestured to the display on her desk. "I have Christmas cards to send home to your parents this afternoon so please be sure you come and collect the one for your family before you leave."

The final day before a holiday was not conducive to work so as the children cut out chains of paper snowflakes and played games, Miss Arnold finished her Christmas cards, with notes of thanks to the parents for their gifts. But to the Dietrichs, she penned an extra long note, full of admiration for their work and for sharing their craftsmanship with their children.

Percy was stricken. When school was dismissed, he pulled on his coat and mittens and waited for the Dietrich trio as Lara helped little Rudi with his boots. Then he fell in beside them as they began the walk home. Although his taunts and insults were less frequent these days, his proximity still made them nervous. Rudi slipped around Lara and held tight to her hand, plodding on, head down, fearing an attack. Lotte and Lara looked straight ahead and waited for the onslaught. But Percy was nervous too, suddenly ashamed of the fear and pain he had caused in the past and unsure how to undo the damage.

"My pa is a blacksmith," he suddenly blurted out. "But he can't make nuthin' like that flower you gave the teacher. How'd you make it?"

"Our poppa showed us how," Lara replied. "He makes all kinds of things."

"So where's your forge?" Percy queried. "Where'd the iron come from?"

"The forge is in the drive shed," Lara explained. "Poppa has iron there too." She still wasn't ready to trust Percy, who had bullied them all mercilessly since school began.

"Could I come and see some more of the work?" he asked boldly. "I never seen nuthin' like that."

Lara and Lotte exchanged glances. Was it safe to bring this bully into their home? What would their parents say?

"Lookit," Percy hurried on. "I'm real sorry about all the stuff I said about youse. I'm sorry I hurt your feelings." He had never imagined he'd hear himself apologizing. Lara and Lotte walked on in silence, with Percy fretting beside them, until they arrived at their own laneway. "You can come in," Lotte said simply.

The rich scent of Christmas spices – nutmeg, cinnamon, cloves – tickled their taste buds as they entered the house. The children removed their boots and coats and hung them beside the door. Percy stood uncertainly just inside the door until Lara said: "You have to take your boots off if you're staying." While he untied his boots and pulled them off, she turned to her mother and explained to her in German who he was and what he wanted.

Olga was well aware of Percy's abusive behaviour – thanks to his insults, shoves and even occasional stone-throwing, her children had arrived home in tears day after day – and she had felt helpless to comfort them or remedy the situation. But he seemed tame enough just now. She motioned to the children to sit at the table where she brought cups of hot milk with honey and a plate of an aromatic ginger cake that Percy had never encountered before, and felt tempted to devour to the last crumb as soon as he tasted the first bite.

He looked around the kitchen. There was wrought iron everywhere. Hooks for coats, an exquisite ash shovel for the stove, a collection of gracefully curved stove-top trivets for hot pots. Beside the stove stood a kindling basket made of interwoven strands of twisted iron, crested with ornate curls. On the table, a long slim tray that must have been meant for bread or fruit was made of braided strands of iron. And then, a vase of flowers on the bureau – wrought iron flowers in an iron vase, but far more elaborate than the teacher's gift. Roses, lilies, dahlias, daisies and more – he recognized many from his mother's garden though he'd never learned their names. But he did identify a perfectly formed and proportioned hummingbird that hovered just above them, supported by a slim stalk that hid amongst the flower stems. He thought it was the most beautiful work he had ever seen.

"Can you teach me to do this kind of work," he asked Olga. "I like it a lot."

She was startled as was Otto who came through the door just in time to hear the boy's request. "You are Percy, yes?" he greeted him. "Your father make good strong shoes for my horses."

"Sure," Percy replied. "But not this kind of stuff. Is it hard to learn?"

Otto removed his boots and coat and sat down with the children at the table. "People make wrought iron since four thousand years, maybe more," he explained. "In Europe, beautiful iron gates and doors for castles and cathedrals. Tables, chairs, lamps, window frames. Nice soft iron, easy to work if you know how."

"That's just it," Percy responded eagerly. "I want to know how." He knew he was on the verge of rudeness, but his desperation to seize the moment drove him on.

Otto looked into the eyes of his children who had been the victims of this boy's aggression. They returned his gaze but their faces were impassive. He looked up at Olga and thought he saw an almost imperceptible nod.

"I will teach you, Percy," he replied at last. "But only if your father say yes."

Percy's face fell. "Oh no, my pa will never let me. Stuff like this," he gestured to the bouquet of flowers with its resident hummingbird, "he'd say that's a waste of time. Women's stuff."

"Maybe he must see it first, see how we make. Then maybe he like," Otto argued.

"Oh no please, Mr. Dietrich. He'll be mad. He says I don't make horse shoes well enough. He'll make me do them. He won't let me make anything like this." He looked around at the treasures that graced this simple home and his face reflected his deep sense of loss.

Otto faced a dilemma. As head of his household, he expected his children to obey him. Anything else spelled failure on his part and rebellion on theirs. To give Percy lessons, even in something as inspiring as wrought iron craft, without his father's permission, was a denial of a father's authority. Yet often when he took his horses to the smithy, he heard the father shouting at his son, insulting him, disparaging his work. Bullying him, he thought. Yes, bullying. And in turn Percy bullied smaller children, desperately trying to feel strong and powerful. If he turned his back on Percy, he thought, what was he doing to the lad's life?

He got to his feet. "Come. I show you".

Still limping from the accident he suffered the previous year, Otto led the way to the tin drive shed, where he showed Percy the forge and his stash of iron. "We come here, I find forge and iron in barn," he explained. "Under old grain bags. Very old but still work." They examined the huge leather bellows that pumped by hand, forced air onto the coals to heat the iron. "They look like new," Percy observed. "I make," Otto explained."Old leather very rotten, no good. I cut from cowhide and… good like new." Percy was amazed.

Otto showed him the slim bars of iron that awaited his artistry, the anvil and vices at which he worked the red hot – sometimes white hot – metal. It was all familiar to Percy, yet new, too. He marveled at the tidy rack of ball pein hammers, graduating in size from tiny to the biggest that was still a miniature of the hefty tool used for beating horse shoes. On the work bench he saw a slim vase of twisted iron, awaiting its final touch. His heart raced at the thought of being able to create so much beauty using such familiar everyday tools.

Otto watched him discreetly and saw the excitement in his face, the reverence with which he touched the works in progress – the petals of a rose, the six-petalled lily awaiting its stem, the neat spirals of twisted iron that would become vases or baskets. He made his decision.

"We will have lessons," he said. "But you must find way to come here."

"We got Christmas holidays for two weeks," Percy responded as if he'd already thought it through. "If you have time, I can come every day. I'll pretend I'm going skating."

And so, feeling somewhat a traitor to fatherhood but a champion of his beloved craft, Otto became Percy's teacher.

He was amazed at the speed with which the boy learned. Ruefully he had to admit that the lad was more skilled than his own daughters whom he had been teaching for a couple of years. But, he postulated, Percy was already comfortable with hot horseshoes, with firing the forge and manipulating metal. So he was a splendid candidate for wrought iron.

They began with simple twisting – heating the iron bar to red hot, gripping one end in a vice and using giant pliers to turn it gently into rhythmic spirals. Otto encouraged Percy to keep the final product always in mind, applying delicate strokes for smaller pieces but bolder pressure for larger utilitarian work.

"This feels different from the iron my pa uses," Percy observed. "Easier to work."

"For horseshoes, tools – mild steel – more carbon. Stronger, harder to work," Otto explained. "Wrought iron – less carbon than mild steel, softer."

Percy was impatient to move beyond twisted rods and tackle the intricacies of flowers and birds. Otto stood over him as he began the painstaking process of pounding red hot iron into leaf and petal shapes and when enough were completed, affixing them to slender stems. The little bouquet slowly took shape and in due course, they constructed a vase to hold it.

"For your mother?" Otto asked.

"No, for Mrs. Chandler," Percy explained. "She helped me a lot." He did not elaborate and Otto did not ask, because his children had already told him how Julianna had challenged Percy to abandon his bullying and befriend them. It seemed that a hunk of iron had achieved that final step.

"On the second day of January, with school due to start the next day, Percy collected his precious iron bouquet form Otto's forge and wrapped it in his scarf to carry it to Julianna. She was startled to see him at the door but she welcomed him warmly. They had met several times in the months since her intervention in his bullying and, although she had still sensed some traces of his old behaviour, she had always treated him as a friend. After all, they shared the tragedy of wartime loss.

Shyly, he unwrapped the iron bouquet and set it on the kitchen table. "What is this lovely thing?"

"It's a present for you," he replied. "To say thanks. For…everything."

"Percy, it is simply lovely. Did you make it? Is your father now working in decorative iron?"

"No. And I don't want him to know what I'm doing." Percy looked worried. "Please don't tell him. He'll kill me if he finds out I'm taking lessons from Mr. Dietrich. My pa will say I'm wasting my time and he'll make me quit school and work full time in the shop."

He told her the whole story of the rose for the teacher and how he had begged for lessons and how the Dietrichs were guarding his secret.

"Mrs. Chandler, he makes the prettiest things – flowers and birds and baskets. Things for the house. That's what I want to do too."

"Well, Percy, I'll keep you secret too, but you know – sooner or later, your parents will find out. And they'll be even more upset when they realize that you've been going behind their backs all this time. Why don't you make something pretty for your mother and when you give it to her, you can tell her about your lessons and maybe the two of you can tell your father, and she'll stand by you."

Percy was doubtful but he saw the logic of her argument. He finally decided that something practical might be more acceptable to them than a flower so he crafted a simple hook with elegant scrollwork at its base. And as Julianna had foretold, it worked. He finished it fairly quickly and presented it to his mother a few days later. "Look ma, we can hang it right up here by the stove so yer towels dry quick. Or ya might want it for yer apron. Tell me where ya want it and I'll put it up for ya."

"Did you make this in the shop?" she asked suspiciously.

"No. Mr. Dietrich taught me how to work in wrought iron and I made it there. Ma, this is wrought iron. It's what I want to do. Will ya help me tell Pa?"

At suppertime, Lizzie pointed out the hook to her husband. "Lookit what our boy made," she said proudly. "Isn't that lovely?"

Hector glared. He turned on Percy angrily but his wife intervened.

"Come now, Hector. There's no call for yelling. Lookit the work he's put into it."

Hector raged on. "Why are ya wasting yer time and my iron on this rubbish? You're supposed to be cuttin' horseshoes and the hardware store in town is waitin' on a dozen stove pokers. Who says ya can spend yer time on this kind of trash?"

"Hector," Lizzie interrupted him firmly. "This is not trash. If you look close you'll see how nice it is. And useful too. Besides, just last week you was complaining how business is slow. You said with tractors coming in, some farmers was gettin' rid of their horses so making horseshoes and farm tools will soon be a thing of the past. Them was your very words.

"And I know you're right, Hector 'coz at the Women's Institute, everybody's been talkin' about buyin' tractors and sellin' the horses, just like you said. Before we know it, there won't be enough horse shoein' to put food on the table. Now Percy's gone and found a new way to put blacksmithin' to work."

But father and husband that he was, Heck felt obliged to take a stand. He ranted and roared, bellowed and bawled, fussed and fumed, and finally told his son to find out where to get wrought iron and prepare to work it in their home forge.

And deep in his heart, he felt a swelling sense of relief and pride that his son would never have to suffer a lifetime of the hard slogging that he had endured, that perhaps he himself might be able to abandon the boredom of the ferrier's trade and turn his hand to crafting beauty.

CHAPTER 19

In God's Hands

Ask anybody in our Valley and they'd claim they was faithful churchgoers. Not that we got to church every Sunday. Them churches was a fair ways off in Paxton Ford, so in rain, snow, sleet, hail, a touch of fog, seeding or harvest time, or a hint of flu, we'd stay home. Or, if the cows or sheep or even the wife was birthin'. If the horse was lame or the buggy wheel was loose, if we'd been out and about on Saturday night and felt a bit poorly, or if a fine summer Sunday dawned, all dew and blue skies after a week of hard labour – well then, church had to play second fiddle, as Tommy Flaherty would say.

But we called ourselves believers all the same – Catholic or Protestant, most likely Presbyterian or Methodist that turned themselves into United, a few Baptists, maybe even a few Anglicans, but they was hoity-toity and most likely English, though some people said they might just as well be Catholic and have done with it, what with the incense and the wine and the fancy dress and all that fal-da-rol.

For some reason, the Catholics and the Protestants hated each other, most especially around the Twelfth of July when there was a Orange Parade in Paxton Ford – somethin' to do with the troubles in Ireland. Velma and me never did understand why them troubles didn't stay in Ireland where they belonged. That Orange Walk business never did nothing for nobody except sell a lot of booze and make people hate each other for no good reason. Tho' most of the time we was too busy with farmin' to fuss over religion.

Bert Wilkins now, he got religion in the war, along with a couple of lungs full of mustard gas. Neither one did him much good – he and Edna with their seven youngsters goin' on eight was poor as paupers and proud as Scots. Bert couldn't work the farm so it didn't produce much, they had almost no livestock and any extra chickens or eggs got eaten at home. They was poor, no doubt about that, but they was stiff-necked and afraid of accepting what they called 'charity'. They just kept waitin' for God to provide. Finally, when it got to be a matter of life and death, Julie and Adam pitched in and the neighbours followed suit. But Bert and Edna still gave God all the credit.

Lenny

An urgent knock at the door late one evening revealed Bert Wilkins, sweating and wild eyed. The self-conscious shyness he'd exhibited at the welcome party was replaced by desperation.

"Mrs. Chandler, can ya come and see my wife?" he begged. "She's having a baby and she's been at it now since yesterday. Nothing's happening and she's getting weaker. She can't sit up and she's bleeding. Can ya help her?"

Julianna looked to Adam apologetically but she was instantly on the move. Stocking her trusty black bag with as many remedies as she thought she might need, she pulled on a coat and joined Wilkins in his buggy for the wild ride across the Valley, to their home two concessions away. Hanging on to her bag and her seat, she still managed to ask questions – how old was his wife (thirty-six), was this her first child (no, her eighth), did she have a history of difficult births (dunno – guess not), who attended her previous deliveries (one of the neighbours for the first couple or three but she moved away, so no one at all for the last four). Julie was glad that the darkness masked her growing concern.

Walking into the house, she was struck by the dank smell, but even more by the sounds of pain that emanated from the bedroom beyond the kitchen. The whole family was gathered in the kitchen, wide-eyed and scared, anxiously listening to their mother's groans and screams. Wilkins slumped wearily at the kitchen table and struggled with a spasm of coughing.

"Hello children," Julianna greeted them kindly. "I'm here to help your mother, but I'm going to need help from all of you." She hoped that her confident tone sounded genuine, although they said nothing at all. "Don't be worried – we're all going to pitch in to help your mum get well."

The bedroom was a shambles. Edna Wilkins lay atop a lumpy straw tick, in a tangle of sheets and blankets, soaked with sweat, blood and amniotic fluid. Her body was clammy and her dank hair clung to her skull. Obviously terrified, she moaned constantly and screamed in agony with each contraction.

Julianna had delivered plenty of babies but the fact that labour had already lasted more than twenty-four hours was alarming. Speaking soothingly, she examined Edna's swollen body and with some difficulty made a cursory pelvic examination. The baby seemed to be in a breech position, she soon realized, and it would not budge.

"Edna, we're going to work together now. Try to breathe deeply and relax your whole body. I know it's painful but try."

She rushed to the kitchen and set the children to work, finding fresh linens, preparing warm water and making sweet weak tea for their mother. "Now we need a good load of wood to keep the stove going and plenty of hot water. I need a wash basin and a pitcher of hot water and washing clothes beside your mother's bed right away, and as many clean towels and sheets as you can find." She silently thanked her lucky stars that she had remembered her new rubber hot water bottle, a recent invention that was far softer and lighter than the clumsy stoneware jars of old, and she handed it to Gladys, the oldest girl, to fill with hot water. She asked for more lamps in the delivery room but there were none to be had – at least none containing oil for burning. So she had to make do with the one small coal oil lamp. When Gladys brought the hot water bottle, Julie asked her to stand by to help. Gladys was shaking with fear but she waited stoically for instructions.

Back at the bedside, Julianna checked for progress but there was none. She placed the hot water bottle against Edna's pelvis and covered it with towels to maintain the warmth. "We'll need to keep this bottle warm, Gladys, so make sure there's plenty of hot water on the stove," she instructed. There were ways to turn a breech baby, she knew, but they should have been implemented weeks ahead of delivery, not when it was so far advanced.

She found a tincture in her medical bag and instilled a few drops into her patient's mouth. It was bitter and Edna's face contorted but she had no choice but to swallow it. "That's going to help you to feel calmer," Julie explained. Another dip into the medical bag brought forth a tiny container of oil that smelled richly of unknown herbs. She applied it to Edna's lower belly, massaging thoroughly, and applying gentle upward pressure away from the pelvis. Edna was calmer now and although she was still in pain with every contraction, she was able to swallow a few sips of the sweet tea from the invalid cup that her daughter held to her lips.

"I need you to hold the lamp so I can see better," Julie told Gladys. "Now I know you're frightened but for your mother's sake, you must get control of yourself, so you can really help her. If you feel faint or sick, put the lamp down on the dresser and go outside until it passes. I can only care for your mother at this point – not both of you."

Gladys obeyed, breathing sharply but holding the lamp near Julie's shoulder as she spread Edna's legs and peered into the birth canal, trying to slip her fingers around the baby's body, hoping to help ease it out on the next contraction. But there was no space.

Still another little pot of salve emerged from her medical bag and she applied it all around Edna's cervix. "This will help to dull the pain," she reassured her. She sent Gladys to replenish the hot water bottle and then to find a small stool or box and scrub it thoroughly.

"Edna, I want you to sit up now," Julie told her patient. "I can't," Edna protested weakly. "You must," Julie replied. "I want you up and on your knees."

Together they eased her up to a sitting position and then helped her to turn over onto her hands and knees, resting her arms on the little wooden stool that Gladys had found. "Oh for a birthing chair," Julianna thought to herself. "But this is the best we can do."

She applied more of the heat-generating salve to Edna's lower abdomen, hoping to persuade the baby to turn toward it. The next contraction was a major one but the pain killer seemed to be working. Edna puffed and panted but she didn't scream at all. Julie continued the massage with firm upward strokes. The night seemed endless.

Gladys bathed her mother's face with cool water and administered a few more drops of the relaxant while Julie examined her abdomen. Another mighty contraction and Julie gasped with relief. A tiny foot popped out, closely followed by a second one. Released by the pressure of the feet and legs, the baby's bottom began to appear. Julie grasped the slippery little body and pulled gently, trying to hurry the baby into the world. It was a boy, weak from the prolonged struggle and blue from lack of oxygen. She could not yet determine whether he was alive. Finally free of the birth canal, she held the baby by his feet and gently patted his wrinkled little bum. At last the lad opened his mouth and howled. Quickly, she wrapped him in a tiny blanket and placed him on his exhausted mother's abdomen.

She dealt with the cord and the afterbirth and swabbed away the blood, keeping a close eye on Edna's blood pressure, pallor and breathing. She was very weak and she was still losing a worrisome quantity of blood.

Back in her medical kit, Julie found another compound, an herbal concoction that helped to thicken the blood and control bleeding. She added a few drops to Edna's tea and instructed Gladys and Bert, who had now ventured into the room, to give the patient three drops in a cup of sweetened tea every three hours.

Lifting Edna gently, they turned the straw tick and replaced the sheets. The sodden pillows and blankets needed laundering but Julie saw no tub or scrub board to do the job. "Hang these on the clothes line for now," she instructed Gladys. "And try to find a dry pillow and dry quilts to keep your mother warm." The children scurried off to raid their own beds for dry bedding.

"Where can I find some baby clothes and diapers," she asked Bert. He looked at his boots, embarrassed. "Well see, there ain't much money for such things," he confessed. "She prolly has something in one of them dresser drawers." Gladys dug about and came up with a few little shirts and diapers. "That will do for now," Julie confirmed.

The bleeding still worried her. She could only offer pads of old clothing to absorb the discharge and she asked Gladys to change them regularly and wash them, as well as the soiled sheets. "Hang them out in the sunshine in the morning," she instructed. "The sun will sterilize them…kill the germs."

At last, she asked Bert to drive her home. "That's a nasty cough, Mr. Wilkins," she ventured. "Would you like me to have a listen to your chest before we leave?"

"Nuthin' to worry about," he responded, recoiling slightly from her outstretched hand. "Prolly just dust."

She let the subject drop for now, her mind on Edna and her own lack of sleep.

As the sun rose, she arrived home to find Clara already in the kitchen, brewing strong tea. Julianna carried hot water to her room and peeled off her stained clothing, grateful for a hot soapy wash. Refreshed and dressed, she returned to the kitchen where Adam had just come in for breakfast.

"That family has nothing," Julie told them. "They have no clothing for the baby. No oil for their lamps. I suspect they have precious little food. Something must be done."

Adam attended to his porridge and said nothing. He knew by now that when Julie was formulating a plan, his safest response as to keep the peace and let her proceed.

"Adam, we have so much. I want to go into town today and get some things for that family," she announced.

"Are you sure they want our charity," he asked. "They may be poor, but they're proud. Sometimes charity offends."

She thought about that as she sipped her tea. "You have a point," she replied. "But we can't just stand by and do nothing. Clara, what do you think?"

"I understand what Adam is saying," Clara replied."Believe me, there's nothing worse than Lady Bountiful, dispensing her charity to the poor."

"Adam, they have two sons," Julie ventured. "They're still young but is it possible to give them some paid work to help the family out? Or is there something that the father could do to earn more money? Why are they so poor anyway?"

"Nine mouths to feed," Adam replied succinctly. "And Bert's not a well man.

"But here's an idea," he added. "I recall that Bert Wilkins was a rather good repairman back before the war. He could fix broken machinery, broken furniture, mend harness, replace windows. But there wasn't much work for him around here because the Valley folks don't have much cash. George, do we have some jobs that might help this family out?"

"I could break a few windows," George offered, straight-faced. "Or take an axe to the furniture."

His humour fell flat so he tried a different tack."Say, Adam, don't you need some bee hives and frames? You mentioned in the summer that some of them needed attention. And there's that nice little buggy in the drive shed with a broken shaft. You know I never really learned the skills of repairing things. I regret it, but it was not the kind of work that I was trained to do. So I'd be happy to have a hand with all those little jobs that need attention."

"That's good, George. I'll drive over and ask Bert if he's available."

"Well, let's drive into town first," Julie suggested. "Lady Bountiful or not, I want to get that little chap some clothing and blankets. And I want to check up on Edna to see how she's doing."

The general store and the dry goods shop stocked everything she needed and more. Julie lingered over the little shirts and nightgowns, aware once again of her own unrequited yearning for a baby. Then she scooped up the tiny garments along with diapers and blankets for the newborn plus two dozen pairs of socks in every size and eight pairs of mitts. "The older children are needy too," she rationalized, "and Bert's thumbs were poking out of his mitts." They visited the hardware shop for coal oil and stopped at the grocer's for oatmeal, tea, bread, butter, jam and a tin of peanut butter, the newest food fad in the city but relatively unknown in the Valley. And off they went to the Wilkins farm.

"God bless you," the new mother murmured weakly as Julie entered. Edna was still in bed with the baby beside her and the sheets were already darkened by her blood. Julie wished she had brought sheets and blankets from the well stocked linen closet at home.

"I've brought a wee gift for your new baby," she announced cheerfully. She laid the package down on the bed but did not open it. "I see you're still bleeding. May I have a look?"

Now that the birthing ordeal was over, Edna was reluctant to uncover her body but

Julie finally persuaded her. Sure enough, there was still too much blood and the examination, which Edna found intensely painful, convinced Julia that the long and arduous labour had caused serious internal damage.

She perched on the side of the bed and took Edna's hand. "Edna, you're still losing blood and I'm worried about you. I think it would be wise for you to see a doctor."

Edna responded with a small moan. Julie realized that she was too weak to take in the full meaning of her words.

In the kitchen, Adam and Bert had finished their business and sat companionably at the kitchen table enjoying a cup of tea. Julie laid the second package on the table. "Mr. Wilkins, here's a little gift for all the children. They've all been so brave and helpful during this ordeal. You have a lovely family, you know." She dug out the mitts and socks and arranged them neatly, placing the adult sized mittens before him without a word.

"I thank you," he said quietly. "God bless you."

"Mr. Wilkins, I have to talk to you about Edna," Julie began. "I'm worried about her because she is still losing a great deal of blood, which tells me that her internal organs were damaged during her labour. I think she needs to see a real doctor – a surgeon – and decide what to do."

"We ain't got no money for a doctor," Bert replied. "She's got over it with all the others so she'll get over it this time too. God will take care of her, like He always did."

"I don't think so, Mr. Wilkins. I think Edna needs surgery very soon or her life will be in real danger."

He looked up at her briefly and then away. "Your husband has just offered me work," he said quietly. "And I'm grateful for it, especially coz I know that you don't really need me…that you're doing this just to help us out. And I appreciate it. But as hard as I work, I can't make enough money to pay for no doctor. She's in God's hands now. There's naught we can do but pray."

"I doubt that prayer is going to be enough," Julie replied, ignoring Adam's warning glance. "She needs skilled medical care that is beyond what we can safely do here at home. Without it, she may die and leave eight children without a mother.

"I believe that she needs a hysterectomy which is an operation that removes the womb. That's where the bleeding is coming from. And the result of this is that she will not have any more children. Which is just as well, because even if she recovers somewhat from this past labour, another pregnancy could kill her."

He was startled but resigned. "Nuthin' I can do. I already told ya – she's in God's hands."

"No, Mr. Wilkins, she's in my hands. I'm the one who delivered this baby. And I'm the one who sees that your wife is bleeding heavily and she could die within days, leaving eight little children with no mother. I don't want that on my conscience and I'm sure you don't want it on yours. The way out is to take her to hospital and have the surgery performed, as quickly as possible."

He stared at her but said nothing. "Bert, we'll arrange for your wife's surgery," Adam urged, "and when she is well and you are back on your feet, we'll work out some way for you to repay us."

He sat slumped over the table, a man defeated. "Bert," said Adam gently. "If the tables were turned, I'll bet you'd do the same for me or any of the neighbours. Now let us lend a hand when you need it. Your children need their mother and you need your wife."

Wilkins nodded mutely and Adam briefly laid his hand on his shoulder. "Good man," he said.

"We need a wet nurse for the baby," Julie pointed out. "Let me drive over to Mrs. Hooper's place right now – she may have enough milk for her own baby and yours."

She rushed out and returned within an hour to find Adam and Bert still sitting quietly in the kitchen. "It's all arranged," she announced. "Mrs. Hooper can look after your little one until Edna recovers. Mr. Wilkins, we'll take her this afternoon – there's no time to waste. The baby needs feeding and Edna needs help."

"You know the Hooper family is Catholic," Adam commented as they hurried home.

"Now you mention it, yes, I recall seeing a crucifix in the bedroom."

"So when Bert Wilkins recovers from his grief and confusion, he may object to having her wet-nurse his child."

"Oh Adam, don't be ridiculous. His wife is dying, his baby will die without proper care and you are telling me her milk is the wrong religion?"

"A lot of folks here in the Valley think so. There's still plenty of ill will between Catholics and Protestants, Well, ill will doesn't even cover it – it's blind hatred and superstition that's a spillover from the Old Country. You've seen the July 12 parade in Toronto and the fights that always break out afterward. And it's just as bad around here on King Billy's day. Catholics and Protestants are like oil to water – they just don't mix. Not even here in the country. It's an unwritten rule."

'Well, the Wilkins baby and Mrs. Hooper are about to break the rule," Julie retorted. "Can you drive a bit faster? We haven't a moment to lose."

Julie set Clara to work rounding up bedding and nightclothes for their patient while she telephoned the surgeon at Morganston hospital, the closest one to Paxton Ford. Then they hurried back to Edna, to find her almost unconscious. With the older children away at school, she missed Gladys' help but she managed to bathe Edna quickly and dress her in one of her own warm flannel nighties and wool socks. She collected the baby's sparse wardrobe and wrapped him in his new little blankets while Adam pulled the automobile up close to the front step and carried Edna out the door. Julie tucked her snugly into the blankets with a hot water crock at her feet and a hot water bottle at her chest and blankets plus a vast bearskin rug over all. Wilkins had scarcely moved but now he rose slowly to his feet and holding the four youngest children close to him, came to the door to see them off. He did not speak to his wife or touch her.

The Hooper farm was on their route to the main road. Although she was eager to deposit the baby with his foster mother and hurry away. Julia was too concerned with Edna's condition to worry about the baby's religious affiliation or its chances of survival. Mrs. Hooper had already nurtured four children of her own, including the youngest whom Julie had delivered some three months earlier, so no doubt her skills would extend to this one. All the same, as she cuddled the tiny creature who kept turning toward her breast in search of milk, her throat tightened and her heart ached to keep him all to herself.

Her telephone call to the doctor had alerted the party line. As Adam and Julia drove as swiftly as they could to the hospital, their neighbours reacted to the emergency at home. By the time Edna was in a hospital bed and being examined by doctors, the Wilkins' table was filling up with soups and stews, fruit and jams, cakes and breads, that set the children's mouths to watering and their eyes to shining.

When the older children arrived home from school, Bert Wilkins gathered his family around the kitchen table and told them about their mother. "Your ma's at death's door," he said. "She's in God's hands. All's we can do now is pray." Obediently, with tears streaming down their cheeks, the children knelt down on the kitchen floor and prayed with their father for their mother's recovery and safe return. Then with the little ones clamouring to wear their new mitts all through supper, they dove into the feast that God and their neighbours had provided.

The doctor in Morganston agreed that the situation was urgent. There was no time to try to revive Edna's strength; it was draining away more dangerously with every minute that passed. So the invasive surgery was performed that very evening. The doctor was not encouraging but "while there's life, there's hope," Julie told herself. She stayed at Edna's bedside and sent Adam home with a message to Wilkins that his wife was holding her own. Sleeping in a chair beside the bed, she roused frequently to wet Edna's lips with a little water and check on the bleeding. By morning, it had abated somewhat and Edna was half awake, but still unaware of her surroundings or what had happened to her. Julie talked to her gently, to help her regain consciousness. When the doctor made his rounds, he was mildly pleased with her condition. "She's not out of the woods yet," he told Julie. "But she has no fever and the bleeding has let up somewhat, so I'm optimistic."

And optimism prevailed. As the day wore on, Edna continued to revive so by evening Julie was able to give her a little clear soup and several sips of sweet tea. Edna slept throughout most of that night and Julie gratefully snoozed in the chair beside her. They awoke together the next morning with Edna wild with worry over her children, especially the newborn, and the cost of the surgery. "The children are doing just fine," Julie comforted her. "Gladys is so very capable – you've raised a lovely daughter there who knows how to take charge of a household. The baby is safe with Mrs. Hooper who just happens to have enough milk for two babies. The hospital bill is being taken care of. And I think you'll find when you get home that your pantry is well stocked, thanks to our wonderful neighbours."

Late that afternoon, Adam arrived with Bert. Never having darkened the door of a hospital, he was visibly nervous. He searched the ward for Edna, and when at last he saw her he hurried to her bedside, bowed his head, and sobbed. Julie swiftly pulled the curtains around the bed and she and Adam left them alone.

"How is she?" Adam asked when they were out of earshot.

"The doctor thinks she's doing fairly well," Julie reported. "She's a strong woman but she couldn't have survived that heavy bleeding for much longer. I think she'll need to stay here for another couple of weeks to get her strength built up again, and then we can bring her home."

They found a corner in a lounge and sat for a while in loving silence. As they strolled back to the ward, Julie recognized a familiar face – Betsy Donovan in a starched snow white uniform with a little cap perched on her head. Betsy had finally realized her dream of becoming a nurse.

"Betsy," Julianna called. "Wonderful to see you."

"What brings you here?" Betsy asked. "Is something wrong?"

"Yes, we brought Mrs. Wilkins in. Do you remember her? They live over on the third line." Betsy's face registered momentary distaste but Julianna hurried on. "In fact, Betsy, if you could look in on her from time to time, you would be doing us all a huge favour. She just gave birth to her eighth child and she had to have a hysterectomy. She's had a really hard time and she's worrying intensely about her children at home. She'll be here at least two weeks. I'm absolutely sure that seeing a familiar face who's also a medical expert would be a comfort to her."

"I'm just on call now but I can come and see her in an hour or so," Betsy replied, basking in the 'medical expert' label.

Julie and Adam paused before entering Edna's curtained alcove to ensure that all was well. Bert was kneeling beside the bed, praying with Edna. "Thank you, Lord, for this gift of life," he intoned. "You have given us a miracle."

"Humph," Julia whispered crossly. "I thought the doctor and I had something to do with it."

"Julie, my dearest," Adam turned to her. "You are the miracle. And I can't help but marvel at it every single day."

CHAPTER 20

A Man-Made Miracle

In them days, neighbours helped neighbours. No ifs, ands nor buts. Didn't matter if ya liked 'em or ya didn't like 'em – if they was in need, ye'd lend a hand. If a farmer broke his leg or lost his horse, the neighbours was there to help out whether it meant milkin' and feedin' the stock or providin' a horse, or even seedin' a field. If the missus was sick or givin' birth, the women set about bringin' food or cleanin' the house or carin' for her and the youngsters. If they was on in years, they'd more'n likely find a casserole or a fresh loaf of bread in their kitchen many a mornin' or hear the sound of chopping and find a flock of the young lads laughin' and choppin' up their fire wood for winter. 'Course there was the heavy work too – everybody pitched in for the threshin' with that big machine rollin' along from farm to farm and the men and boys followin' along and the women headin' for the house to help with the big meals to feed them all when the job was done. And then in winter, they're back again when the sawyer drags in his big saw to cut trees down into stove lengths. Quiltin' bees too – the women would get together and quilt all day and by nightfall they'd have a nice warm quilt. People who come to the Valley from away sometimes was uncomfortable with all this neighbourin'. If they was poor, like Bert Wilkins, they was often ashamed of themselves and felt like it was charity, forgettin' that they would have plenty of chances to give back when another neighbour was in need.

Lenny

One miracle was not enough. Another miracle was enacted at the Wilkins home when Tommy Flaherty stopped by to deliver a loaf of his wife's fresh bread and a pound of butter. Bert greeted him at the door, grateful but still shamefaced as he thanked Tommy for his largesse.

But Tommy was intent upon a different mission. "Bert, I got a proposition for ya," he began. "Just between the two of us, not a word to anyone else." Bert waited, polite but puzzled. Tommy's fun-loving manner always seemed to brighten the day but now he was looking serious.

Tommy settled himself in a kitchen chair and removed his venerable tweed cap, a sure sign that he intended to stay a while.. "Now as I recall ya went off to the war to fight fer yer country," Tommy continued. "You was brave enough to enlist right away – ya didn't wait to be called up. And back ya come wounded, as sure as if ye'd been shot in the leg, ya was wounded by that there mustard gas."

Bert looked embarrassed and turned away, stifling a cough.

"Now Bert, hear me out," Tommy persisted, leaning across the table. "You're a good man and ya deserve better than what the army handed ya – a set of lungs that give out on ya whenever ya need 'em the most. You've a fine family and a lovin' wife, all in need of a husband and father.

"So Bert, here's my proposition. How'd it be if ya rent me your land? I'll work it and plant it and harvest it. You and Edna will hang on to the house, of course, and the orchard and a nice big garden plot and the woods back there so's youse can sell lumber and harvest wood for the stove. It'll never make ya rich, Bert, but it'll keep the land worked and that's important."

Bert nodded. Farm work generated dust and dust set off the wracking cough that left him gasping for breath and too weak to walk.

"And here's the rest of my idea," Tommy rolled on. "Ya know Bert; you're a real smart fella with yer hands – specially when it comes to fixin' things. I seen ya replace a broken chair leg as neat as a pin and repair broken harness and machinery. And metalwork – I mind that time ya fixed Otto Dietrich's harrow after his team run away with it and just about busted it to smithereens. Good as new it was when ya got through with it. And as I recall ya never took a penny for that job.

"And am I right in believing that you made the chairs we're sitting on here and the table too? Good sturdy furniture it is, and it'll last a lifetime.

"So here's what I'm thinkin'. Why don't we finish off one of them big box stalls out in the barn and set up a workshop there. Ya could be working at somethin' you're good at, right close to home. Ya could even have a couch in there to take a rest if ever ya need it. I'm willing to bet ye'd end up putting in more hours that way and making a decent living while you're at it."

He paused to let it sink in. "I'll think about it, Tommy," Bert finally allowed. "But I don't feel good about accepting charity. I know we're real hard up but I should be able to manage and feed my family on my own."

"This ain't charity, Bert. This is a business proposition. It's makin' sure ye'll be around a good long time to take care of your fine big family. And it's giving the Valley something we all need – I mean to say a place where we can get good furniture and get things fixed. It's no money out of my pocket – just a little time to help out, the way you would yerself if a neighbour needs a hand. The way ya did when you fixed Otto Dietrich's harrow and wouldn't take a cent for it."

Bert still looked doubtful and discomfited by the fulsome praise.

"I'll leave ya to think it over," Tommy added. "But mark my words; I'll be back tomorrow, ready to start on yer workshop."

Bert walked Tommy out to his buggy and thanked him for his visit. Slowly returning to his shabby house, he gazed around at his children who had assembled silently in the kitchen, hungrily eying the banquet that neighbours continued to provide. Tommy's arguments had made sense to him. Surely it was God's will that he accept charity to help feed his family. Jesus accepted charity, he recalled. Surely it was not dishonourable to accept Tommy's offer and make a better life for all of them. And it was true – he had offered his help many and many a time when neighbours or even strangers were in need. Surrounded by his family, Bert and his children knelt down and offered thanks for neighbours, friends and their bountiful generosity.

Tommy wasted no time. He persuaded his long-suffering wife to take care of Bert's youngest children while the men applied themselves to the new workshop. It materialized quickly. The field stone foundation, six feet high and two feet thick, was sturdy and firm, needing only a few dabs of pointing to fill the cracks. And the concrete floor provided a solid base. The two men scoured the premises in search of lumber and found a surprisingly large stash in the rafters above the drive shed and more in the peak of the woodshed, left over from long-ago construction projects. "We'll start with the ceiling," Tommy suggested, "coz of the dust from the threshing floor and straw that drifts down. We don't want ya breathin' that."

Bert tied a polka dot handkerchief over his nose and mouth and together they framed the ceiling and walls with two-by-fours, cladding them with the good dry boards, finally covering the seams with narrow strips of lath to discourage dust. The deep hay manger that stretched wall to wall at one end was covered in broad thick boards to make an impressive work bench. From Tommy's drive shed they hauled over a sturdy cabinet with a heavy-duty work surface on top and shelves below for supplies. Bert screwed rows of hooks into the walls for his tools and attached his trusty vice to the work bench, ready for action.

Tommy insisted on frequent work breaks, devising consultations and errands to lighten Bert's fatigue. Covertly, he kept an eye on his neighbour and noted with satisfaction Bert's growing involvement in the job and his look of unabashed pleasure as it neared completion.

"Ye'll be needin' warmth in the winter," Tommy reminded him. "Now then, my stable's gettin' a bit crowded so if ye'll agree, I'll bring my heavy team over to keep yer Sally company in them empty stalls. The three of them should be able to pump out a pretty good supply of heat, t'say nuthin' of a good supply of manure for the garden."

He left Bert to arrange his tools on the walls and returned with his team of massive gray Percherons. They thundered into their new stalls, eliciting excited neighs and nickers from Sally, who was unaccustomed to such mighty company. And just like people, the three began to bond as they settled down to a good meal.

Bert Wilkins, Esq., Furniture and Repairs, was open for business.

CHAPTER 21

Joe's Life of Crime

We never had no crime in our Valley, nuthin' to speak of. Not unless you count them Smith brats stealing the watermelons from all our gardens every summer or tipping over our backhouses on Halloween. So when Young Joe got in big trouble with the law, we was shocked, even though everybody knew he was a brute. No question about it, we felt bad but then again, Old Joe had managed to offend every single one of us more than once so sympathy was kinda in short supply. Mostly we was worried about Rita. We hardly ever seen her outside the house except she was runnin' to the garden or the henhouse. She already looked poorly after Chrissy left but now she was facing all kinds of new troubles. Velma said she seemed like she was hidin' – she even stopped goin' to the Women's Institute meetings and just stayed in the house there all alone.

Of course Gossip Gertie picked up a good story when Rita Dunning died and she made the most of it, addin' juicy little bits and pieces every time she retold it. I hate to think what she'd a done with our story if she'd ever found out about Annie's secret or Tommy Flaherty's deal with Joe.

Lenny

Julianna was not accustomed to being hated. She had often faced people who disagreed with her radical points of view or opposed her ambitions. And in the years since she arrived in the Valley, she'd been the target of plenty of juicy gossip, most of it amusing. But hatred was new and it was not fun.

Far from feeling grateful that the Chandlers had taken Chrissy and her unwanted pregnancy off their hands, the Dunning family was angry, resentful and spiteful. They never spoke to Adam or Julie or even to the Coopers, but their baleful stares when they met on the road or in town said it all.

Julie was especially uneasy about young Joe, "a loose cannon with too much brawn and too little brain," as she described him to Adam. Fortified by strong drink, as he was much of the time, he was completely lacking in common sense or fear.

And sure enough, as she worked one afternoon on the flower beds that rimmed the front lawn, there he was swaggering purposefully down the lane. And as he approached, she could not mistake the savage ill will that imbued his entire being.

Julianna found the vegetable patch a challenge but she loved the flower gardens, where she felt more at home because she had worked alongside her mother and her Auntie Margaret on their flowerbeds for years. The day was sunny, the ground was moist from a recent rain and she had the friendly company of Fogo, dozing in the shade of a huge snowball bush.

"Good morning, Joe," she greeted him cordially. "Lovely day today."

"Nuthin' luvly about it," he growled. "Who the hell do ya think ya are buttin' into our family business? Why don't ya go back to yer damn city where whores like you belong and mind yer own business?"

"I'm sorry if you think I'm interfering, Joe. I took care of Christine because she was badly hurt and she couldn't go back home. I simply wanted her to have proper medical care so she could recover from all her injuries and get her life back again."

"That little slut got just what she deserved," Joe snarled. "And yer gonna git the same." He lunged toward her but she was on the alert and, armed with a long-handled hoe, she rammed the flat blade into his ample gut. He grunted and pulled back only long enough to catch his breath.

"Go home, Joe," Julie ordered sharply. "You've caused enough trouble already. If you keep this up, I'll have you charged with assault and mischief."

"Oh yeah? Try'n stop me." He leapt forward again but another belly-full of hoe slowed him down just long enough for Fogo to take action.

The big dog's well-tempered nose had picked up Joe's crude scent well before he approached Julie. No doubt remembering their encounter at the wedding party, Fogo knew he had a job to do. In two leaps, he was on Joe's back, his teeth firmly planted in his well-worn overalls, which tore neatly down to his buttocks. Fogo let go and nipped again for a better grip. This time, he tore away the button-up trap door of Joe's combinations, stained brown and reeking, to reveal his plump buttocks. Fogo seized the moment – or rather the buttock – and managed a strategic bite that actually drew blood.

Joe wished heartily that he'd brought a club or a gun with him but it was too late now. With his torn overalls and underwear flapping around his bare bum, he hurriedly abandoned the assault and took off for home. Fogo followed him, barking fiercely, as far as the road, then trotted happily back to Julie, huge tail wagging, tongue lolling as if to say: 'That was jolly good fun.'

Julie was still shaking but she patted his head and scratched his chin and told him what a good, brilliant dog he was to save her from Joe. She took him up to the house to find him a suitable treat – his fondness for shortbread cookies and buttered tea biscuits was legendary – while Joe made it to the road and hustled on toward the Dunning farm.

But he did not go unobserved. Gertie Biggar – Gertie the Gossip – returning from a trip into town to deliver fresh beef to the grocer, happened along just in time to witness part of the show. Urging her horse to a brisk trot, she overtook Joe on the road and pulled up to a walk beside him, the better to view the entire vista.

Her smile as their eyes met was almost beatific. This was the best bit of gossip she'd encountered in years. The bare bottom, the torn overalls and the stained underwear were too much happiness and just retribution for the snubs and insults she had endured from the Dunnings in the past. She clucked up her horse and galloped home to call up the party line. When the Valley phones sounded their familiar jangle indicating a call coming through, nearly everyone picked up their receiver to listen in, even Rita Dunning. She listened with growing horror and then quietly hung up, dug out a bottle of Old Joe's rum, and poured herself a hefty drink. That night, father and son faced an empty table and neither Joe's bluster nor his fierce fists could get Rita out of bed and into the kitchen.

Rita had never been a drinker but now the burning rum became a solace that she frequently turned to as each new embarrassment overwhelmed her. The never-ending abuse that Joe inflicted upon her, the shocking behaviour of both father and son at the wedding party and afterward, and now Christine's pregnancy and banishment from home – it was all too much to bear. Until now, she had often submerged her pain and embarrassment in stitchery, spending countless hours with appliqué and embroidery transforming mundane quilts into works of art that no one ever saw. But now, more often than not, she simply took to her bed in late afternoon and stayed there until morning. Sometimes she would throw a handful of oatmeal into a pot of water and leave it to steam on the back of the stove. If she thought of it, she would poke into the pantry and find an old lard tin, filled with fried pork preserved in its own grease, and leave it beside the porridge and the tea pot. It was a far cry from the plain but hearty meat and potatoes and pie that she used to prepare. As the meals became sparser and the house dirtier, her husband became angrier and more threatening, nurturing his anger with rum ever more frequently and expressing it with slaps and beatings.

Young Joe, as usual, knocked back a few good snorts before heading into town on Saturday night to join his cronies. He hoped they had not heard about his butt-baring incident, but if they said anything, he was prepared to shut them up. In fact, he was bristling with nervous energy and longing for a fight. He drove into the livery stable and tied his horse, forgetting to loosen the bit or the girth to make the long wait more comfortable. The horse snorted and stamped, but Joe walked away, intent on an evening with his pals, perhaps culminating in a visit to Myrtle's house, which passed for the town's brothel.

Paxton Ford was a small town, its single street unpaved and dusty, lined on either side with the usual shops – a general store that sold just about everything, a hardware, a grocery shop and further along, the post office, the grist mill, a couple of churches and a few homes. Everyone knew everyone – and to Joe's despair, everyone knew Gertie the Gossip and had heard of Joe's ignominious retreat, with underwear flapping, from the Chandlers' zealous dog. His gaggle of cohorts waited for him under the bridge where they were unlikely to face an encounter with the town's lone police officer.

"Hey Joe, ya got your pants back on?" Pete Duff guffawed. "Musta been real breezy on the ass, runnin' around with yer flap down."

"Prolly improved the smell though," quipped another great wit.

"Better stay buttoned up from now on," crowed Herbie. "If that dog had gotcha frontwards instead of backwards, you'd a lost more'n yer underwear."

"C'mon, Joe. Show us your battle scars," urged Pete. "Don't be shy. Jest drop yer drawers."

Joe could tolerate no more. "Shaddup, ya jerk," he shouted. "Keep your fat yap shut an' mind yer own business."

"Aw Joe," Pete persisted. "It musta been a dandy show. If I can find a dog, would ya do it again?"

Enraged, Joe turned on Pete and pushed him sharply. None too steady on his feet, Pete tried to swing back at him but Joe was ready with his fists and landed a hefty blow to the jaw. Pete's staggered backwards, hitting one of the metal bridge supports. He fell hard and his head cracked against the concrete abutment. He lay very still, his head at a peculiar angle, one leg twisted beneath him. His blood began to pool on the concrete. He did not move. Joe and the gang stared at him for a moment. Then they turned and fled.

In a town of that size, there are few secrets. Two small boys who had been hiding behind another stanchion in hopes of hearing or seeing something forbidden, rushed up to the street and into the general store. "Pete's hurt," one of them panted to George Kirby, the store owner. "He's laying under the bridge and he ain't movin'."

"You boys stay right here," Kirby ordered. "Here, have a peppermint and sit right there on them boxes and don't move." He called his helper to run to the police house and within minutes, Sergeant Collins came puffing along, his official jacket still unbuttoned after a hearty dinner at home. One look at Pete was enough. He sent the shop assistant for the doctor and ordered the store owner to call several deputies to help him deal with the first murder ever recorded in Paxton Ford.

The gang had swiftly dispersed and Joe headed back to the livery stable to get his horse and set out for home. But his need for speed was his undoing. A horse and rig proceeding at a gallop down the main street was an attention-grabber and several people glanced up expecting to see a runaway. When the police officer emerged from the store where he was questioning the two small boys, they were quick to identify Joe and some of the gang. The troublemakers were well known in Paxton Ford and the lawmen first went in search of those who lived in town. Denying all knowledge of the crime did them no good. They didn't stand a chance in light of the people who had observed them emerging from under the bridge and hastily scattering toward their homes. The two junior witnesses, enjoying a brief moment of glory, were able to identify each one of them, complete with names. Joe's cronies, at first arrogant, then nervous and finally caving under the officer's stern questioning, all finally agreed on one point – the fight was between Pete and Joe and it was Joe who had struck the fatal blows.

"That Dunning lad is dangerous," Collins told his deputies "and so is his father. We'll need extra manpower." Driving a black police wagon and with three more volunteers mounted, he rode out toward the Dunning farm. Young Joe had already arrived home, hastily stabled his horse and thrown himself into bed. When the banging began at the door, he heard it and dug deeper into his blankets while Old Joe, with his customary bad temper, headed downstairs to ward off the intruders. He was shocked to see the police officers and furious when he was informed that they needed to see Young Joe about a fight in town. "Youse got the wrong man," he argued. "He come home early. He wasn't there long enough for no fight."

"We need to see him now, Mr. Dunning. Would you please go and find him."

Old Joe was ready to fight but the sight of three deputies backing up Officer Collins cooled his ire somewhat. He marched off up the stairs and eventually came back with his son, still drunk, sulky and loudly declaring his innocence. "I don't know nuthin' about it," he shouted. "I only went into town to get some tobacco and I come home right away. I didn't see no fight."

"Three of your friends have told me that you were with them down below the bridge and that you were the chap who hit Pete Duff."

"They're liars," Joe bawled. "I wasn't there. I went for tobacco and come straight home."

"Where are the boots you were wearing," the officer enquired politely. Some of Joe's bravado faded.

"I dunno," he stalled, and then sensing escape, "Mebbe I left 'em down at the stable."

"Odd place to leave your boots," Collins commented. "Well then, off you go down to the stable and bring them here." Joe rose uncertainly. "My deputies will go with you to help you search," he added, aware that Joe might try to run if allowed outside.

"There's no need. Here they are." It was Rita, who had quietly come downstairs, now proffering Joe's stained boots.

"Are these the boots you were wearing tonight?" the officer enquired. Joe nodded mutely. He knew he was trapped.

The boots had been none too clean in the first place but several dark stains did look like blood. Sergeant Collins rubbed his finger over one of the stains and it came away dark red. He showed it to Joe. "Where'd the blood come from?" Joe's dim brain could no longer concoct a response. He simply shrugged and sank lower in his chair.

The formalities didn't take long. Within hours, Joe found himself in one of the police station's two cells in town. The next morning, he was transferred to the county jail in Morganston, where he was formally charged with murder. It was clear to everyone, even Joe, that he'd be staying out of trouble for a good number of years.

Old Joe returned to the house alone. He sank into his usual chair at the kitchen table and stared at the cold stove, as if willing it to warm up and produce a meal. Then he remembered his favourite sustenance and hauling himself over to the bureau, he dug out his bottle of rum, returned to the table and began drinking it straight from the bottle. Before long, the bottle was empty and Joe was unconscious in his chair.

Rita Dunning died a few months after the trial. When she failed to appear downstairs one day to make either his breakfast or his dinner, Joe angrily climbed the stairs. He charged into the spare bedroom where she now slept, ready to slap her awake, only to find her gray and cold, her mouth open, her eyes staring. "Need a drink," he muttered as he retreated downstairs. Several hefty draughts later, he was snoring in the kitchen arm chair, where he spent the night. Next morning, still bleary-eyed, he ate some of the slimy porridge from the back of the stove and then suddenly remembered Rita. Was it a dream or was it real? He stumbled back upstairs and there she was, just as he had left her, only colder and grayer than before.

His booze-addled brain wasn't helping. He couldn't think what to do. Finally, he pulled the sheet over her face, fortified himself with another hefty swig and headed for the stable. He harnessed up his last remaining horse – the others had been sold one by one to pay for the rum – and headed down the road to the Biggar house. Peering out her kitchen window, Gertie saw him coming and, sensing disaster and a good story to tell, hurried out to meet him.

"It's Rita," Joe gasped. "I think she's died."

"Come inside, Joe," Gertie urged. "Herb's in there cutting meat. Ye can talk to both of us."

Having extracted as many details from him as he was able to remember, Gertie asked him about a funeral. "I ain't never done a funeral," Joe whined. "I dunno where to start."

"Leave it to me, Joe," she replied. "I'll fix everything for you."

The party line quickly delivered a squad of neighbour women – Velma Findlay and Lizzie Hawkins and Mabel Flaherty and Gertie herself – who agreed to meet at the Dunning home. Herb drove Joe back home and stoked up the fire, put the tea kettle to boil and heaved a huge tub of water onto the stovetop. Then he and Joe drove off to Foreston to buy a coffin.

It was an unspoken rule that when anyone died in the Valley, their neighbours, whatever they may have thought of them in life, would respectfully prepare their bodies for burial. The women were no strangers to death and they set quietly to work to cut away Rita's filthy clothes and bath her worn-out body. But they paused in shock to stare at the raw abrasions and ugly bruises that discoloured her shoulders, back and legs.

"She didn't get them from bumping into no furniture," Lizzie remarked. "I guess we have Joe to thank."

"I knew it was bad," Gertie commented. "But not this bad. I seen the bruises and the black eyes."

"That Joe should be arrested," Velma protested. "He deserves to be in jail just like his son."

"Maybe that's what he deserves," Mabel observed. "But it ain't gonna happen. Men beat their wives all the time. And lookit what he did to Chrissy. Nobody cares."

They worked on, softening Rita's dry, scaly skin with goose fat and although her matted hair resisted every attempt to tame it, cutting away the worst snarls and brushing it flat. Her wardrobe was sparse and shabby but they chose her best dress and together, they lifted her and slipped it over her body. When the men returned with the coffin, she was ready.

The party line had done its job and already the kitchen table was filling up with food fit for a wake.

Hector rounded up a group of strong young men with shovels to dig the grave and they set to zealously, in the family grave site at the foot of Joe's old orchard.

Neighbours began to arrive as soon as the chores were finished, shaking Joe's hand and then arranging themselves in the chairs that ringed the parlour, facing the coffin and chatting quietly. Many of them approached the coffin and gazed at Rita's ravaged face, some saying a silent prayer before returning to their seats. "Poor soul," murmured Andy McTavish whose love for his wife, Jean, his partner in life and Scottish dance for 54 years, had never wavered. "She's far better off now than ever she was with him."

Joe heard, but he no longer cared.

With no preacher to conduct the service, it fell to Adam to muster a few kind words about Rita, followed by the usual platitudes that are supposed to provide comfort for the bereaved. In this case, the bereaved was so inebriated that he had to be propped up on the couch to keep him moderately upright during the brief service. When it was over, Adam suggested that everyone bow their heads and say a silent prayer for Rita. And that was that.

Six of the strongest young men, who had already dug the grave, hoisted the coffin and carried it down to the orchard, with the handful of neighbours straggling behind, all but Joe, who had slumped down on the couch the moment it was over.

The funeral was brief and while the evening was still young, the coffin was lowered into the grave and covered with earth. Rita's pain was finally at an end.

Joe was still asleep on the couch but Tommy Flaherty roused him. "All right Joe, that's enough," he bellowed. "Up ya get and greet yer neighbours." He applied a few slaps to Joe's shoulders and Joe blearily sat up and tried to focus on what was going on.

As always, the neighbour women had stocked the table with sandwiches and cakes and great pots of tea. At many a wake the post-funeral party got noisy and upbeat but this time, the group was quiet and a bit embarrassed. Before long, the chief mourner fell asleep again and his neighbours quietly headed for home.

CHAPTER 22

The Lay of the Land

That Tommy Flaherty was full of surprises. Just goes to show yeh can know a man all yer life and yet not know him at all. He was jolly and friendly, but he knew plenty of secrets – he musta knew more about some of us than we knew ourselves. But he never tattled about other folks behind their backs and he never said nuthin about his self. Sure enough he'd come from Ireland a while back – he still talked like an Irishman and he looked like an Irishman, with his old tweed cap and his fancy vests. He was a bootlegger but he didn't charge much for his drink. He said it was a service not a business. He was a pretty good fiddler and he played at just about every party in the Valley and beyond, with Mabel, his wife, playing the piano if there was one to be had, or sometimes a tin whistle. If it was an important wedding or a banquet, the host might slip them a dollar or two but Tommy said they was mostly playin' fer the fun of it and from the look of them, they sure was havin' fun.

My dear wife Velma was pretty pally with Mabel but she was another one who kept herself to herself. One time when Velma was admirin' some of Mabel's fancy embroidery, she asked where she'd learned it and Mabel said: "In the convent." Velma was fit to be tied. "What was you doin' in a convent," she up and asked. "Goin' to school," was all Mabel would say. Well she also said that's where she learned music. Velma was all shocked. She was real fond of Mabel and they spent a lot of winter afternoons together, sewin' or knittin'.

"D'ya think she's Catholic?" she asked me. "My pa would roll over in his grave if he knew I was sittin' around bein' friendly with a dogan." Well, we talked it over a good bit just like we did everything. "If they're Catholic," I sez to her, "why aint' they got any of them crucifix things hangin' around. Catholics always have them things and I never seen one any time I was inside their house." Velma agreed with that – she was a smart woman. "And they never go to church," she sez to me. "Not that we do, but Catholics have to go to church or they'll be excom… excommun… well, kicked out anyways."

So then Velma sez, "I wonder why the Catholics and the Protestants hate each other." And I sez. "I think it started in Ireland and the English was to blame." "Well," sez Velma, "I kinda hope Tommy and Mabel really are Catholics. Then we can show folks that we're all friends and good neighbours an' that's what matters." And she was right, of course. She most always was. Tommy never preached at nobody, never told nobody what to think or do. He just went ahead doin' good on the quiet, like he did for Bert Wilkins and then for Old Joe Dunning and later on, for Velma and me.

Lenny

Tommy Flaherty had seen a lot in his life and he was not easily shocked. But today, as he told Mabel, he was fit to be tied by the sight and smell of Joe's house and the fellow's general disarray. He and Joe went back a long way – some might say they were friends, a relationship that was acutely lacking in Joe's life. But then Tommy was everybody's friend. Tommy's low-level bootlegging was a sideline that put actual cash in his pocket and he had become Joe's number one source of rum,. But now he saw that booze was killing Old Joe and he didn't want that on his conscience.

'Can't cut him off entirely,' he thought to himself. 'But he needs to get a grip.' To Joe's dismay, Tommy's rum deliveries became fewer and further between while regular visits brought a pot of soup or a loaf of bread. However, the result was not sobriety – Joe would be desperately waiting for Tommy to arrive, bearing the coveted drink. He would snatch it up and guzzle down a substantial quantity then and there. If no bottle materialized, he would treat Tommy to a stream of abuse that later merged into a whining, begging diatribe. Tommy stood firm.

In due course, Tommy formulated a plan and hastened to Joe's place to present it. As usual, he stopped at Joe's old tin mailbox to collect whatever was there – the monthly copy of the Farmers Advocate and an occasional tax bill or Eaton's catalogue – and walked into the Dunning house without knocking. Likely as not Old Joe would be passed out in his rocking chair or on the couch, he thought, and sure enough, there he lay, snoring, drooling and smelling of bad hygiene and rum.

Tommy checked the stove and stoked up the fire. He filled the tea kettle and carried the tea pot to the back door to empty its month-long accumulation of tea leaves. He poked around for tea and finally located the canister atop the warming oven. "No clean cups," he grumbled to himself. "No clean nuthin." So he did the unthinkable – he reached into Rita's china cabinet and removed two of her best cups and saucers from her Blue Willow wedding set and carried them to the kitchen table.

Now it was time to rouse his host. Tommy shook Joe's shoulder. "Here now, Joe, time to wake up," he demanded. "I've come for a visit and it's kinda hard to visit with a chap that's snorin' loud enough to raise the roof." Joe twitched and opened his eyes a slit. "Didja bring me a bottle?" he asked through a parched throat.

"No, Joe. No bottle just now. You an' me, we're gonna have a chat. So we'll have some good strong tea instead. Now get yerself up an' wash yer face an' get ready to talk."

It took some persuasion but Joe finally heaved himself upright and staggered over to the wash basin to splash dirty water on his face. He slumped into a chair at the table and waited without interest for whatever was to come.

Tommy poured the tea, adding copious amounts of sugar. "Joe," he began. "Yer not in too good shape. Looks to me like ya ain't eatin' proper and ya ain't takin' care of yerself, ever since Rita passed away."

Joe stared at him through bloodshot eyes but said nothing.

"Awright Joe, so I'm gonna make ya an offer. I wanna buy yer farm."

Joe looked sharply at Tommy, struggling to pay attention.

"Can't sell the farm. Noplace else to live," he replied.

"Well now, Joe, what I'm proposin' is ya stay right here. I'm offerin' to buy the farm for one dollar an acre – that's more'n yer pa paid for it back in 1900. Back then it cost ten dollars a hundred acres. But on top of that, I'll make sure ya have wood for the stove and food fer the table fer as long as ya live. Right here in yer own house."

He paused to let it sink in. Joe's brain was fuzzy but now he was trying hard to focus. "Pa only got crown land," he replied. "Nuthin' but trees. Got a house now and barn too. And forty acres cleared for crops."

"Yer right about that," Tommy agreed. "But the price of land ain't gone up – in fact, its akshully dropped a bit since the war. It's damned hard to make a livin' with farmin', what with the price of everything from seed grain to tea goin' sky high but the price we get fer our milk and our livestock droppin' day by day.

"Besides, I'm thinkin' ya ain't took a close look at yer buildings lately. Yer barn there, the stone foundation's fallin' down, and the roof leaks. Has been leaking' for quite a while, I'd guess, from the amount of damage. And it looks like the roof is leakin' here on the house too."

Joe slurped his tea and stared into his cup.

"And keep in mind," Tommy forged ahead, "yer in no shape to take up farmin' again. You've no livestock left, no hay or straw in the barn and yer fields haven't seen a cultivator in a good three years. I'm offerin' ya a walk down easy street, Joe. I supply ya with a good meal every day that Mabel cooks – and ya know, she's a fine cook – and wood for the stove, and a helpin' hand when ya need it for as long as you live. You turn over the place to me and I'll send a man to farm it and plant and harvest it and look after repairs."

But Joe had another objection. "What about Joe? My son gotta have somethin' to come home to once he gets outta jail."

Lord love us, Tommy thought to himself. He doesn't even know about Joe. He prolly never read the letter. He glanced up at the muddle of mail that had piled up on the kitchen bureau. Weeks back, he'd collected Tommy's mail as usual and noticed a letter from the Department of Justice. Curious, but also concerned, he'd slit it open to find a formal notification that Joe Junior had died in prison. A report from the prison warden recounted the circumstances – a brawl in the exercise yard involving a group of inmates, several of whom attacked Joe, who later succumbed to his injuries. "We sincerely regret, etc. etc."

Tommy was reluctant to break the news to Joe but it had to be done. He walked to the bureau and shuffled through the mail until he found the letter. He laid it before Joe and waited for him to read it. "What's this?" Joe demanded. "What's it say?"

"Joe," Tommy spoke gently. "It says yer son passed away in prison over three months ago. It says he got in a fight with some other prisoners and he was killed. I'm real sorry, Joe. This letter's been here for a month or more – I figured youdda read it."

Joe peered at the letter and then at Tommy as if none of this made sense. He picked up the letter and tried to read it himself but suddenly his eyes filled with tears. Laying his head down on his arms, he began to sob. "There ain't nuthin' left," he mumbled. "Nuthin' left. Joe gone. Chrissy gone. Rita gone."

Tommy waited quietly for Joe to calm himself. "Joe, we won't talk about the farm any more just now," he said gently. "Ya just take some time to think about all this – it's a big shock, I know. And I'll come back tomorrow to see how ya are."

Without another word, he pushed another sheet of paper across the table but Joe paid no attention. It was his offer to purchase, neatly written in Mabel's hand – like many girls in the Valley, she'd had more schooling than her husband and was thus the designated family scribe. It simply stated that he offered to purchase Joe's farm for one hundred dollars and to provide him with food and a roof over his head for the rest of his days.

Tommy poured another cup of strong sweet tea for Joe and quietly left the house.

His next stop was the Chandler household and as luck would have it, Adam was home and enjoying a cup of tea in his own cozy kitchen. "I been tryin' to make a deal with Joe Dunning," Tommy told him. "Need yer opinion." He handed Adam a copy of the purchase offer and sat quietly sipping his tea, as he waited for him to read it.

Adam sighed and handed it back. "It's really sad that he's come to this," he commented. "But this is a generous offer. And you're a good man, Tommy. I know you'll keep your word about taking care of him. But what about his son?"

"He died in jail in a fight." Tommy told him all that he knew. "He was always pickin' fights, y'know, but looks like he lost that one. And Chrissy wants nuthin' to do with the place. So it's free and clear."

"And what was Joe's reaction?"

"He didn't know til just now that his son was dead. He was real upset. I said I'd come back tomorrow. And I'm hopin' ya might go with me to witness this, if Joe does sign. Which I think he will."

The next morning, Tommy arrived at Joe's house bearing chocolate cake and a flask. He was followed by Adam, with a plate of Clara's oatmeal cookies and a tin of honey. With shaking hands, Joe reached for the liquor but Tommy was too quick for him. He found a glass and poured half a finger of dark rum, which Joe dispatched in a single gulp.

"Now Joe, we wanna talk about the offer I made yesterday and ya need to be cold sober to think it through," Tommy told him. "Mister Chandler here has come along to make sure it's all on the up and up." Joe nodded, but his eyes were on the booze bottle. "So Joe, are ya satisfied with me offer? Are ya ready to sign?"

"Joe," Adam spoke firmly. "I want to be sure that you understand this offer. Tommy is offering to take over your farm, to run it as a farm, but also to give you the use of the house for the rest of your life. He's also offering to provide you with a good meal a day and with firewood for the stove."

He paused to let Joe think it over but he was rewarded with an indifferent shrug.

Tommy laid a straight pen and a small blotter on the table and uncorked a bottle of ink. He carefully dipped the pen into the ink and handed it to Joe. Joe was thirsty and he did not hesitate. He grabbed the pen and painstakingly scrawled a shaky signature, managing to add a couple of splatters which Tommy blotted up. Tommy signed underneath and pushed the paper to Adam, who added his name. They repeated the process on the second copy and Tommy placed it atop the pile of mail on the bureau. Joe reached for the bottle.

The deed was done. Old Joe died less than a year later. There were few mourners.

Rita's Legacy

Come winter, all the women in our Valley made quilts. They'd save up every scrap of cloth they could find – worn-out shirts and dresses and once in a while a bit of a remnant they'd buy from a pedlar or from Eaton's catalogue. Then they'd cut and stitch to make a dozen or so quilt blocks from patterns they'd got from their own mothers or grandmothers – Log Cabins or Dresden Plates or some such. Next thing, they'd sew the blocks together for the top of the quilt and they'd make the backing from flour or sugar bags. And in between they'd lay out batting if they could afford it, or sometimes just more old cloth. Then they'd invite the neighbour women for a quilting bee that generally lasted right through the day. In our house, I always had to help Velma set up the quilting frame. It stretched from one end of the sitting room to the other and we had to lace the quilt to the frame so it was pulled tight. Then the women would sit themselves down all in a row on each side and stitch and gossip and drink tea, and roll the quilt, and stitch and gossip and have a good lunch and stitch some more until every inch of it was covered with their tiny stitches – twelve to the inch, Velma said, but not many of them can manage that. Considering how little they had to work with, they sure made some pretty quilts. Little girls started making quilts as soon as they could be trusted with a needle. They was stockin' their hope chests against the day they'd marry and set up house somewheres else. Lots more stuff like crocheted doilies, towels, dishes and fancy nighties went into them hope chests – which was usually cedar boxes made by their father or, if they had money, the woodworkers over to Foreston. So quilting was important, but it was nuthin' special. It was just somethin' that the women-folk did.

Lenny

Julie had no intention of sharing her call with the party line. She sat down at her desk and carefully composed an urgent note.

"Dear Chrissy:

"I'm writing to ask you to come for a visit as soon as possible. There are some important family matters that we need to discuss and I cannot deal with them without your help. Could you spare a couple of days? We can meet you at the train and of course, you'll stay with us. Please say 'yes'. And please give my love to Auntie Margaret and my Father. I hope to see you very soon."

She signed it: With fond love, Julie."

Soon after Joe's death, she and Adam had a hurried visit from Tommy Flaherty. "There's somethin' ya need to see over to Old Joe's house," he announced urgently. "And I think Chrissy should see it too."

"Whatever can it be?" Julie asked. "Did you find a buried treasure?"

"Ya might call it that," Tommy replied mysteriously. "When can ya come and have a look?"

"Right now," Julie replied, pushing her tea cup aside and reaching for her coat. "I do love a good mystery."

They entered the silent house, still redolent with the stench of neglect, but at least warmed by the fire Tommy had started in the wood stove. "In here." He headed toward the parlour. Like many farm homes, the parlour had an extra room at the back – the parlour bedroom, used only for visiting dignitaries such as the minister or an honoured relative. The Dunnings had neither, so the parlour bedroom had been closed up for years. Or so it seemed.

"I had a time getting in here," Tommy explained. "It was locked up tight and I couldn't find no key. Finally found it in that there fancy bowl by the window." He retrieved the key from its lair and unlocked the door.

The room that awaited Julie was a shock. The first surprise was the smell – a gentle lavender scent that was a welcome respite from the lingering stench that permeated the rest of the house. But the real surprise was the contents. The room was chockablock with quilts. A full-size quilting frame reached almost from wall to wall, an unfinished quilt stretched and rolled across it, thread and thimbles in a small basket and a threaded needle piercing the fabric next to the last stitch. By the window, a table that obviously served as a preparation surface displayed shears, chalk, templates and fabric scraps, all neatly arranged.

But the most remarkable sight was the quilts themselves. Hanging from the walls, draped over racks and stacked on shelves, were quilts and more quilts – two dozen or more creations the like of which Julie had never seen. In the years since she'd moved to the Valley, she had begun to learn about quilting and to respect the fine workmanship that it demanded. But most Valley quilts were hard-working utilitarian bed coverings, cobbled from whatever scraps and remnants a woman might salvage from worn-out clothing – traditional patterns, occasionally pretty, but rarely spectacular.

But here was a visual feast: lush fabrics, rich colours, spectacular motifs. No

Dresden Plates or Log Cabins, no Flying Geese or Evening Stars. Each quilt appeared to be an original design, embellished with Rita's unique touches: velvets and silks contrasting with simple cottons, delicate embroidery peeking out unexpectedly from complex medallions, colourful oriental motifs accenting dramatic borders, clever appliqué creating depth and texture. She took down a quilt from the shelf and shook it open over the quilting frame, catching her breath as its full vista was revealed – a stunning velvet creation of deep burgundy, dark green and bright navy blue, adorned with three-dimensional rosebuds made of carefully folded and pleated pastel satin. She chose another and found it crafted with layers of fabric, softly folded and stuffed to suggest clouds above, rolling fields below, with sunflowers in the foreground, each petal lightly puffed to create a three-dimensional effect.

On the wall opposite the window hung a stained glass window, entirely made of fabric. Each panel depicted a flower, a butterfly or a bird, crafted in bright rich colours against a background of muted blues, greens, purples and golds. Enhancing the stained glass concept, each figure was outlined in tiny black satin stitch and facial features were executed in cross stitches and knots. A deep black border, accented by lines of gold embroidery, framed the panels to complete the window effect. Julie stood before it, truly in awe of the hours and hours of eye-straining, finger-cramping stitchery that it must have demanded but even more the charming motifs and colours that bespoke the creative output of a true artist.

She was overwhelmed. Never had she imagined that lowly quilts might emerge as dramatic and artistic as this collection. And how was Rita, heart-broken, browbeaten and abused, able to plumb her imagination and energy to conjure these brilliant creations? And why were they hidden away? What was Rita's motive?

"Tommy," she spluttered. "How can this be? How could she manage all this? And why was it all locked away like this?"

"Dunno," Tommy replied. "But for sure she didn't want Joe to know about it, an' I can't say I blame her. But look – there's some papers in this here case. I didn't look at them but maybe they'll explain some of it." He handed Julie a very old, very battered leather portfolio.

Julie peeked into the case and pulled out a sheaf of official-looking documents – certificates of some sort. Some had ribbons attached – red and blue mostly – and Julie realized that she was looking at prize presentations from the Canadian National Exhibition and the Royal Winter Fair. Rita had entered her work in the two major quilt competitions and won – repeatedly.

"To think that she never told a soul," Julie remarked to Tommy. "The top quilter in the country year after year and nobody knew or cared."

She riffled through the notebook and saw that it contained not only notes describing the quilts and a record of fabric purchases, mostly from Eaton's catalogue, along with some jottings of poetry and prose. "I'll take this home and go through it more carefully," she said. "Maybe it will offer up some clues."

She looked around one more time, absorbing the artistic wealth that imbued the room. Then she waited for Tommy to lock the door and return the key to its hiding place.

"Tommy, you're the owner of this farm so all of this technically belongs to you. But I'd like Chrissy to see it. I have a feeling that she didn't know about her mother's private life either."

"Far as I'm concerned, it's all for Chrissy," Tommy replied. "Maybe it'll be a comfort to her…let her get to know her ma a bit better. Ya know where the key is. Whenever Chrissy comes to visit, just bring her in and tell her all these quilts belong to her. I won't touch nuthin' in this room."

And so it was that Chrissy returned home, none too willingly but bowing to Julie's insistence.

"It's about your father's farm," Julie began.

"I was afraid of that," Chrissy replied. "I don't want anything to do with the farm. My so-called brother can have it. I never want to see it – or him – again in all my life."

"Chrissy, there have been some developments since you went away. Maybe I should have kept you informed but I didn't, because I knew that talk of the farm and your family would be deeply upsetting for you. But here's the picture."

She turned to Chrissy and held both her hands. "Your step-brother is dead. A while back, he got into a fight in town and killed a young man and he was sentenced to twenty-five years in prison. But in prison he got into another brawl with other inmates and he was killed. I think your mother died of a broken heart along with the abuse she suffered from her husband. And after her death, Tommy Flaherty made a deal with your father, to buy the farm and let your father live there for the rest of his life. Tommy made sure he had food and firewood and so on and he looked in on him every day until he died.

"So Tommy owns the farm. But he found something that he wants you to see."

With Chrissy wide-eyed and tense beside her, no doubt reliving the agonies she had suffered there not so long ago, Julie drove up to the rarely used front door of the Dunning house, avoiding the shabby kitchen and sitting room, and led Chrissy straight into the parlour. She unlocked the bedroom door and stood back for Chrissy to enter.

At first, she did not understand what she was seeing. She studied the unfinished work on its frame, looked around at the glorious finished quilts on the racks and stood before the stained glass creation, obviously impressed by its beauty and perfection. She turned to Julie. "What is this? Are these your quilts?"

"No, my dear, they are yours. They are a legacy from your mother."

"But …she never did this kind of work. She made quilts like everybody else but they were just ordinary – nothing like these. And she always had the quilting frame set up in the sitting room, not in here. In fact, I never saw this room open, now that I think of it. We were never allowed in the parlour."

"That's just the point, Chrissy. It was her secret. Her quilts expressed all her artistic impulses, all the love she felt for you. She captured some of the beauty she saw around her and used it to turn her back on the pain and fear she had to face every day. This room was her haven. And she made quilting an art form."

Julie flipped open some of the quilts but Chrissy stood with her hands tightly folded, refusing to touch anything. Julie pointed out the painstaking stitchery of the stained glass and the exquisite satin roses on their velvet background. She pulled out a quilt that she hadn't previously investigated and found a glorious rainbow arcing from earth to sky, a backdrop for various birds in flight, displaying fanciful and colourful plumage. Chrissy attended to all the details that Julie pointed out but she still seemed not to comprehend the significance of what she was seeing.

"Time for tea," Julie suggested cheerfully. "We can come back tomorrow, if you want to, and look at all the rest."

Settled at the Chandlers' kitchen table, the comforting cups of tea steaming before them, Julie handed Chrissy the leather portfolio she'd brought from Rita's secret haven. Once again, Chrissy was reluctant to touch it so Julie pulled out the sheaf of certificates testifying to Rita's prizes and spread them across the table.

Without a word, Chrissy examined each one. She blinked back tears as she looked up into Julie's kind eyes. "How did she do this without getting caught?"

"She was a very clever lady. She was secretive because her life depended on it."

"Oh yes. My mother suffered in some ways more than I did. I saw how my father treated her, but we never talked about any of it. She never complained about her pain and she never let me talk about mine. And she never shared this strange compulsion of hers."

"I suspect it all started on a small scale and then she became obsessive about secrecy," Julie suggested. "These prizes from the CNE date back several years. So she kept her secret for a very long time. And her notebook tells the same story."

She opened the little scribbler at the first page and laid it before Chrissy. "She often mentions your name."

At last Chrissy allowed herself to touch the booklet and turn its pages. It opened with simple financial records – neat columns of costs of fabrics, thread and batting and the value of prizes won. Then it provided carefully coloured sketches of each quilt with detailed accounts of when and how each one was made, the specific fabrics and stitches used, the contests to which it was submitted and the prizes won. Most pages contained an inscription, a few lines of poetry or a quotation.

"A glorious rainbow for my darling daughter."

"Heaven and earth for Chrissy."

"In memory of my dear lost girl."

"She walks in beauty, like the night of cloudless climes and starry skies. And all that's best of dark and bright meet in her aspect and her eyes."

"My dearest daughter, lost to me, lives in my dreams and memory."

There were many more and Chrissy read them all without a word, while Julie busied herself with dinner preparations.

The sound of an auto in the lane interrupted both of them. "Oh Chrissy, could you answer the door please," Julie asked. "I'm up to my elbows in biscuit dough."

Chrissy opened the door and stood transfixed, looking up into gray eyes that were solemn and hopeful, a friendly but serious face – the face of Willie Donovan. "Chrissy," he said hesitantly. You're here. When did you come? I was afraid I'd never see you again."

She stared at him, speechless. She had not expected to see him, now or ever again. Suddenly she reached up to him and kissed him. He wrapped his arms around her and they clung to one another. In that moment, all Chrissy's tension and anger flooded out of her. She laid her head on his chest and cried uncontrollably, great wracking sobs that slowly receded to leave her red-eyed and exhausted. And Willie wept too, overwhelmed by joy and relief. Willie's parents, waiting discreetly in the car, held hands tightly as they watched the drama unfold, before joining Julie in the kitchen.

Chrissy and Willie wanted only to be together yet they were suddenly shy. Hand in hand, they strolled along the laneway, marvelling that their paths had crossed again. "You've grown so tall," Chrissy remarked. "I hardly knew you at first."

"You've changed a bit yourself," Willie countered. "You've grown too."

"And grown up, I guess," she replied. "But Willie, I've finished high school and I'm going to go to University next year. I want to be a writer. Now tell me what you've been up to."

"I'm finishing high school this year," he reported. "During the week, I live in town with my grandparents and come home on weekends. It's been awkward at times, but luckily, I've been able to finish all five years in four so my purgatory will end soon."

"Purgatory? Was it that bad?"

"Well at the start, I ran into a few bullies. I was at a disadvantage, you see, because my parents were my teachers and they didn't exactly follow the normal primary school course of study. So when I got to high school I was way ahead of the other students in every subject. I tried to keep my head down but a couple of the teachers kept singling me out, so before long I became known as the class egghead. And that brought out the bullies, especially one fellow named Walter Peabody. Almost from the first day of school, he'd walk up beside me in the halls and give me a push or elbow me. And it got worse every day."

"So what happened? Did you report him?"

"Not exactly. One day as we were changing classrooms, he moved in on me and the math teacher, Mr. Harris, was standing in his doorway watching. Peabody pushed me once and as he came at me again, I just put a foot in front of him and pulled his arm up behind his back. Hard. He went down on his knees, yelling that I had attacked him. Mr. Harris saw what happened and he took us both into his classroom and told Peabody he'd seen the whole thing and to mind his manners or he'd have him expelled. And it worked. After that Peabody and his cronies more or less left me alone."

"I'm amazed. Where did you learn to fight?"

"Well, that's not fighting – that's just a wrestling move that my Dad taught me, to take control of a person without really hurting them. He learned wrestling when he was in the army.

"But what about you?" he deflected the conversation. "What made you decide to be a writer?"

"It started when I moved to Toronto," she began and then paused, embarrassed, wondering whether he knew the circumstances that had driven her away from home.

"I know about that," he said, clasping both her hands in his. His compassion brought tears to her eyes.

"Well, Julianna took me there and I was really scared and hurting inside and out. So when she was leaving, she gave me a little notebook and asked me to write in it everyday. All she wanted me to do was write down three good things I could remember about each day. At first it was really hard. All I could think of was my own problems. But after a while, I started seeing so many good things – Julianna's aunt and her father who were so kind to me, their homes and gardens, the city itself and eventually other people that I met. I started writing more and more and before long the book was full. So Auntie Margaret – that's Julie's aunt – she took me down to Eaton's and bought me another bigger book, a diary, and some notebooks for writing down my stories. And one thing led to another and believe it or not, I have a little book of poetry that may just get published sometime soon."

Willie was amazed. "Chrissy, that's wonderful," he exclaimed. "Am I allowed to read it?"

"Maybe. I'm still a bit shy about it. But if we go ahead with the book, I guess I'll have to get over that. Besides, Julianna isn't shy about her book, so why should I be?"

"Julianna has written a book?"

"Yes, and a good one too. It's all about women's health. When she first came here to the Valley, she had just published a very small edition of it – you won't remember, but she gave copies to everybody at the Women's Institute and it caused quite a fuss. And since then she has published a new edition, much bigger and more detailed than the first one, and now she's working on a huge new edition – 400 pages at least."

"Women's health. Why would that cause a fuss? I'd have thought the Women's Institute would be interested."

"Oh they were," Chrissy laughed. "Very interested. And very shocked. It contains quite explicit information about reproduction and birth control, and most of the older members thought it was obscene. They put them in the stove and burned them. But younger women realized that they needed to know more about their own bodies, and she became their heroine."

"She's my heroine too," Willie confided. "She gave me back my voice. I will never be able to thank her enough." He recalled Julie's therapy and his slow but sure recovery.

"Isn't it wonderful, Willie? She saved both our lives. Whatever we're able to do in the future will happen because Julianna picked us up and set us on the right paths. Let's go and tell her that."

Willie paused mysteriously. "Let's tell her something else."

She sensed his meaning. "Let's tell her we're going to get married."

They laughed and again suddenly shy, headed back to the house in silence.

Willie and Chrissy spoke simultaneously. "We wanted you to know…" "We have some news…" "Oh Willie, you go first…"

Willie got right to the point. "Chrissy and I are going to get married," he announced.

"Not right away," Chrissy added. "But someday."

They waited. Everyone looked at everyone else. Finally Julie and Rachel made the same move. They wrapped their arms around the young people and each other, laughing and shedding tears of happiness. John and Adam whooped their approval over the din.

"They're so young," Rachel thought to herself but recalling the challenges that each had already overcome in their young lives, she set aside that worry, exchanging a long look with Julie that reinforced her sense of the rightness of it all.

In the joy of the reunion, the quilts were forgotten. But in the days ahead, Chrissy and Julie returned to Rita's retreat, wrapped each quilt carefully in a clean sugar bag and carried them home to the Chandlers' attic, where several sturdy steam trunks provided storage.

"I don't know what to do with them," Chrissie commented as she surveyed the substantial stack of quilts, "but I'll try to decide soon and take them off your hands."

"Well, it's a big attic," Julie reminded her. "They're safe here. And they'll be waiting for you whenever you're ready for them."

"I'll take the rainbow home with me." Chrissy decided. "I need it to help me get to know my mother."

CHAPTER 24

Annie's Secret

Every fall, Annie would give us a few bottles of her herb tonic – she said it was good at warding off colds and the flu. Well sir, it pretty well warded off anybody who tasted it – bitter as poison and burnin' all the way down. But sure enough, if we felt a cold comin' on, we swallowed it down and it worked. We slept like babies and the babies did too when we give it to them. She also made a liniment that cured man or beast – she called it pigeon milk but I never knew of no pigeon that produced stuff like that – stinkin' of turpentine and pine resin and goodness knows what else. But ye'd rub it on and it cured every ache or pain. I mind usin' it more'n once when one of the horses took lame and in no time they was right as rain. We never give much thought to how she made the stuff: she and Oscar was odd, kinda gypsy-like, and there weren't no point in wonderin' much about them. So we just thanked her and dreaded the day when we needed to swallow any of her medicine.

But then when we come upon her fruit cellar, we sure wished we'd asked more questions.

Lenny

One bitter morning, Lenny glanced down the road toward Annie's house as he usually did, keeping an eye on her. It was too quiet. No smoke rose from the chimney and there was no sign of Annie, rushing out to feed her chickens or water her horse. Lenny finished his porridge and checked again. Still no smoke. "I think I'll just go down and have a look," he remarked to Velma.

By the time he had walked the quarter-mile to Annie's place, Lenny's ears were complaining of the cold, in spite of the heavy wool cap he wore all winter. He knocked on the door but all was silent. He walked along to the kitchen window and peered in. There sat Annie at the kitchen table, her head on her arms as if she were having a good cry. And close beside her on the table was Araby, her vast white cat. Lenny rapped on the window. The cat stared at him but Annie didn't stir. He shouted but still no response. So he returned to the kitchen door and tried it. It was unlocked and he walked in.

"Annie," he called. "Ya didn't answer the door." She was silent. He approached her gingerly and touched her shoulder. No reaction. He took hold of her arm and shook it. Not a word. He wasn't sure that she was breathing.

He picked her up and carried her to the couch, covering her with a quilt. She was very cold, as was the house. He checked the fire – it was completely dead, which meant she hadn't tended it since the previous day. He set a new fire, pulled the tea kettle to the front and went back to check on Annie. The cat had followed her to the couch and now lay close, stretching its great furry length all along her body. It fixed Lenny with a disconcerting two-tone stare that seemed to say: "She is mine. Stay away. I will take care of her."

Lenny was no expert on emergencies so he did what he always did in crisis. He went to get Velma. Sensing that something was wrong, she was already on her way and together they hurried back to Annie's. She hadn't moved. "Is she dead?" Velma whispered. "I don't think so," Lenny replied. "I thought she was breathing."

"Better go get Julianna," Velma urged. And he did.

Julie arrived with her black bag and went straight to Annie, checking for a pulse and nodding to them when she found one, taking blood pressure and looking worried. She spoke softly to the cat who permitted her to examine Annie's head, shoulders and arms for blood in case she'd fallen, but she found nothing. "She's very cold, Velma. Does she have a foot warmer or a hot water bottle, do you suppose?"

Velma had never been inside Annie's house. She searched but found nothing. Velma found some towels and plucking a lid from the now-warm stove, wrapped it and laid it at Annie's feet.

"Lenny, would you please go up to our house and ask Clara for the foot warmer and my new hot water bottle? And Velma, would you please make up a batch of that amazing oatmeal gruel of yours. Cook it 'til the oatmeal disappears but keep it very thin.. When she wakes up, she'll need some good nutrition." Velma's famous gruel, laced with blackstrap molasses and various undisclosed extras, was much coveted throughout the Valley, almost on a par with Annie's own tonic as a remedy for myriad ailments.

Alone with Annie, Julie reached into her bag and withdrew a flat tin of a strong smelling paste which she applied to Annie's temples and throat. The cat recoiled from the smell, hopping up to the back of the couch to keep a wary eye on the proceedings. Julie removed Annie's shoes and stockings and massaged the paste into the soles of her feet. She talked constantly. "Annie, it's me, Julie, your neighbour. You were not feeling well so Lenny and Velma asked me to come and try to help. You're going to be just fine, Annie, it looks as if you just had a bit of a fainting spell. I'm applying this salve to your nerve centres now. It's wonderful stuff. The Indians make it from herbs and it helps to get the blood circulating and pump up your heart rate."

Lenny and Velma returned and with them, Adam, bearing the foot warmer, a heavy stoneware jar, flat on one side, a cork on the other. Velma filled it from the kettle and tucked it under Annie's feet, returning the stove lid to its rightful place on the stove. She had never before encountered a hot water bottle and viewed it with suspicion until Adam explained that it was softer and more comfortable then the awkward stoneware jar. It too was pressed into service.

They stood beside Annie and looked down at her shrunken body, her wrinkled face still tanned from summer days in the garden, her hands calloused by hard work, her hair a tangled mess. "Pathetic old thing," Velma remarked. "She must have been so lonesome."

While Julie kept vigil, Lenny went off to see to Annie's livestock. Sure enough, Dobbin had not been fed and he was fretting and stamping in his stall. Lenny led him out to water and then returned him to the stable with fresh hay and oats and a few kind words. He found the hen feed and gave the cackling flock their breakfast, gathering fresh eggs at the same time. Velma crumbled some bread into Araby's dish and added milk. After a show of utter disdain, hunger prevailed and he lapped it up before returning to Annie's side.

She was beginning to stir. "Who's that," she demanded. "What are you doing in my house?"

"Just taking care of you, Annie," Velma soothed her. "You maybe had a fainting spell. Julie came along to help. Here – I made you some oatmeal porridge. You must be hungry." She tried to feed her, but Annie pushed her away. "I'm not a baby," she protested. "I'll feed myself." She sat up a bit and tried to slurp up the porridge, a good deal of which landed down her front. Lying back on her pillows, she sighed deeply and seemed to be dozing.

Just as Lenny returned from the stable, Annie gave a little gasp and began clutching at her quilt. She began to mutter to herself but neither Velma nor Julie could understand what she said. Lenny would really have preferred to be anywhere else but he came close to her and knelt down beside the couch. "Annie, don't try to talk now," he said. "Just stay quiet so you don't upset yourself." He looked helplessly at Julie who was holding Annie's hand.

Suddenly Annie seemed to rally and she stared at Lenny as if she were seeing him for the first time. She continued to mutter but one word seemed to emerge – tea. "Tea," Lenny repeated. "I think she wants some tea." The kettle was singing quietly on the back of the stove. Velma hurried to find the tea pot and the loose tea. She opened the little pantry cupboard behind the stove and found numerous tea canisters. "I never dreamed Annie drank so much tea," she muttered to herself. She chose the one nearest to her, scooped some loose tea into the pot and added boiling water.

"It'll be ready in just a few minutes," she told Lenny. Annie was still struggling to speak. "I think she said 'tea can' but I'm not sure why." Julie said

Annie wasn't giving up. "Tea can," she said clearly. "Look." She waved vaguely toward the cupboard where Velma had found the tea. "Maybe she keeps things hidden in them tea canisters," Velma suggested. She went to the cupboard and pulled a large tin off the top shelf. It was stuffed with money. She gulped and replaced it, then checked another…and another. They were all full of cash. She brought one back to the couch and showed it to Lenny and Julie. "Y'mean this here tea can,?" he asked Annie. She reached out and grasped his wrist – a surprisingly strong grip, he thought to himself. "Tea can," she said. "You keep. All."

"You want us to take this money?" Lenny asked in amazement. "Annie, this looks like a lot of money." He met Velma's gaze. She nodded toward the cupboard. "Lots more," she whispered. "You keep. All," Annie commanded.

"Now then Annie, don't do nuthin' rash. We'll just put this back in your cupboard and it'll be waiting for ya when you're feeling better," Lenny assured her.

"Will," Annie managed to say. "Tea can. Will."

"Maybe she's telling us she has a will in one of those tins," Julie surmised. "You'd best go and have a look."

Velma opened tin after tin, each one stuffed with money. She had never seen so much cash in her life, never dreamed of owning such wealth. Her throat felt dry and her hands were shaking. Finally, she opened a tin that contained documents. It looked like the deed to Annie's farm, Oscar's citizenship papers, his death certificate, some old photographs and yes – a will.

She brought it to Lenny who held it open before Annie's eyes. "This looks like yer will, Annie. Do ya want me to read it to you? I don't think now is the best time to make changes."

"Read," Annie ordered.

This is the last will and testament of me, Anna Emily Walters," he read. *"Upon my death, I leave all contents of my house and cellar and all goods and chattels of my farm, including my horse to my friend and neighbour Lenny Findlay, except my husband's violin which I leave to Willie Donovan. I leave my farm jointly to*

Christine Dunning and Willie Donovan. They can share it or sell it or keep it, as they see fit. I feel ashamed for all that they have suffered at the hands of insensitive and cruel people. When I was Christine's age, I suffered the same as she did. Willie's friendship has brought me true joy. I am proud that each of them overcame the hardships that life gave them. Araby belongs to them." It was signed Anna Emily Walters and witnessed by someone named Ralph Peters, Morganston, Ontario. Beneath his signature, Annie had written: 'Cousin'.

Lenny could think of nothing to say. He waited for some comment from Annie but none was forthcoming. Finally Velma took Annie's hands in hers and said quietly: "Annie, ya need to get yerself better before ya start worrying about wills and money and such. Now ya just lay yourself down quiet and we can talk about all this tomorrow if ya want to." Annie glared at her, then at Lenny. "Tea can," she said fiercely. "You. Keep." They were her final words. She nodded off soon afterward. Toward midnight, she opened her eyes wide and gasped. Then she stopped breathing.

Lenny and Velma gazed at one another, unsure what to believe. "What should we do," Lenny asked Julie. "That's more money than I ever seen in all my days and it's hard to believe that Annie gave it to us." They had no idea how much money was stashed in the tea cans, but they knew it was more than they'd ever dreamed of owning.

"I suggest that you go home and get your horse and cutter and pack it all up and take it home tonight," Julie advised. "I am your witness, both to the will and to the removal of the tea cans. They are rightfully yours – take them."

Together, they gathered up the hefty cans and transported them home to their own place, feeling a bit like thieves, but remembering the terms of the will.

In the morning, Adam and Lenny drove to the casket maker in Foreston where they chose a simple pine box for Annie's burial, knowing that's what she would prefer. It fell to Velma and Julie to prepare her body for burial. In her bedroom, they searched the closet and bureau for appropriate clothes. There was not much to choose from until they poked into a large travel trunk that contained a lavishly embroidered garment, more like a kimono or a ceremonial robe than a dress. "I think it's from Turkey," Julie surmised. "Or it could be Morocco. Maybe not quite right for a funeral but it obviously meant something important to her." They cut away Annie's old clothes and stuffed them in the stove, then bathed her with soap and water, brushed her hair and dressed her in her elegant gown. In the sleeve, Julie found a note: "To my beloved Annie, the most beautiful gown for the most beautiful woman in the world. All my love, Oskar."

"Yes," she told Velma. "This is the dress she would have wanted."

They gently lifted her tiny body into the casket. Then they were ready for the wake.

"You must be exhausted," Julie said, noting the dark circles under Velma's eyes. "I'll go home and telephone the neighbours. But are there relatives?"

"That cousin down Morganston way that witnessed the will," Lenny replied. "Name of Ralph Peters. I never heard of him before – maybe the phone company can find him. She never mentioned nobody else."

"And there's Willie and Christine," Julie added. "I'll call Rachel first. Maybe she'll come and take poor Araby home." The cat was perched on the back of the kitchen couch, disconsolate and worried.

"I'll just bank the fire and make sure there's water and wood for later," Lenny offered. Velma filled several pots with water for the gallons of tea the neighbours would drink at the wake. She tidied the couch and table and swept the floor. Then she and Lenny made a tour of the house to see what 'goods and chattels' Annie might be leaving them. Furnishings were sparse and well used. A couple of beds and dressers upstairs, the kitchen table and chairs and the wood stove downstairs, and a mighty pile of books, many dealing with life in foreign countries, several in languages they could not identify.

Lenny opened the cellar door and encountered total darkness. "I'll need a lantern to see what's down here," he said. He found one in the woodshed and lighted it. Together they descended the stairs.

The sight that awaited them was not what they expected. Nor was the smell. They stood at the foot of the stairs and peered into the shadows. This was no ordinary cellar. Of course it had shelves of preserves, like every other farm house in the Valley. But they were puzzling preserves. Rows of wooden shelves were packed with stoneware jars and a few glass bottles, carefully corked and sealed with wax. Each section was labeled. Stomach Bitters. Herbal Tonic. Cherry Cough Syrup. Plum Roborant. Raspberry Cordial. Fruit Elixir. Parsnip Physic. Apple Cider. And in much larger jars, Potato Spirits.

"Well, I'll be jiggered," Lenny remarked. "Lookit, there's that there tonic she gave us each winter, but what's all this other stuff."

He examined the well-stocked shelves and then looked beyond them to a low bureau. Atop it was an open notebook, filled with records of fruit harvested, processed, bottled – and sold.

Even more puzzling was a stone wall behind them, fitted with a polished wooden door, fit for a parlour. They opened it and ventured inside. Lenny lifted the lantern to penetrate deeper into the darkness. They were in an immaculately clean room with a floor of carefully fitted flagstones, plastered walls and a ceiling of patterned tin. Before them they saw a gleaming copper pot attached to a complicated array of copper pipes. Two padded rocking chairs with footstools stood before it and on a small table just to the right, a small bottle of Annie's Raspberry Cordial along with two stemmed crystal glasses that glimmered on a silver tray in the semi-darkness.

They stared at the contraption, trying to decipher its secrets – walked all around it, touched its polished exterior and examined the pipes and tubes that protruded from it. Then they sat down in the two padded rockers that faced it and stared some more.

"Whadya suppose it is?" Velma wondered.

"Dunno," replied Lenny. "Never seen such a thing in my life."

"But it's warm. Is it some kind of a stove?"

"Could be. But it's a dang funny place for it down here in the cellar."

"Maybe it's cooking something inside itself," Velma suggested. "There's a smell…"

Lenny inhaled deeply. The air in the little room was rich with some unknown aroma, something that tickled his nostrils and made him feel a bit hungry. But all the same, he was stumped.

"I'll just take another look at that book," he said, making his way out to the bureau and returning with the recipe book.

He moved the table closer and set the lantern on it for better light.

"I think I'll just have a drop of this here Raspberry Cordial," he suggested to Velma. "It's been a long day and my throat's feelin a bit raw."

Splitting the wax seal with his pocket knife, he worked the cork out of the bottle and poured a half glass for each of them.

"I dunno," Velma demurred. "Whatdya suppose is in it?"

"Well, prolly raspberries," Lenny allowed. "And some of them herbs – she always had a garden full of herbs, one kind and another."

He took a sip and coughed. He held the glass up to the light and looked at it intently, as if to decipher its mysteries, and ventured another sip. "That's a fine drink," he announced. "Throat feels better already." He topped up his glass. "Try it, Velma. It's real tasty and it sure will ward off a cold."

Velma unwillingly touched her lips to her drink, savouring its myriad flavours. Then she tried a full-scale sip and nodded her approval. "Very tasty indeed," she avowed. She held out her glass for a drop more.

Lenny studied the notebook and began to read the entries: Start date, variety, quantity of fruit, date bottled, quantity bottled. Amount received. And at the back, a roster of recipes and instructions for each product, carefully written in Oscar's hand. A separate set of instructions covered fermenting potatoes and distilling the mash. Lenny suddenly realized what he was smelling. He also realized what he was drinking – and the bottle was now at least half empty.

"This here's likker," he gasped. "Annie was makin' booze. I always figured her for a teetotaler.

And I'll bet that's where all that money in them canisters come from."

They stared at one another in amazement and at their glasses, recently topped up with the raspberry elixir.

"What we gonna do with it all, Lenny," Velma asked.

Lenny allowed himself another sip and carefully considered her question. "Well, we'll drink some of it," he replied. "And we'll store the rest of it."

They sipped again, both deep in thought. When they glanced up, they realized that they were being watched. Araby had leapt silently onto the table and sat glaring at them. He did not look friendly.

"That cat. Sure am glad he's not part of the goods and chattels she give us." He reached out a hand but Araby recoiled from his overture and leapt to the floor, hunkering down near the door, still glaring at them with his unnerving bi-coloured eyes.

"Guess we'd better be off home," Velma suggested. "I'm feeling a bit dizzy – prolly not enough sleep." In fact, climbing the cellar stairs was a greater effort than they expected and they leaned on the door jamb briefly when they reached the kitchen, giving Araby an opportunity to slip through and station himself on the couch. Lenny closed the cellar door and noticed a key, hanging on a nearby nail. He swiftly locked up and pocketed the key.

Annie's secret was finally revealed. And now, for better or for worse, it belonged to them.

CHAPTER 25

A Wee Drop a Day

Tommy Flaherty, our Valley joker. Always a grin. Always tippin' his old tweed Full of stories and music. But behind the jokes and the smiles, there was a darn smart fella that most folks never knew. See, in them days, them Yanks started this here Prohibition that was supposed to stop people from drinkin'. Booze, I mean. Well sir, it didn't stop nuthin' – the Yanks wanted their booze, law or no law, and they got it by the boatload from Canada. It started a big business that they called rum-runnin' – boats full of booze slippin' south across the lake to New York State in the dead of night. And some of our mighty big booze makers got their start with prohibition money. Canada tried Prohibition for a bit but then I figger them government guys got thirsty so they changed it around and set up some 'wet' places where booze was legal and some 'dry' ones where it wasn't. That opened the door to a lot of bootleggers, some of 'em greedy buggers, but a few, like Tommy Flaherty, just tryin' to look after his friends. Our county was 'dry' and Tommy did his bit to dampen it, if ya follow me. He kept his secret well hidden but a few folks in the Valley got a glimpse of him, including me and Velma, and we was amazed.

Lenny

Prohibition was the problem and crime was the remedy. When Temperance fever swept across North America like a new religion or (some said) an epidemic, many a fine man – and plenty of women too – turned to crime to thwart Prohibition. And Tommy Flaherty was one of them.

The hail-fellow-well-met life of the party and unsung helper of many a neighbour in need, he had always been relied upon to provide alcohol discreetly to the Valley's tipplers. While booze barons, supported by death-defying rum-runners, were accumulating family fortunes by shipping alcohol across the border to thirsty Americans, Tommy's business was decidedly low-key. He often drove far afield, past Paxton Ford, which was 'dry', to Morganston, which was 'wet', where he'd fill up the back of his buggy with bottles and jugs and trot off home. But Tommy was a bootlegger with a difference. He took only a small profit on his stock, yet over the years, those profits added up, especially since Tommy himself rarely touched a drop.

So it was that Lenny, whose experience with alcohol was almost non-existent except for a single and amazingly restorative bottle of raspberry cordial in Annie's cellar, stepped up to Tommy at the grist mill one day and asked if they could have a word in private.

"Ya see, Tommy, I've come into an inheritance and I don't know just how to handle it," he began mysteriously.

"An inheritance! Ya don't say!"

"Well, ya might call it that. Not money, mind you. No siree." Lenny had no intention of publicizing his new financial status.

"So if ya didn't inherit money, what'd ya inherit?"

"Booze," Lenny blurted out. "Annie Walters left us all her likker."

For once, Tommy was speechless. Briefly. "What kind of likker did Annie have?"

"Well, ya recall she made all them tonics that she passed round to some of the neighbours if they was feelin' poorly."

"Yeah, so?"

"Well, y'see, when she died her cellar was full of the stuff. All kinds of drinks she called elixirs and cordials made from fruit. Very tasty, some of it, but likker. And along with that, there's a dozen or more jugs of some sort of drink with no flavour at all but a heck of a kick. I reckon she made it from all them potatoes she grew every summer. Velma and me, we used to wonder what she did with so many potatoes. Now we know.

"And we found her account book too that shows she sold the stuff to a guy down to Morganston – name of Ralph Peters – and she made a fair bit of money from it.

"This Ralph Peters, his name was witness to her will – she called him cousin – but Mrs. Chandler couldn't find hide nor hair of him. The phone companies don't know him neither. And anyways, I'm not so sure about him coz I ain't had no dealings with him before."

"Well, I have," Tommy ventured. "And you're right to be careful. But how'd it be if I come round to your place this afternoon and have a look at what ya got and see what we can do about it."

"Something else," Lenny added. "Annie had this here cookin' contraption in her cellar – prolly used it to make the booze. I took it all apart and took it home but I don't know what to do with it."

Velma joined them, when they met that afternoon, worried about the legalities but excited by the potential value of their windfall. She produced a small bottle of the raspberry cordial along with the record book and Tommy sipped appreciatively and studied carefully, especially the financial parts.

"She wasn't getting near enough for what she sold," he told them. "This stuff is worth a fortune. In New York, they'd make it into cocktails and sell each one of them for five or ten dollars, even with just half an ounce of this here juice. You play your cards right and you folks are gonna get mighty rich with this here windfall. Now let's have a look at that still."

Lenny and Velma were in shock but they obediently led Tommy to the cellar and uncovered the dismantled still, all shining copper and mysterious pipes.

"Luvly," Tommy affirmed. "A nice clean well maintained still. Where ya gonna set it up?"

"Oh I'm not so sure …" Lenny began.

"We wouldn't have any kinda idea how to use it," Velma added.

"Well I think we can figger it out," Tommy said, tapping Oscar's book. "Everything we need to know is right here. Even tells ya as how ya should throw away the first few ounces that have the poison in them. Methanol, it's called. Oscar knew exactly what he was doin'. He's writ the book for ya."

"But it ain't legal," Lenny argued. "And we don't even drink the stuff, except for medicine and that once at Annie's when we didn't know what it was."

"All the more reason to make it," Tommy responded. "If ya don't drink it, ye'll have more to sell."

"Well, we'll have to think about it for a bit," Lenny said, glancing at Velma, who nodded silently.

But they did agree to sell Tommy their current stock of nearly 200 bottles of elixirs and cordials, along with a dozen gallons of potato-based alcohol. "No Tommy, ya can't pay that much for it," Lenny protested when his neighbour peeled off a wad of bills. "It can't be worth so much."

"Ah but it is," Tommy argued. "And when I sell it on to some of my dealers, I'll make a nice wee profit too, so we'll all be happy.

"And when you're ready to proceed, I'll be glad to stop by and help set up the still. And take anything ya make off your hands."

Velma held the money in her two hands as if it were a dove that might take flight.

But it didn't fly away. It went into the same tea canisters that Annie had given them and added up to a fortune such as they had never imagined. "Enough to send Liam to that Agriculture College up to Guelph," Lenny crowed. "He's always wanted to go there, just like Adam. And we can buy Bernie his own farm so he can start workin' for his own self." The fact that their older son had hired himself out to a farmer several concessions away, working to save money for his own place, was a constant source of worry to them.

"And enough to buy room and board in town for the girls to go to high school like Liam did," Velma added, still a bit miffed that their younger son was accorded an education whereas the two girls were expected to stay home and wait for husbands to materialize.

"That too, sure enough," Lenny agreed diplomatically. "And how about electricity in the house? And running water in the barn?"

"Not just the barn. Running water in the house too," Velma allowed the dream to expand and envelope them all. "And a toilet right inside the house like them folks in town."

"Say, Velma, we could even take a trip," Lenny added. "How about a visit to Niagara Falls? Adam says it's a grand place. And maybe the Royal Winter Fair in Toronto? Adam goes every year."

"Oh, I dunno about that," Velma demurred. "I'd hafta have a new dress."

"Ya kin have a dozen new dresses," Lenny roared. "We kin have anything we want."

They gazed at one another in shock and wonderment. "It's agin the law," Velma whispered.

"Didn't somebody say somethin' about the law being an ass?" Lenny retorted.

They decided to delay the assembly of the still until after their three younger children were away at school and a farm had been found for Bernie. All very well to thwart the law, Lenny thought, but we don't want the youngsters to pick up our bad habits.

Since her hefty supply of potatoes was part of the 'goods and chattels' that Annie had bequeathed them, Lenny bagged them up in denim sacks and brought them home to their own cellar, to await the day when the still would spring into action.

"Who'da dreamed," Velma ruminated, "that a few tea canisters could change our lives. But that Tommy – he's a caution."

And that he was. In fact, he was already embarked on a new venture that rewarded both his generosity and his propensity for playing tricks on his neighbours. One day at the grist mill, where the men gathered to gossip as they waited for their grain to be ground into meal, he encountered Dave Dempsey, wheezing and coughing, his eyes and nose running. Dave was the local thresher who trundled his unwieldy machine from farm to farm each summer, threshing the summer grain to separate the oats from the straw. It was a dusty job; every man who participated in the threshing – and it was always a community effort – was soon coated in dust from hair to boots and deep into his nose, throat and lungs as well.

"That's a nasty cough ya got there," Tommy commented.

Dave mopped his nose and eyes and found his voice. "Hay fever," he replied hoarsely. "Never used to get it but now it comes every summer."

"Can't ya do nothing for it?" Tommy asked sympathetically. "What's the doc say?"

"Ain't seein no doc," Dave growled. "Never do no good."

"Well, Dave, the wife makes up a real good medicine that might help. It's her old grandma's recipe – she made it for years and years and Mabel's ma made it and now Mabel makes it too. And it really works. It'll clear up your breathing problems in summer and then in winter, if you get a cold, ya can use it again."

Dave immediately perked up. Valley folk generally believed that home-made medications were far superior to the commercial varieties. "I could bring along a wee bottle of it if ye'd care to just try it," Tommy offered. "Just a wee drop a day."

"Need to do something'," Dave replied. "I got another month of threshin' to get through."

"I'll be along this afternoon and see if this stuff can help ya," Tommy promised.

Good as his word, he trotted up the Dempsey laneway a few hours later and handed over a small bottle of dark brown brew with a hand-written label: 'ELIXIR for colds and sneezes. Take half a glass at bedtime.' The bottle was remarkably similar to Annie's stock.

"Now then, Dave, ye'll be sure to follow the directions," Tommy warned. What he was thinking but not saying was that the product was not suitable for a man who was operating a monster machine that had no regard for the safety of life or limb. Furthermore, it might not meet the criteria of a professed teetotaler, whose wife enthusiastically espoused the doctrine of the Women's Christian Temperance Union.

But the medicine worked. Only a week later when their paths crossed at the grist mill, Dave Dempsey was awash with gratitude. "Cleared it right up," he shouted. "No cough, no runnin' nose. Cured the lot. I'd be grateful to ya, Tommy, if ye'd let me have another bottle and let me pay ya for it." And Tommy obliged.

Many there were in the Valley – mostly Scots – who were fiercely opposed to alcohol consumption in any form. Many of Irish descent held more liberal views. Some 'talked out of both sides of their mouths', as Tommy liked to say, publicly deploring drinking but privately tippling. All the same, they all got on well in the intricately interdependent way that isolated farm communities did in those days, depending on one another for midwifery, sickroom care and labour for harvest and wood cutting, listening in on the party line to keep up with the news, attending each other's house dances, quilting bees and funerals and in general knitting an impenetrable support system that could withstand most pressures.

Blissfully unaware that most of the medicines they purchased from trusted travelling salesmen comprised as much as ninety per cent alcohol, they knocked them back and fed them to their children, and thought nothing of it. If there was one point on which all agreed, it was the efficacy of home-made medicines and no one questioned their contents. Least of all Dave Dempsey who was overjoyed at his new-found return to health.

The bubble burst a few weeks later, when Rose Dempsey's young brother, Jimmy, came for a visit. Jimmy saw himself as a man of the world, having once left home and ridden the rails all the way to Saskatchewan to work in the wheat harvest, returning with improbable yarns of a land without hills or trees, where thousands upon thousands of acres of wheat stretched to the far horizon and beyond. Nobody believed his tall tales but they helped while away a winter evening. Now Jimmy was job-hunting and proposing that Dave take him on as his threshing partner, a move that both Dave and Rose viewed with grave mistrust.

But their reluctance only made Jimmy more insistent. "Look at ya, Dave," he proclaimed. "Always choking' and coughing' with the hay fever. Ya need somebody to take it over for ya. Ya can't do the job if yer sick all the time."

"Well, I'm not sick," Dave argued. "I got this here new medicine and it's cleared it up just fine. So thanks, Jimmy, but I don't need a helper right now, nor can I afford one."

Jimmy eyed the medicine bottle with interest. "What's in it?" he enquired.

"Secret recipe that Tommy Flaherty's wife got from her mother and her from her grandmother. Started takin' it a month back and haven't coughed since."

Jimmy snatched up the bottle, uncorked it and sniffed the contents. Then without asking, he tipped a dram into his cup and downed it. "Some medicine," he snorted. "That's likker."

Dave rose to his feet, headed for the door, bottle in hand, where he heaved it across the laneway and into the cedar hedge beyond. Jimmy quietly made a note of the probable location, intent on retrieving it after dark and enjoying what was left, out behind the barn.

Dave's hay fever returned a week or so later, worse than ever. With streaming eyes and wracking cough, he realized that he was no match for the thresher, especially its vicious hundred-foot belt that could chop off a horse's tail or a man's arm if they got too close. Jimmy continued his campaign to move in permanently and take over the threshing business. Dave was torn. Yet in spite of his views on alcohol, he refused to accuse Tommy Flaherty of leading him down the path of slipper slope.

Finally, it was Rose who resolved the quandary. She sat him down at the kitchen table and stood over him. "David, this has got to stop," she ordered. "We don't even know for sure that Jimmy's tellin' the truth. But the fact is, that medicine of his works. Sure enough, it's a sin if ya drink up all your money and get drunk and let yer family starve. But I'd say it's a bigger sin to stay sick when there's somethin' close to hand that can cure ya."

"But Rosie," Dave wheezed. "What's that saying' you have? 'Lips that touch likker shall never touch mine.' Where's that leave me? If drinking hard likker is wrong, I shouldn't be doin' it."

"Them's just words, Dave. That little bit of Tommy's medicine that ya swallow every night don't make ya a drunk. It made you stronger and better and able to do your work like a man. So I say, drive on over to Tommy's right now and get a fresh supply. And while you're away, I'll just have a few words with Jimmy. When ya get back, ya can drive him to the train and he'll be gone."

Dave never suffered from hay fever again. And thanks to Tommy, he and Rose even had a new slogan. "A wee drop a day keeps the doctor away."

CHAPTER 26

Adam's Dream

So it was a horse that finally done Adam in. Or almost. I always figured them wild horses he bought at the auction that he thought he could tame would be big trouble. And I was right.

By then, all the gossip had died away and Julie was friends with everybody in the neighbourhood. Even Gossip Gertie turned to Julie when she tripped in the garden and twisted her ankle real bad. She never said nuthin' good about Julie but at least she let up on the insults.

Julie and Adam was different from the rest of us but we quit thinking about that – they was just part of the Valley and if we thought about them at all, it was to ask their advice or get help on something medical, or something legal, or some important letter we had to write, or enjoy their anniversary party each fall. They was always there, like a rock-solid foundation. We couldn't have carried on without them. But we had no choice.

Lenny

In his dream, Adam was four years old again. He was crying and covered in blood.

Uncle Joseph was standing over him, looking annoyed. "What have ya done to yerself, laddie?" He sounded angry. "Ya should know better than to climb on that wire fence?"

Adam didn't try to answer – there would have been no point. Uncle Joe believed that children should be seen but not heard so even when he asked a question like that, he would not permit an answer.

Uncle Joseph was tall and serious. He hardly ever smiled though his blue eyes were sometimes warm and twinkly. This was not one of those times.

"Get on up to the house," Uncle ordered. "Get your Auntie to look after ya and clean ya up. And mind ya stay off that wire fence like I told ya time and time again."

In his dream, Adam staggered a bit as he headed up the path to the house. Blood was pouring down his leg and into his sock and boot. When he had fallen, he had not only gashed his leg but smacked his head on the hard ground. Blood was everywhere. When he swiped at his tears, his hands came away bloodied. He was scared.

Aunt Sarah, busy with the baking, didn't look up when he came into the kitchen. Then she heard his sobs and turned to look at him. Her floury hands flew into the air. "Heavens above, Adam, what have ya done to yourself? Come over here into the light so I can see ya. No, you're messin' up the floor – go back to the summer kitchen and stay quiet."

Adam stood miserable and sobbing in the chilly summer kitchen. He was very cold and feeling dizzy. His head had begun to ache and his leg was hurting fiercely.

"What happened to ya," Auntie demanded. "You've surely made a mess of yourself."

"I climbed up the fence," Adam sobbed. "And my coat caught on a wire and I fell."

"How often have I told ya not to climb fences," Auntie scolded. "You're a very wicked boy. Now look at the mess you've made of your clothes and boots. And the mess on the floor and all the extra work…"

Her voice trailed off as she realized the depth of the leg injury. She spread some sugar bags on the couch and lifted him by his armpits to lie there. Then she used torn strips of sugar bags to bind up the leg wound and stanch the bleeding, and turned her attention to his head. His forehead was bruised but his cheek was cut and bleeding. She made a pad of cloth and ordered him to hold it firmly over the wound.

"Now stop that crying," she snapped. "It does ya no good. Lie still so's not to make more bleeding."

"I want my mommy," Adam sobbed.

Auntie's eyes hardened and her mouth formed a straight angry line. "You're a nasty ungrateful boy," she flared. "Ya know very well that yer ma didn't want ya then and doesn't want ya now. Uncle and I took ya in and we care for ya and give ya everything you need. Instead of complaining, ya should be thankful for your blessings."

She left him there, shivering and still bloodied, and stormed back to her baking.

His teeth chattered, from cold and fear. His head throbbed. But he lay still for a long time, cowed by Auntie's wrath and longing for his mother. He hadn't seen her since coming to live with Auntie and Uncle but he still remembered her plump warmth, her strong arms holding him, her hand brushing back his hair and wiping away tears, her funny little songs that made him laugh while she laughed along with him.

The dream seemed to fade yet he couldn't wake up. He struggled to find consciousness but it eluded him. The pain in his head was brutal, just like the one so many years before when he fell off the wire fence, the one in his dream. He felt lost and he tried to call out for help.

Immediately his mother was beside him, her cool hand on his cheek, speaking gently.

"Adam my dearest, you're awake at last," Julie said. "Don't try to talk, dear, and don't move. Just lie still if you can. I'm right here beside you."

Adam opened his eyes. Just for an instant, he was disappointed. This was not his mother. And then he recognized Julie, her loving smile, her soft voice, her gentle touch and a wave of gratitude washed over him, so powerful that he wanted to weep.

He tried to speak but his throat was too dry and constricted. And the headache was so intense that he had to close his eyes.

"Adam, my love, let's try a drop of water for your poor parched throat." She held the tiny pitcher to his lips and he managed a sip. Then she gently patted his cracked lips with glycerin, sponged his face with a warm cloth, and measured his blood pressure and temperature, recording them on a hastily improvised chart.

Her father looked in on them. "Any progress?" he asked.

"Yes, he surfaced briefly," she replied. "And I gave him a sip of water. He seemed to be having a bad dream before that though. Maybe it was just pain, but he seemed to be sobbing and shivering. Would a drop of morphine be safe?"

Dr. Brightson checked the chart. "The morphine would keep him still and perhaps even dreamless," he commented. "But we must be wary of it, you know, because he needs to wake up. So we'll try to strike a balance between being conscious and controlling the pain. Let's have a look at that head wound."

Adam's face and upper body were purple. His broken right leg rested in a plaster cast and his broken ribs were bound with bandages. His thick black hair had been cut away and a light bandage covered his head wound.

Julie gently removed the bandage to reveal a broad gash across his skull, stretching down across his forehead and ending in a deep scratch on his right cheek.

"His face is beginning to heal," Dr. Brightson observed. "I doubt he'll even have a scar on the cheek." He peered at the head wound and nodded. "This will take a bit longer but you can see – it looks dry and clean. Shall we continue with Dr. Rankin's excellent salve?" Julie nodded. Using a tiny wooden paddle that the Indian doctor had also supplied, she applied the dark brown paste to the wound and fashioned a fresh bandage to cover it.

"I'll mix up one of Dr. Rankin's pain killers," Dr. Brightson said. "It can be administered with a dropper or the invalid pitcher if he's able to swallow." He disappeared to the dispensary and returned with a beaker of clear fluid. "For the pain," he explained.

"You'd best get some rest, my dear," he suggested. "You've been beside him for almost two full days and a night now. If you exhaust yourself, you'll be no help to him when he needs you most. And I'll need you too," he added, "because we mustn't let a patient with a head injury like that remain unconscious."

"I'll stay right here," Julie replied. "If he has more bad dreams, I need to be here. I can sleep in the rocking chair."

Her father paused at the door. "As a wife, you're a fine doctor," he quipped. "And as a doctor, you're a fine wife."

Was it only yesterday, Julie wondered to herself. It seemed like an eternity. But also just a quick minute. The time since Adam's accident was a blur – of fear and worry, of struggling to stay calm and make the right decisions, of the comfort of being back in her father's house, knowing that Adam was receiving the best possible care in Dr. Brightson's Toronto clinic.

Yesterday morning had been cold and bright as Adam headed for the stables to 'commune with his beasts' as he liked to say, and Julie settled down to train her recalcitrant fingers to use her new Underwood typewriter, in hopes of completing revisions to her medical book. It was slow going as her attempts at touch typing tangled the keys and produced lines of incomprehensible gobble-de-gook. She was about to give up and make some tea when she heard Fogo barking frantically at the back door.

"What's that about?" she wondered. Fogo rarely barked unless he was delivering a message or a warning.

She opened the door but he refused to come in. Instead, he continued to bark and run to and fro, a few yards from the door and back again. Something was wrong. She pulled on her coat and boots and followed Fogo toward the barn.

First she caught sight of her own black mare, Cleo, a gift from Adam more than a year ago. Out of respect for Cleo's volatile temperament and sharp hooves, Julie had managed to avoid driving her, much to Adam's dismay. Now she saw Cleo standing in the stable yard, shivering, her lead trailing the ground.

And then she saw Adam, lying on a patch of ice that had formed beside the watering trough. He lay on his face with one leg twisted beneath him. She could see blood already pooling around him.

"Fogo", she called, pointing to the stable. "Find George."

Fogo approached Adam and nosed his body. "No, Fogo, find George." She pointed toward the cow barn. "Go. Find. George."

Fogo was reluctant to leave his master but he trotted off in the direction she had pointed and then she heard him bark. He had found George.

"We have to move him, George. He's unconscious and icy cold and he's losing a lot of blood."

"Give me a minute," George replied. While Julie pulled off her coat to cover Adam, George ran up the gangway to the granary and hauled out a wide board that served as a tabletop for bagging and weighing grain. Together they eased Adam's inert body onto the board. Blood oozed from his face and head, staining the wood.

Fogo ran ahead of them to the back door and barked again, alerting Clara. Without taking time for a coat, she hurried down the path to meet them and together they carried Adam into the house. They were all breathless when at last they laid the makeshift stretcher on the kitchen table.

The kettle was boiling and Clara prepared a basin of hot water and washing cloths. She refilled the kettle, along with a copper boiler and set them to heat on the stove before delving into bureau drawers to find towels and bandages. Julie handed her a cloth pad to try to staunch the head wound, while she examined the rest of his body. His right shoulder was dislocated and his right leg was broken just above the knee. And a cursory examination revealed at least four broken ribs.

"The bleeding is the most urgent," she told Clara. "Just keep gentle pressure on that gash and I'll collect my medications." Once again, she snatched up the gold-imprinted black bag that had served so many of her neighbours and would now serve Adam. From her pharmacopeia in the pantry, she chose several bottles and tins and returned to the kitchen.

"George, we'll need your help in a few minutes to move him to a bed," she advised. "But I saw Cleo in the stable yard, shivering. Would you kindly look after her? I suppose Adam was leading her to water or exercise and she must have reared and crashed down on him.

"And George, bring Fogo in. He deserves a very special treat."

The scalp wound needed stitches, a procedure that Julie performed delicately, after filling the wound with an herbal tincture provided by Dr. Rankin. Clara, who had never before seen stitches in human flesh, turned away to pay close attention to refilling the wash basin with hot water, willing herself not to be sick.

The dislocated shoulder was relatively easy to remedy but the heavy femur was more challenging. With Clara's help, Julie managed to set the bone and apply a plaster cast. "Not much I can do about the ribs," she told Clara. "We'll just bind them up so they won't hurt so much when he moves. Or coughs, heaven forfend."

When George returned, he proceeded to stoke up the stove and make a pot of tea, keeping his worry at bay with busy work and in fact, providing some nerve-calming brew precisely when it was needed. Fogo threw himself down under the kitchen table, a great black bundle of worry, somewhat comforted by the two buttered biscuits that Clara administered.

Adam was still on the granary board, and still unconscious. "The parlour bedroom?" Clara asked.

Julie shook her head. "Too far from the kitchen. And it's cold. We dare not try to move him upstairs. If we slipped or bumped anything, we could do him more harm. Let's make a bed for him right there in the sitting room. George, you know there's a single bed in the third bedroom upstairs? Could you dismantle it and bring it down? And Clara, could you please find some old sheets or sugar bags that we could use until the bleeding stops?"

While her helpers rounded up bed and bedding, Julie took Adam's blood pressure and noted without surprise that it was low – a natural reaction to blood loss. Then she sat down by the telephone and rang the operator, asking for her father's number in Toronto. "That number is busy," came the friendly response. "Would you like me to keep trying it and call back when they answer?"

"No, I'll try my aunt instead – 4464," Julie replied.

Aunt Margaret answered promptly.

"Hello, Auntie Margaret," Julie greeted her.

"Julianna," her aunt exclaimed. "What a pleasure. I was just thinking about you and wondering when you and Adam will be back here for a visit."

"Not soon," Julianna replied, her voice trembling a bit as she found herself longing for her favourite aunt's comforting presence. "Adam has had a bad accident. I need to talk to Daddy right away but his line is busy. Could you please ask him to call me?"

"Oh my dear, I'm so sorry. I'll run over this minute and tell him. And we'll talk later, you and me."

Her phone rang within minutes, the familiar one short, one long, one short, alerting the Valley's party line to a not-to-be-missed call to the Chandler house. Several neighbours heard the news as Julie relayed it to her father, and it spread like brush fire.

Clearly and without emotion, she described the wounds and reported the procedures she had taken. He listened in silence, reviewing in his mind the possible treatments and probable outcomes. "You seem to have taken all the right steps, my dear," he said at last. "But I don't need to tell you – that blow to the head could have very serious consequences. In spite of the pain, we need to bring him back to consciousness as soon as possible."

"What do you suggest?" Julie asked. And then her voice caught. "Oh, Daddy. Could you possibly come and see him?"

He heard the fear in her voice and instantly made his decision. "I'll be there," he promised. "I think I just have time to catch that afternoon train."

"Oh, Daddy. Thank you. Thank you. George will be waiting for you at the station."

The bed was already prepared and now they moved Adam's inert body, covering him gently and adding the foot warmer, the hot water bottle and even a couple of spare lids, hot from the wood stove and wrapped in sugar bags, to combat the chill that pervaded his body. George moved a rocking chair to the bedside and brought Julie a steaming cup of tea. She collapsed gratefully into the chair and then reality hit home. After two hours of unemotional analytical management of the situation, she finally allowed herself to burst into tears, sobbing uncontrollably. Clara pulled another chair over and sat close to her, an arm around her shoulders, tears streaming down her own cheeks.

And all across the Valley, their neighbours sprang into action, doing what they always did in an emergency, the women whipping up cakes and casseroles, the men making plans to pitch in with milking and barn chores and wood chopping, rallying in support of the family that, they realized anew, were the best friends that Valley folk ever had.

By the time her father arrived, Julie had regained her composure but seeing her red eyes and puffy face, he wasn't fooled. He hugged her long and warmly and then matter-of-factly examined their patient.

"You've done a very good job, Julie," he praised her. "Now our challenge is to wake him up. You'd think that staying unconscious would be preferable but we do know that he cannot live without water for very long. And we also know that for some reason, patients with head injuries need to wake up sooner, rather than later, if they're to have any hope of recovery."

He opened his bag and dug out a brown bottle that, when opened, emitted a rich complex scent that Julie recognized – a combination of eucalyptus, pine and other herbs from the forests and fields. He soaked a piece of cotton with the tincture and held it to Adam's nose, removed it, returned it – over and over again, willing him to blink.

"Julie, I'd like to move Adam to the clinic in Toronto," he announced.

"But how can we? Surely it's more dangerous for him to travel than to stay here."

"Well, you remember my old friend, John Sylvester – he's the head man at Canadian National now. I'll call and ask him to arrange a private carriage for us. And I'll have an ambulance meet us at Union Station. The biggest challenge will be to get him from here to the train because we can't bend that leg – he must remain prone and the automobile doesn't have the space. So we'll rely on George for the softest sleigh and the gentlest team and we'll transport him on that same board. We'll need plenty of blankets and bed warmers to withstand the chill. Oh yes, and we'll need padding and pillows to keep him absolutely secure and motionless. Once we arrive, I'll have access to colleagues with specialized knowledge of head injuries."

It was the longest journey of Julianna's life – lengthened by the slow drive on snowy roads to the station, the three-hour train journey and half-hour ambulance ride to Dr. Brightson's clinic, part of his sprawling three-storey house in Parkdale.

And at last they were there – Adam safely in bed in the clinic, Auntie Margaret standing by to help and comfort, Dr. Brightson administering an aromatic mixture that finally restored Adam to the waking world. Julie took up her post in a rocking chair beside the bed, ready for whatever challenges lay ahead.

CHAPTER 27

The New Family

Just like Adam to buy a wild horse and then fall under it and get his head smashed. After his accident we never seen much of him. He took his time getting well and he stayed in the clinic with Julianna's father and then with Julie's aunt. I'd venture to say that everybody in the Valley was worrying about him and bothering George and Clara for news. Julie called Clara a few times and Rachel too so the party line was able to pick up and listen to the news. But we all worried and wondered if they'd ever come back to the Valley. And that big black dog of his worried most of all.

Lenny

The phone jangled in the hall and Julie padded toward it in her slippers and dressing gown, toast in hand.

"Julie," her father said urgently, "I have two emergencies on my hands and I'm hoping you can help me with one of them."

"Of course, Daddy. What's happening?"

"I need you to attend a young mother at 299 Sloman Street. Her name is Vera Ambrose. She already has two small children and a third one almost ready to deliver. I've only seen her the one time, three days ago, and she is on my schedule for today because her situation is urgent. The problem is that she's on her own – her husband was killed in a factory accident only a couple of months ago. They appear to have no money and no family so it's a challenge all 'round. Can you see her?"

"I'll be on my way in 15 minutes," Julie responded. Since returning to Toronto she had been keen to help her father, as she had done in the old days before her marriage, but he was reluctant to take her away from Adam, who was still recuperating from his accident. "Adam will be fine," she reassured him. "Auntie Margaret is here and she keeps feeding him."

"He's a lucky man," her father responded. "I have to deal with what presents as a ruptured spleen so I don't know when I'll be back. But I'll check in with you as soon as I can."

She said good-bye and reported to Adam and Auntie Margaret who were enjoying a leisurely breakfast in the dining room. "I'll try not to be too long," she promised. "But with Auntie Margaret you're in good hands."

"And if all else fails, I do know how to boil water and make tea and toast." Adam quipped. "You taught me well."

Her black bag was packed and ready as always, so she was soon out the door and into a cab. The car crawled along Bloor Street and then turned north to a part of the city that had never been fashionable and was now decidedly down at the heels. The street was lined with a shabby row of narrow houses. There were no sidewalks. She approached the door and knocked but there was no answer. Tentatively she tried the door and found it unlocked. "Hello," she called, stepping directly into the kitchen. "Anybody home?" A weak voice responded: "In here." A doorway opened off the kitchen and she moved through. A pale young woman lay on the bed, with two toddlers beside her. They stared at Julie in total silence. "Dr. Brightson asked me to come and see you," Julianna announced. While some patients knew that they were father and daughter, the two always maintained a formal relationship in the company of their clientele. "I'm Julie Chandler. How are you feeling?"

The woman seemed almost too tired to respond. She gazed at Julie for long seconds and then replied: "I don't know quite what to do." Julie noted her almost transparent skin with its sheen of feverish perspiration. Her swollen belly contrasted oddly with her skeletal body. Her pulse was weak and her lips were beginning to crack. There were no glasses of water, no cups of tea, no dishes in the room. Absolutely nothing.

She noted the children's apathy and silence. "They are starving," she thought to herself. She hurriedly checked the kitchen for a bit of bread or oatmeal – anything she could provide to stave off their hunger, but she could find absolutely no food. She found a cup and filled it with water but her patient was too weak to raise her head and drink. Julie dug into her black bag and found her invalid's cup, with a spout on the side. She was able to give Mrs. Ambrose a few sips and then she held the cup for each of the children to drink.

"Do you have any family who can come and lend a hand?" Julie enquired. "Any neighbours to help you?"

The woman shook her head. The younger child crawled to his mother's side and tried to nurse but she feebly pushed him away and turned her head to the wall in despair.

Julie sized up the situation swiftly and silently agreed with her father's assessment. This woman was seriously ill, her children were hungry and too tiny to care for themselves and with her husband gone, there was surely no money to hire help or even to buy food.

"Mrs. Ambrose, I want to take you to Dr. Brighton's clinic to help you get your strength back," she announced. "We'll find a foster home for your children and when you're strong enough, you'll all be together again."

Mrs. Ambrose wanted to protest but she had neither the energy nor an alternative. She simply waited while Julianna decided what to do.

"First, we'll get all of you to the clinic. Then I'll make arrangements for your children while the doctor looks after you. Don't be anxious. You'll be in very good hands and so will your little ones. Now just stay as you are for now. I'm going out to hail a cab in the street and then I'll be back to help you."

Not many cabs roamed the streets in that neighbourhood but eventually Julie found one, a surly driver who was none too pleased to be transporting a sick woman and two tots. When Julie waved a bill under his nose, he relented somewhat.

She brought the two toddlers to the car first, spreading an old blanket before placing them in the front seat next to the horrified driver. They both began to cry. "Do you have any cookies or bread?" she enquired. "These little people are starving." His grimace of distaste said it all, yet he rifled in his lunch box and came up with an oat cake which he broke in half for them. She left him to admire their dirty faces, runny noses, and smelly diapers while she hurried back to the house where Mrs. Ambrose was beginning to fret over her brood. "No worries," Julianna reassured her. "A nice cab driver is looking after them and he's waiting for us." Helping her up to a sitting position, Julianna tried to get her to her feet but the woman was too weak. She was so thin that she seemed to weigh almost nothing so Julie simply pulled a grubby blanket off the bed, wrapped it around her patient, scooped her up in her arms and carried her to the automobile. The cab driver was shocked at the sight and sprang to open the door, lending a hand to place her across the back seat. He was well on his way to becoming downright respectful.

Julie climbed in front with the two little boys, now hungrily eying the cab driver's lunch box in hopes of more snacks, and they were on their way. "Drive very gently," Julie ordered.

He was well rewarded for his help. When finally they reached the clinic, he carried the two soggy toddlers into the building while Julie again scooped up Mrs. Ambrose and carried her inside.

Her father was still out on his call but Miss Jefferson, his very competent nurse, was ready to pitch in and within minutes, Mrs. Ambrose was settled in a clean dry bed. Julie took the two little ones across the road to Auntie Margaret. "I know I'm imposing on you," she began, "but these little folk are very hungry. I've brought their mother here to the clinic but she's too sick to look after them. Could you please help us?"

Auntie Margaret inspected the newcomers with a mixture of pity and distaste that slowly turned to concern. "Good thing I never throw anything out," she commented. "I still have diapers that I bought when Christine was here." They both knew what she meant. Christine's baby died at birth so the diapers were never used.

"Auntie Margaret, you're a marvelous Margaret," Julie crowed, recalling a favourite expression from her youth. "Thank you. Thank you. I'll be back as soon as I can." With a quick peck on the cheek, she was gone.

Back at the clinic, she checked on Mrs. Ambrose before invading her father's kitchen to make some sweet tea and toast. Wonder of wonders, she found chicken broth in the icebox so she warmed it on the stove, and took the meal to her patient. She propped her up a bit on the pillows and fed her the soup by the spoonful, handed her the toast to feed herself and offered her the tea in her invalid cup. The food made a difference – Mrs. Ambrose was looking a bit brighter, a bit stronger and much more optimistic.

"Your little boys are just fine," Julie reported. "They are across the street right now being fed and given baths and put to bed. Now that you've had some sustenance, I'll give you a bath and then you can tuck in for a good sleep. Dr. Brightson should be back soon and he'll be taking charge of your care. But Miss Jefferson is marvelous – she's been with him for years. And I'll be nearby too."

Mrs. Ambrose listened quietly. "I thought I was going to die," she whispered. "I thought the babies would die too…starve to death."

"No more worries, Mrs. Ambrose," Julie reassured her. "You're in good hands now and so are your little ones."

The sponge bath gave her an opportunity to examine her patient's emaciated body and try to determine the state of her pregnancy. Now a little stronger, Mrs.Ambrose revealed that her baby was due within three or four weeks. "That's too many babies so close together," she confessed. "We decided we'd have to find ways to avoid . . . you know . . . after this one is born. But now my husband is gone . . . " She had no need to finish the sentence.

"How old are your children?" Julie asked. "And what are their names?"

"Michael is the oldest. He'll be three on January 14. Davey is fifteen months. His birthday is June 10. If this one's a boy, we wanted to call him Peter. If it's a girl her name will be Emma. Do you think the baby is all right?" she asked anxiously. "I know I haven't been eating right."

"Babies are amazingly resilient, Mrs. Ambrose. While you've been losing weight, your baby has been growing. He's not a very big baby, but I expect he – or maybe she – is perfectly healthy."

With her patient in Miss Jefferson's care, she crossed the street to see how the little ones were faring. As she expected, they were fast asleep, the bigger one in a spare bed, the little one in a huge cardboard box, fitted out with warm blankets. "Aren't they beautiful," she remarked. "Amazing how their cheeks start to turn rosy as soon as they're fed and safe."

"And clean," Adam added. "Much easier to love with the grime scraped off."

The phone jangled again. It was Dr. Brightson, back at his office, looking for more information about Mrs. Ambrose. Julie reported her own observations. "She's so thin and undernourished. I hope that baby holds off a bit until she gets some strength back."

But it was not to be. Late that night, the phone summoned Julie again. Mrs. Ambrose was in labour and since Miss Jefferson had left for the day, could she come and assist?

"About two hours ago," Dr. Brightson brought her up to date. "Took me by surprise, really, because I thought she was stable for a few days yet."

The patient was semi-conscious, her pains tempered by an herbal tincture that was a secret between Dr. Brightson and his Cree shaman friend, Dr. Rankin. Her breathing was shallow, interrupted only by her contractions. "Her pulse is weak," Julianna reported. "And blood pressure down too. What do you suggest?"

"With the pain suppressed, she should fare better," he replied. But she continued to weaken, unable now to put any effort into her contractions. Finally, as her baby girl slipped into the world, her breathing ceased.

Dr. Brightson was haggard and suddenly exhausted. "Two patients lost in a single day," he mourned. "My spleen patient bled out. I didn't dare move him here to the clinic but he bled to death anyway. And now this poor young woman with her three orphans." He turned away and stood with his hands on his instrument table, propping up his weary body. Julianna dealt with the cord and afterbirth and wrapped the tiny waif in a blanket. Then she moved to his side and waited, her hand on his, sharing the grief that they both felt. At last her father took a deep breath and turned back, once more in control of himself and the situation at hand.

"We'll need a wet nurse for the infant," he began. "I have several nursing mothers on my list who may be able to supply milk or foster the baby for a while. But for tonight, we'll start her on barley water. She's undernourished, for sure and she'll need close attention. Can you stay, Julie, to take care of her?"

"I'll take her home," Julianna volunteered. "Auntie Margaret will help me."

"But first, we'll move our patient." They wrapped her frail body in a sheet and together carried her to the doctor's cold room, where he stored medications and ingredients but rarely dead bodies.

"I'll arrange for her to be picked up by the university in the morning," he told Julie. "We need more cadavers for teaching anatomy to first year students. And her vital organs will be used for research. Mrs. Ambrose lost her life but in the long run she may save many more."

Julie scooped up the tiny infant, and cradled her gently. Her heart ached for the baby, who seemed too weak even to cry, and for herself, still childless despite her happy marriage. "You're coming home with me, Emma," she whispered. "Maybe we can save your life."

Adam was already asleep when Julie slipped into the house but her aunt was waiting for her. She peered at the infant and waited for Julie to explain. "She died – just as the baby was born," Julie explained. "It's too late to find a foster home or a wet nurse at this hour, so I brought her back to care for her "til morning." She looked down into the tiny face and sighed. "Isn't she perfect?" she commented. "If only she weren't so thin and weak. Whatever is going to happen to her?"

Auntie Margaret laid a loving hand on her shoulder.

"You could keep her yourself."

Julie stared at her in amazement. She could think of nothing to say. The suggestion was preposterous but – was it?

"You could keep all three," Auntie Margaret added. "The perfect little family that you've always wanted."

"Is it allowed?" Julie wondered aloud. "Is it legal?"

"I'm not suggesting that you steal them," her aunt replied. "Adoption needs to go through the proper channels. But these children have no parents and to the best of our knowledge no relatives to care for them. They desperately need parents and good food and care. You desperately want a family – I see it in your face every time we pass children in the park or on the street. Is this not a match made in heaven?"

"But I know nothing about them," Julie argued. "There's no opportunity to study the family's background or medical history or…"

"No, they don't come with a pedigree," her aunt agreed. "But how many of us do? We do well because we're well nourished and loved and… lucky. This could be their stroke of luck – and yours.

"Now let's find a bed for that little rosebud and get everybody tucked away."

While Julie fed barley water to the baby, Auntie Margaret disappeared briefly, reappearing triumphant with a cradle, another reminder of Chrissy's heart-wrenching pregnancy. Deftly fitting it with flannel sheets and blankets, she carried it to the spare room to await Julie's arrival with the baby.

Julie was exhausted. Her body cried out for sleep. But her mind was racing, tumbling and diving around the possibilities and the challenges of this ready-made family. And during the rare moments when she did doze off, Emma wakened for nourishment.

In the morning, she changed the baby and carried her, along with a bottle of barley water, to Adam's bedside. He was awake and sipping the tea that Auntie Margaret always brought to start the day.

"Adam," she began. "Something happened during the night."

He looked up expectantly.

"I had a baby. In fact I had three of them."

He laughed aloud and waited.

"What would you think about adopting this entire little family? Michael, David and Emma. They need parents. And I think we need a family."

She perched on the side of his bed and they sat together in silence, each acknowledging the other's deepest yearnings.

CHAPTER 28

And Then There Were Five

Everybody in the Valley wanted Adam and Julianna to come home. The women was missing Julianna, especially if they was in a family way and needed her there for the birthing. That woman caused a right lot of fuss sometimes but she was always on the spot for anybody that broke an arm or had a baby and she always knew the right thing to do. And Adam – he was quiet and smart and wise. I guess they was kinda like royalty. The Valley sure was different without them – kinda empty. We was worried about Adam but we didn't hear much from them even though we pestered George and Clara for news. So when the news come, we was fit to be tied. They was comin' home. And what's more, Willie and Chrissy was comin' too. It felt like the Valley would be complete again.

Lenny

Whatever happened to peace and quiet and a chance to read a book right through to the last page, Julie wondered. Her days were so packed that she could scarcely breathe and there seemed no respite in sight.

But there was joy.

Imagining the children's faces when they saw their first-ever birthday celebration, she swirled a final dollop of icing onto the cake and added five bright blue candles, two for David, and three for Michael, whose January birthday had got lost in his mother's illness and death. Julie covered the cake and hid it away in the pantry to await the little family party. Then she carried a tea tray to the garden where Adam was puttering in the flowerbeds.

"Just what the doctor ordered," he commented as he sipped. "Where are the troops?"

"One asleep just there in the sitting room, two of them off to the park with their commanding officer," she responded. "Auntie Margaret is a very fine sergeant-major."

"We'll miss her when we move back home," he said matter-of-factly. "We'll have to hire a local girl to help you take care of them. Can't expect Clara to be as keen as your aunt is."

"It's hard to imagine being back at the farm with three children," Julie replied tentatively. "The longer we stay here, the more I think of this as 'home' and the farm as a distant memory."

"Maybe for you, Julie, but not for me. That farm is my responsibility and I need to get back there and take care of it.'

"Besides, all my memories are there – of Uncle and Auntie… my horses…the neighbours. I really miss them. Y'know, I've been thinking a lot about the Valley… the way people look out for each other …the way they rally 'round anyone in need. Whether it's a barn burning or bad health or some other disaster, they rush in to help with chores or finish the harvest or bring food – whatever's needed, just as they did when I was hurt. You don't see that in the city."

"Well, keep in mind that you haven't seen real city life yet, because you've been busy recuperating," she argued. "When you're able to be out and about more, you'll see that communities and neighbours pull together here too. Not the way they do on the farm, of course – we don't have much hay to mow or cows to milk. But taking care, all the same."

"Perhaps. But then there's the matter of having a purpose. I don't belong in the city – I have no job, no purpose, no future. I just wander around the garden, nipping off the occasional dead bloom or pulling a weed. It's time to get back to the farm and do some real work."

Instinctively he touched the scar on his forehead, a souvenir of his skittering horse's sharply shod hoof. Occasional ghost twinges from his smashed ribs and broken leg, and his general malaise were receding day by day, but that scar remained as a dramatic reminder of his brush with death.

"Adam, you've been recovering from a very serious accident," Julie reprimanded him. "You're homesick. But you're not ready yet for a full day's work.

"But here's something to take your mind off it – maybe my father mentioned this to you… there's a gala evening coming up next month in support of the Royal Winter Fair – a big dinner and entertainment at the Queen's Hotel. Daddy has asked us to go if you're feeling up to it. Shall we give it a whirl?"

Adam brightened at mention of the big fair that celebrated farms and farmers. He'd attended it annually for years and it was at just such a dinner that he and Julie had first met. "I'll be well enough," he promised grimly, "even if I need a stretcher."

"Well…maybe a stick with an 'orse's 'ead 'andle instead," Julianna quipped.

They heard Auntie Margaret at the gate with the two children in a push-chair. She joined them for tea while the little boys raced and toddled around the garden, chasing a ball. Julie's heart swelled at the sight of them, now so rosy and healthy and adjusting beautifully to their new family life. She thought back to the first few weeks when the youngsters never spoke, never smiled, never played – in fact, never even moved unless told to do so. Now they were on the run, laughing and chattering. Only baby Emma seemed slow to thrive.

Margaret's joy in having a house full of children was positively contagious, Julie thought to herself. They're never too noisy, too sleepless, too grubby, too soggy or too hungry for her. She feeds them, bathes them, dresses them, walks them, plays with them, reads to them and tucks them in at night. Or she would if Julie didn't wade in to take charge at least some of the time. Her frequent offers to hire a nanny to shoulder some of the work were always flatly refused.

She'll be devastated when we move back to the farm, Julie thought. IF we move back to the farm.

"Time for lunch and a nap," she announced as she rounded up the children and headed for the house. "And that includes you, sir," she smiled at Adam. "Come along."

With the children tucked in and Adam settled in his favourite chaise lounge on the verandah, Julie checked in with her father in the clinic. It was an unusually quiet day so she turned her attention back to the evening's festivities. And help appeared in the persons of Willie and Chrissy, laden with gifts for the little folk.

"Dr. Chandler, I presume," Willie intoned grandly, bowing over his extended hand. "I trust that your brand new medical degree meets with your approval."

"Oh indeed," Julie laughed. "Prettiest piece of paper I've ever seen. Though I suspect that the bigwigs at the University were none too happy to hand it over to a mere woman."

"We're so proud of you, Julie," Chrissy enthused. "You've fought a long battle for this."

"Well, I have my father to thank. All those years of practical experience working with him were what equipped me to write the medical exams without actually having attended classes. And now I'm so glad to be able to practice medicine with him because the powers-that-be still aren't keen on women doctors. And the sad fact is that many of the patients, even women, also want nothing to do with a woman doctor.

"They're making some good inroads at Women's College Hospital but I think I'll stay right here and try to lighten Daddy's workload."

"Old prejudices die hard," Chrissy remarked. "When you've been told from birth that girls are inferior or useless, you're inclined to believe it."

Julie stopped to give her a hug. "Well, my dear, you don't believe it anymore, do you? Tell me about your studies and your book. How are you folks finding university life?"

"Wonderful," said Willie. "Exciting," Chrissy added. "And I have Aunt Margaret to thank – with all my heart – for keeping me there. Did you know that she quietly approached the IODE on my behalf and they've given me a scholarship for the rest of my tuition? It's wonderful."

Now happily married, they were embarked upon separate learning programs at the University of Toronto – Willie at the recently formed Faculty of Music, abetted by private lessons at the Royal Conservatory of Music, and Chrissy intensely involved in literature at Victoria College.

"Is the university giving you any grief about being married?" Julie enquired. "Married women are not considered good risks."

"What the university doesn't know won't hurt it," Chrissy replied sharply. "As far as they're concerned my name is Dunning – though all I want is to be Chrissy Donovan." She and Willie exchanged a loving glance. "I don't wear my ring and I don't share my private life. I don't like to be deceptive but…"

"I'd do the same" Julie replied. "As long as small-minded men try to deny women their rights, we have to fight with whatever weapons we have available."

"But really," Chrissy added enthusiastically, "my professors are amazing – men and women – and every week that goes by I'm introduced to some new author or a new genre of literature. Sometimes I feel my mind is exploding with new ideas and I wonder if I'll ever catch up."

"The world is changing so fast," Willie chimed in. "In music, in literature, in science – new ideas are bursting out everywhere. Jazz, for example. That chap Gershwin in New York sounds like jazz but he's as classical as they come. And think about the gramophone. Now we can hear all the greatest music and musicians right in our own sitting rooms. But the fact is, we'll never catch up and I'm not sure I want to. All we can do is keep ourselves open to those new ideas and let our minds expand with them."

"Willie has written the most beautiful concerto for violin and orchestra," Chrissy announced proudly. "Debut performance in the fall, probably. You must come."

"I wouldn't miss it for the world," Julie promised.

Willie did a fair imitation of looking modest. "It's just a short one," he countered. "But while I was writing music, Chrissy was writing amazing poetry. Wait 'til you see the new book."

"Also a short one," she shrugged. "Willie and I seem to specialize in short works of art."

"But what about you, Julie," Willie asked. "What's the latest on your new tome?"

"Just off the press and ready to go," she reported. "All four hundred pages of it. What a relief to have it over and done with."

"Is there all that much to say about women's health?" Willie enquired half-seriously.

"Well, it's a long way from that skimpy little book I was so proud of when I first moved to the farm," Julie replied. "That one concentrated chiefly on gynecology but the current edition looks at subjects like diseases of the heart and the blood, thyroid and goitre, digestion – the entire spectrum of ailments and diseases."

"But surely they're not unique to women," Willie argued.

"Some are. But in other cases, the symptoms and the way they affect women are different than men. Until now, it was assumed that illnesses such as heart attacks, for example, presented the same in women as in men. But both physiology and life style can make a difference. You spoke about the challenge of keeping up. Believe me, in the medical field new research and medicines and techniques are hailing down upon us thick and fast. Even while the book was on the press, some of its content became, if not obsolete, at least outdated."

"And yet – let me share a secret with you. The book is being considered as a standard text on the curriculum of the Faculty of Medicine – the very place that refused to admit me as a student just a few years ago."

"That's wonderful, Julie. Congratulations," they cheered almost in unison. "But you should be the professor who introduces it," Chrissy added.

Julie smiled and busied herself with dinner. The second half of her secret could not yet be revealed – that she had indeed been invited to join the Faculty that very autumn as a professor in women's health. Now with Adam fretting to get back to the farm, that door might be slamming before it even opened. She put the thoughts aside and set the young people to counting out silver and china.

They seemed to be in an especially sparkling mood tonight, she noted. And in a moment, she learned the reason.

"But Julie, we have some big news," Chrissy said. "You remember Mr. Flaherty, the fiddle player? He died a few months ago – heart problems, apparently. Well, years ago, he bought my father's farm. And when he died, he ordered that the farm be sold and he left the proceeds to us in his will. I never wanted anything to do with that farm again but the money will let us buy a house here in Toronto. No more rent! Isn't that wonderful?"

"Wonderful indeed!" Julie enthused. "I hope you plan to stay close to all of us." They discussed the city's housing options as they mixed the fruit punch, ladled out the salads and sliced the roasted chicken. The world seemed limitless in its possibilities.

It was a merry party and all the family enjoyed it. The children greeted their presents joyously, especially three cuddly teddy bears, sized to fit each little set of arms. But they were struck dumb by the sight of the cake and its candles. "Make a wish, Michael, and blow out the candles," Chrissy urged, but he just continued to stare at them wonderingly. "Come on, I'll show you," she offered, blowing gently on the candles. "Can you do that?" Suddenly he drew in his breath and blew a great blast that extinguished all the candles at once. Immediately he burst into tears, grieving for the flames he had destroyed. "Don't cry, Michael," Willie comforted him. "Look. We'll bring them back to life." He found matches and lit all five again. Michael's face registered wonder and love. He climbed into Willie's lap and gazed up at him, the man who made fire, with unabashed hero worship.

"He may be three," Julie remarked quietly, "but certainly this is his first birthday."

****

The prospect of the Royal Winter Fair gala evening boosted Adam's spirits and seemed to accelerate his recovery. In fact, the two of them were a picture of glowing health and wellbeing as they entered the hotel's lavish dining room, she in a floor-length ivory dress with her burnished hair piled atop her head, he in black tie and dinner jacket and sporting an elegant brass-feruled cane. To Julie, he seemed handsomer than she'd ever realized.

"Here's our table," Dr. Brightson pointed out. "We'll be joining Gordon Buchanan and his entourage."

"The minister of agriculture?"

"The same. Have you already met?"

"Only in a receiving line at last year's fair. I doubt that he'll remember me."

But he did. Buchanan had already heard about Adam's accident and asked after not only his health but that of his farm. "I'm lucky to have a really dependable farm manager," Adam explained. "But I do need to get back. George can oversee most of the work but I'm concerned about my bees and my apple trees. I've always taken charge of those myself."

"Bees and apple trees," the minister nodded sagely. "I understand your concern. Apples and honey are the two major crops on my farm too. I have a hundred acres out west of the city, at Oakville and we grow several apple varieties for market."

It was a smooth road from there on in. The two men were instantly deep in discussion about the relative merits of various apple species – those suitable for home use and those, like Buchanan's, rugged enough to stand up to the stresses of the marketplace or the canning factory. And honey was not forgotten – the much coveted apple blossom honey of springtime, the clover honey from white and purple clover planted in orchards to keep the bees busy as summer wore on to buckwheat honey, dark brown and aromatic.

Julianna turned to Buchanan's wife, expecting to encounter a self-important and somewhat dull politician's wife. Instead she soon found herself engaged in a lively discussion of medical matters in which her companion seemed well versed and interested in Julie's involvement. She asked countless questions about the new book, how it had been researched, how the illustrations were done, and where it would be available. To her surprise, Julie found herself telling Mrs. Buchanan about her first Women's Institute experience when most of the older members objected to her frank discussion of reproduction. "Definitely still a problem," Mrs. Buchanan noted. "There's a huge education job to be done, Mrs. Chandler – forgive me – DOCTOR Chandler. Surely you'd be the person to do it."

"Well, I have three children now," Julie explained. "We adopted an entire little family, earlier this year. They were terribly undernourished, especially the youngest – she's only five months old and she still has a long way to go. I'm so fortunate to have my father close by and my aunt as well, but I need to be nearby for them."

Dr. Brightson was very quiet, tuning in first to Adam's talk with the minister, than to Julie's conversation with his wife.

They all parted friends but Buchanan's last words to Adam were the evening's highlight. "You know, Chandler, the Department of Agriculture needs people like you. Major changes are happening in farming – the crops, the machinery, the markets. We need men who know the practical side of farming but also have the education and world experience to steer those changes in the right direction.

"Would you care to stop by my office later in the week and talk about the possibilities?"

Julianna looked away, pretending difficulty with her coat buttons. Dr. Brightson, Julianna noted, looked like a cat that'd swallowed a canary.

And so it was that Adam was offered a post in the Department of Agriculture, expected to lead to a position as deputy minister, with particular responsibility for maintaining the integrity and profitability of small farms. And he accepted.

At last Julianna could share her surprise. "Adam, I've been offered a professorship at the University – in the Faculty of Medicine."

"And did you accept?"

"No, I was waiting and, quite frankly, hoping that you'd decide to stay in the city."

"Well, I will and I won't," he replied. "They've hired me because I'm a farmer and a farmer I shall remain. So come summer, we're off to the farm and in fall and winter, we'll attend to our city duties. I'd call that 'the best of both worlds', wouldn't you?"

Julianna rocked Emma in her arms and looked down at her pinched little face. If this baby lives, she thought to herself, then we will indeed have the best of all possible worlds.

Lenny carries on...and on

Well, that was long ago. Gettin' on to forty years since Adam and Julianna came home with their new ready-made family and every neighbour in the Valley out cranin' their necks trying to take a peek. And plenty has happened since then. A lot of the old folks gone to their graves, a lot of farms bought up by city folks pretendin' they're farmers. A lot of the youngsters gone to the city – and some of them missin' the old days and comin' back.

Adam and Julie moved back and forth from the farm to the city a couple of times a year. In winter, Adam's work took him all over the province and Julie was teaching at the University. But in summers they belonged to us here in the Valley. Adam would wander around among his bees and his apple trees and Julie would go visiting all her lady friends or invite them over for tea. Velma was always on the list and she brought home plenty of merry tales about the two little boys and how Julie got them. And sad tales too about the baby girl that died – Emma was her name – and how broken-hearted Julie was to lose her.

Then the bombshell. The second summer after they come home, Julie arrived back in a family way and later that summer, her father came for a visit just in time to deliver the new baby. Thank goodness it was a girl that Julie wanted so badly. They called her Bella and she grew up as healthy and happy as the two boys and as pretty as her mother.

Willie and Chrissy had babies, too. Along with his music and her poetry books, they still had time to raise four little ones. And along with Willie's parents, they often visited at Adam and Julie's place. And as if that wasn't enough, the farm managers George and Clara up and had a baby too, a bit late in life, but a bright little chap that kept them on the run. I'll tell you it was like a circus over there with eight youngsters on the rip and three mothers ridin' herd on them, but they got along just fine.

Rachel Donovan eventually went back to teachin' – at the same school where Willie was treated so bad on his first and only day. Percy Hawkins taught his father how to make flowers and frills out of iron and as tractors moved onto the farms and horses moved off, their smithy turned into a kind of fantasy place. And very profitable too. They was sellin' regular to Eaton's in Toronto and that big flower shop – Tidy's, I think was the name – and after a bit, they started settin' up a booth at the CNE and the Royal Winter Fair and Toronto folks was wild over their ironwork. The Dietrich family did well too – the three youngsters all went to college but they come back to live near their parents. The boy, Rudi, he helped his father run the farm. And every one of them worked in iron like their father and did woodworking and embroidery and made real good food.

Tommy Flaherty never told a soul about all the good he done for his neighbours, but Bert Wilkins told his family the whole story about how Tommy had got him through his darkest days by helping him build his workshop and make a livin' even in spite of the mustard gas. And those youngsters never forgot. As Tommy was getting' on in years, still wearin' his old Irish tweed cap, they kinda adopted him like he was their grandfather and they couldn't do enough for him. But Tommy still had one last favour up his sleeve. When he died, his will left his farm to the Wilkins family but he ordered the Dunning farm to be sold off and the money to go to Chrissy and Willie. By then it was worth a sight more than he'd paid for it so when they put that money together with the price of Annie's old farm – we'd bought it from them for our lad, Liam – they had enough to buy a nice place in Toronto.

Liam got off to Agricultural College just like Adam and come home with a load of new ideas and some of them actually made sense. He's got a wife and youngsters now, all living over to Annie's old place where we can still glance out each morning like we did for her, makin' sure there's smoke comin' out of the chimney and they do the same for us. We also set our older boy, Bernie, up with a farm of his own, down the next concession south of here and both the boys pitch in to help with our farm. The two girls both went in for nursing and now they're married with youngsters of their own. That gives us quite a family – fourteen grandchildren, last time I counted.

That doctor lady from Toronto, Doctor Butters, she finally had enough stories to make a book so I don't hear from her no more. But on her last visit, she gave me the recording machine and a box of tapes as a farewell gift, and told me to keep on tellin' my yarns. And so I do.

Velma and I hang on here, enjoying our family and our neighbours. And all the problems, all the disasters fade away as we remember them days, them good old days, when the Valley was young and we was too.

⚓ THE END ⚓

In Them Days – An Appreciation

Isobel Warren writes engagingly and all-knowingly about 'them days' because she grew up there, in a later generation, when the remembered gossip, prejudices, superstitions, hatreds and hero worship were as vivid on her elders' tongues as they were on her child's ears. Indelible, unforgettable, waiting to be transformed into art as Isobel does here. The variety of characters in this well-wrought novel, the richness of Ontario rural and agricultural life from horrific barn fire to the rhythms of courtship, marriage, birth and death, the overall panorama, are true to life as only a fellow countrywoman could know them. Read this novel to be moved, to experience a specific Canadian past that is not so long ago, and to learn what streetlights and highrises will never teach you about your country.

Dr. Joaquin Kuhn
PROFESSOR ENGLISH, EMERITUS
UNIVERSITY OF TORONTO
[CO-EDITOR OF THE HOPKINS QUARTERLY]